NIGHTWIND—THE DOOMSDAY WEAPON THE AMERICANS HAD LEFT BEHIND

For journalist Joe Kendall the memory of that day on Hill 651 was a personal nightmare . . . his fair share of the hell that was South Vietnam. He had run from the bombs and death . . . run from the shattered bodies and, twelve years later, he was still running.

But now the FBI was asking questions about the American courier he had met and the mysterious canisters he had seen that day, and suddenly he was involved with something more horrifying than the memory of his screams.

They told him it could kill millions. They told him to stay out of it. But he had run once before and paid the price. So, for Joe Kendall, it was time to turn and fight.

NIGHTWIND

Mark Washburn

A DELL BOOK

Published by
Dell Publishing Co., Inc.
1 Dag Hammarskjold Plaza
New York, New York 10017

Dell ® TM 681510, Dell Publishing Co., Inc.

ISBN: 0-440-15757-9

Printed in the United States of America
First printing—November 1982

For Karen Keating

1968

Chapter One

There was no room for doubt. Second-guessing was not his style. He would leave that to the Harvard historians, who knew in their hearts that nothing he did could possibly be wise or good. They had all the answers. They understood everything because they understood nothing.

They didn't know what it was like, how it actually felt, to be the living embodiment of all the pride and power of the greatest nation in the history of the world. They had never walked alone through the haunted hallways, in slippers and robe, to the Situation Room, or stared for hours at the splotchy, multicolored maps, all because there was nothing else to do at 3 A.M. except lie in bed and listen to the uncertain thump of the presidential heart. They never had to sort through the unending stacks of aerial photographs and decide which bridge, which warehouse, was to become a target, or to wonder if this would be the one that triggered it all, the one that was half a mile too close to Hanoi, the one that brought in the Chinese and the Russians, the missiles and the nukes and the end of everything.

The decision was made. The Harvards wouldn't like it, but it wasn't their decision to make, it was *his*.

He pressed one of the many buttons on the big desk. "Send him on in."

The door to the outer office opened almost instantly. The young man who entered took two steps in and then stopped as the door swung shut behind him. His eyes roved uncertainly around the room until, like a compass needle registering the presence of a lodestone, they came to rest on the President.

He felt it. They all did—the first time, at least.

Lyndon Johnson rose to his feet, circled around the desk, and grabbed the young man's right hand. "You're Turner Poole," he said as he pumped and squeezed. Poole had the odd feeling that his identity had not been official until this moment; he was Turner Poole by presidential fiat.

Still shaking hands, Johnson draped his other arm over Poole's shoulders and pulled him toward a sofa. "Breeze Woodward's told me a lot about you. He and the rest of my friends back in Houston tell me that you're a fine young man. A real comer. They say you cut quite a swath back at Rice."

It had been Baylor, but Poole wasn't about to correct Lyndon Johnson. He let the big man maneuver him toward the sofa and all but shove him down onto it. He still hadn't said a word. His carefully rehearsed line about it being a great honor to meet the President went undelivered. Somehow, that much seemed to be taken for granted.

"You're a bourbon drinker, aren't you?" Without waiting for him to nod, Johnson went to the door and called out the order. Poole looked toward the door and the lights outside and felt as if he had left his ego out there. Inside the Oval Office there was room only for Lyndon Johnson's immense personality.

Johnson returned to the sofa and sat down uncomfortably close to Poole. At this distance it was impossible to focus on the whole. It was like watching a CinemaScope movie from the first row. Poole could only look at part of the President, at the long legs stretched out in front of the couch, pant legs hiked up to reveal an inch of pallid calf above the stockings, or at the wrinkled forehead, the west

Texas squint, or—most riveting of all, strangely—the huge, fleshy left earlobe.

"You ever been in Washington before?" Johnson asked him.

"No, sir," Poole answered. "This is my first time."

"I'll never forget my first time," the President said. He paused and smiled. "It was 1931 and I was green as the grass. I was an aide to a congressman, and there were hundreds of other aides around, and damn near all of them were Ivy Leaguers who figured they already knew all they needed to know. But I was just smart enough to see how ignorant I really was, so I did the only thing I could do. I worked my tail off. From the minute I got up in the morning to the time I turned out the lights at night, I was out there working and learning. And those other aides were so impressed that they elected me Speaker of the Little Congress when I was only twenty-three. What are you, Turner, about twenty-five?"

"Uh, no sir. Twenty-eight."

Johnson scowled. "You look twenty-five," he said.

A Filipino servant entered the office and placed a silver tray on the table in front of the sofa. His exit was as unobtrusive as his entrance, a practiced display of functional invisibility. Johnson plunked some ice cubes in the glasses, poured the bourbon, and handed Poole his drink.

"Here's to being a young man in Washington for the first time."

"I'll drink to that," Poole responded, forcing a smile.

"Of course you will," said the President. Poole took a healthy gulp of the bourbon and tried to relax while the warmth spread through his gut.

"I've got a lot of respect for young people," Johnson said. "Most of the old farts in this town forget all about the young folk as soon as they get themselves elected. And then, ten or twenty years later, those same kids they ignored for so long vote 'em out of office. I've seen it happen dozens of times. So I've always made a point of getting to know the young people, and I'll tell you something—I like 'em. I truly do. Even these hippies and

11

demonstrators and beatniks who want my scalp aren't so bad. I understand them. Hell, if I was a kid today, I'd be pissed off, too. Shit, I *am* pissed off. I hate this war even more than they do. I mean, do they think I like sending American boys out to die in some stinkin' jungle ten thousand miles away? Do they think I like that?"

Poole wasn't sure if the President wanted an answer or not.

"Hell, no!" Johnson declared, relieving Poole of the need to respond. "I hate it! And if those kids just understood that, they'd support me. I know they would. But the professors hate me because I'm not from Massachusetts, so they spoon-feed these kids a lot of communist bull, and before you know it, we've got riots and draft dodging and people spitting on the American flag."

Johnson put his drink down and idly fingered the Silver Star ribbon on the lapel of his jacket. For another man it might have been an unconscious gesture, but Poole was already beginning to doubt that Lyndon Johnson ever did anything unconsciously.

The President turned and looked directly at Poole, their noses no more than a foot apart. Poole had never seen a face that looked so sincere.

"I know I can count on you, Turner." Johnson clapped his left hand on Poole's knee and gave it a firm squeeze. "I know you won't let me down."

"I won't, sir."

"I guess you know why we need all this secrecy. Coming in the side door in the middle of the night and all. That's the way it has to be right now. But I promise you, if you do this job for your President, the day will come when you'll walk in the front door of this place in broad daylight, and everyone will say: 'There goes Turner Poole. He's the man who helped Lyndon Johnson win the war.'"

"Yessir."

"But for now," Johnson went on, "all this is top secret. There aren't ten other people in the world who know about this. Now, I know it'll be a temptation for you to tell people about how you sat down in the Oval Office with the President of the United States and had a drink with him. There are people who work here who do that all the time. They go up to Georgetown and tell the pretty girls about how important they are, and how they talk with me all the time, and those girls just lie down and spread their legs for 'em. They think I don't know about that, but I do. I know who those people are, and I make damn good and sure that they never hear a thing in this office that's really important. But I know I can count on you."

"You can, Mr. President."

"That's what Breeze told me. He just thinks the world of you, Turner. I'll tell you exactly what he told me. He said, 'Mr. President, if there's one man in the world I'd trust with my life and my wife, it's Turner Poole.' That's how much he thinks of you."

Poole realized he was getting the Johnson Treatment. But the mix of bourbon and presidential flattery was a heady brew. Breeze had warned him about it the way the Coast Guard warns about Gulf Coast hurricanes; you could duck, but you couldn't hide.

"Breeze has been like a father to me," Poole said, knowing it was the sort of thing Johnson would like to hear.

Johnson nodded, as if his own impression had been confirmed. "Breeze is a good man," he said. "That's why I went to him when I needed to find a trustworthy and patriotic young man for this job. You can see why I couldn't use anyone on the staff here, or even anyone who's been in this town longer than a week. Hell, it'd be on the front page of *The New York Times* tomorrow morning."

"You can rely on me, Mr. President." Poole was beginning to catch the rhythm of the conversation. In college he had played clarinet in a Dixieland band, and this had much the same feel to it. You let the brass do the talking until you sensed the right moment to come in with the fills and grace notes.

"And I couldn't leave it to the military for the same reason," Johnson continued. "Some of them are just flat against this operation. They canceled the whole business six months ago, did you know that? Didn't even bother to tell their President. So I didn't bother to tell them when I revived it. Just a few of the people who had to know. Sometimes a President has to do things on the sly, especially when your own people are against you. Like that damned Clifford. Did you see how he slipped it to me the other day up on the Hill? I put him up for secretary of defense, and what does he do at the confirmation hearing? He says that we'll allow 'normal levels' of infiltration on the Ho Chi Minh Trail. Now, who the hell told him to say that?"

This was clearly going to be Johnson's big riff. Poole laid out while the President took another sip of bourbon.

"Normal levels of infiltration! That's like the chief of police saying he'll allow normal levels of rape and murder! But he said it, right there in front of God, the United States Senate, and *The New York Times*, so now I'm stuck with it. That's what my advisers tell me. I just put him up, so I can't repudiate him. I'm the President, but *I* can't repudiate *him*! That's because Clifford's a Wall Street man, and if I want those bankers to support me, then I'm supposed to put up with any amount of horseshit, as long as it comes from one of *their* men. Jesus!"

Johnson finished his drink and stared silently at the empty glass. When he spoke again, his voice was lower, almost conspiratorial. Poole found himself leaning a little closer to the President.

"That's what decided me," said Johnson. "We'll see what those normal levels of infiltration look like after we get through, by God we will. Westmoreland says we can expect a major North Vietnamese offensive any day now. If we'd done this six months ago, we wouldn't have to worry about it. Instead, I've got generals telling me there's no problem, and generals telling me we need more bombing, and advisers telling me we don't need *any* bombing. I've got Republicans calling me another Chamberlain and I've got Gene McCarthy running around in New Hampshire calling me another Hitler. And I've got communist

14

mobs in the streets who want to lynch their President. And I've got Bobby, the crown prince himself, just waiting for the right moment to stick it to me."

"But the people still support you, Mr. President."

Johnson gazed at Poole for a moment, then took his glass away from him and refilled it. "That's not what George Gallup says," Johnson pointed out as he handed Poole the glass.

"The American people have never changed horses in midstream, Mr. President. Lincoln, Wilson, Roosevelt . . ."

"And Harry Truman. Don't forget him. He could've run again in 'fifty-two. But he had a mess in Korea that the people were sick of, and if he had run . . . Hell, maybe Harry had the right idea."

"The people want a strong President. Maybe they get a little restless in an election year, but down deep they know that you're a great President."

Johnson gave him a brief, withering look. "Don't get carried away, Poole."

Poole concentrated on his drink while the President poured himself another. He was overdoing it again. He had to watch that. Sometimes it went over and sometimes it didn't; this was beginning to look like one of the times when it would be smart to keep his mouth shut and not try to be too fancy. Lyndon Johnson was no Breeze Woodward.

"You know about Khe Sanh, don't you?" Johnson asked him, his tone a little sharper now.

"Yessir. Colonel Dickinson briefed me."

"That's right, he did. I've got five thousand marines up there, check by jowl with the DMZ, surrounded by forty thousand North Vietnamese regulars. Westmoreland says we can hold Khe Sanh because we control the air. That's what they all say. But what happens if the weather turns bad, if we can't get any flights in there for a week? I'll tell you what happens—we've got ourselves another goddamn Din Bin Phu, that's what happens! Westmoreland says it won't happen, and he's the commanding general, and generals are never wrong. Just ask them. But if generals are never wrong, then how the fuck did the *first* Din Bin Phu happen? Answer me that!"

Poole had no answer, not that Johnson wanted or needed one.

"Well, it's not gonna happen again, not to me, I'll tell you that. I'm gonna make those generals sign a paper. Every one of them. The joint chief says we can defend Khe Sanh, and I'm supposed to take their word for it. So they can just put it in writing and sign their names to it if they're so damned sure of themselves."

"Yessir," said Poole. "That's only fair."

"You bet," said the President. "And then, when those five thousand American boys are lying dead and butchered in their bunkers, I can go on the television and hold up that piece of paper with all those names on it and tell the people: 'See? It wasn't my fault. I got bad advice.'"

"Uh, yessir," Poole said cautiously. He didn't think the President was listening, anyway.

"Yep, that'll do it, all right. The people will say: 'Good old Lyndon just got bad advice. It's not his fault those boys are dead.' And then they'll go out and lynch those generals—first. *Then* they'll lynch me."

Poole kept his silence and tried to find something in the room to look at, something other than the creased and tormented face of the President. The interview was becoming embarrassing; it was like watching someone throw an epileptic fit on the sidewalk at high noon. There was a ghoulish fascination in it, but it was somehow indecent, a lapse of propriety. Poole stared at the presidential seal on the rug and counted the arrows in the eagle's claw.

Johnson was leaning forward, elbows on knees, face on fists. It was the posture of a man sitting on the can, taking a long, thoughtful dump. The thought was irresistible, and Poole turned his head to take a look, just in time to catch Johnson watching him out of the corner of his eye. Johnson was measuring him. He was still getting the Treatment, Poole suddenly realized, the other side of the polished Johnson coin. He was supposed to feel privileged to be granted a glimpse of the inner doubts and turmoil of the most powerful man on the planet. He would become protective of the vulnerable, private Lyndon Johnson, the man only he, young Turner Poole, had been allowed to see.

Poole almost smiled. He was on top of it now. For the first time since stepping onto the White House grounds, he felt in control again.

"You know what Jack Kennedy told me after the Bay of Pigs?" Johnson asked. His tone was more businesslike now, as if he, too, realized that the head games had gone far enough. "He said: 'Never trust the generals. They're in business for themselves.' And he was right. If he had done things their way during the missile crisis, we'd be sitting in a radioactive crater right now."

Johnson suddenly put his arm around Poole's shoulders and vigorously squeezed the soft tissues above the collarbone. It was a very Texan gesture, one that Poole had always hated.

"Turner," the President said soothingly, "I know you must have some doubts about all this. But this has to be done, and I can't do it without your help."

"I'll do my best, sir."

"I know you will." Johnson completed the shoulder massage and gave him a solid slap on the spine. "You're a can-do fella, I can see that."

"I've learned a lot from Breeze."

"I know you have. You play poker with him, don't you?"

"That's part of the job," Poole said with a laugh. "Breeze figures it's every employee's obligation to give the boss a chance to win back his paycheck."

Johnson studied Poole's face for a moment. Poole tried not to give anything away, knowing that was precisely what Johnson was looking for.

"I don't imagine you lose too much of that paycheck."

"Just enough," Poole told him.

Johnson nodded. They understood each other now.

"Well, you're in a high stakes game now, Poole," Johnson said as he reached for the bottle again. He refilled

17

the glasses and surprised Poole by clinking them together before drinking.

"The problem with a democracy," Johnson began, "is that you're supposed to play with all the cards out on the table, face up. I've got two hundred million people kibitzing behind my back, and meanwhile the other guy gets to hold all the cards against his chest. That's not hardly fair, but that's the way the game is supposed to be played. And the people will expect you to win. Well, we are gonna win, but to do it, I've gotta have a hole card. And it's gotta be right there on the table where I can play it at any time. You understand what I'm saying?"

"You want me to deliver your hole card."

"That's what I want," the President said. "Look, I don't like any of this. Not one bit of it. I hope to God I never have to play that card. I know what people'll say if I do. There are people up on the Hill who'll probably try to impeach me. That's an occupational hazard of southern Presidents named Johnson. You know what I mean?"

The President was smiling grimly. "Yessir," Poole said. "I know what you mean."

"They may not succeed—I've still got a few friends in this town. But it would be a god-awful mess if they even tried it. The President of the United States in the dock, like some damned criminal. But I'll tell you this much. If I'm gonna get impeached, it is sure as shit not going to be because I let five thousand marines get themselves slaughtered. No sir, that's not going to happen. I'm not gonna let those boys die that way. People keep talking about Din Bin Phu, but it wouldn't be like that. The French *surrendered*, damn it. And there's no way those marines are ever going to surrender. It wouldn't be like Din Bin Phu, it'd be like the Alamo. Those are *American* boys, and they'll fight to the last man. And I'm their President, their commander in chief. How the hell can I ask some eighteen-year-old boy to put his ass on the line if I'm not willing to do the same?"

Johnson abruptly got to his feet. Poole was unsure whether to do the same because he didn't think the

President was finished yet. He decided to stay where he was. Johnson looked down at him.

"They're up to something," he said. "It's no coincidence. First this North Vietnamese buildup. Then the fucking Koreans snatch the *Pueblo* on the high seas, like a gang of goddamn pirates. I don't care what they say at Harvard, we're fighting Communists. They're out to destroy us any way they can, and I don't give a shit if they're Vietnamese or Koreans or Chinese or Russians. They all want the same thing. They're gonna spring something on us, and by God, I intend to be ready when they do."

Johnson strode across the office to his desk. Poole stood up, sensing the chord change that would lead to the final eight bars of the session. Johnson picked up the envelope and held it out to Poole.

"This is a letter from me to whom it may concern," Johnson explained. "It's on White House stationery and it's signed by the President and it authorizes you to do whatever the hell you have to do to get the job done."

Poole reached for it, but Johnson withdrew it, leaving Poole with an awkward, empty, outstretched hand.

"Now, I know you're not gonna wave this around and show it to every noncom from here to Da Nang. I know you're gonna keep it out of sight. I know you're only going to use it if you absolutely have to. This is *your* hole card. You understand me, Turner?"

"Yessir, I certainly do."

Johnson nodded gravely, then handed the envelope over to Poole. Poole quickly stuck it into the inside pocket of his jacket, knowing he would have plenty of time later to examine the contents. The President again put his arm around Poole's shoulders and steered him gently toward the door.

"We're going to end this war, Turner," Johnson told him. "One way or another, we're going to end it. I want you to remember that, because you're a part of it now. We're in this together."

This wasn't part of the Treatment. This was something very different, Poole realized. The President of the United

States had just told him, unmistakably, that if he screwed up, Lyndon Baines Johnson was going to take him along, right down to the bottom. All the way with LBJ.

"Have a nice trip," said the President.

Chapter Two

The lieutenant calmly explained the rules to Joe Kendall. "Ten at a time," he said. "Not eleven. Not fifteen. Ten."

"But that ten is really only four," Kendall protested.

"How do you figure?" the lieutenant asked him.

Kendall counted off fingers. "Three for the wire services. Three for the networks. That's six. Six from ten is four."

"The limit of ten includes the wire services and the networks. Six plus four is ten. You want to be one of the ten, put your name down on this list."

"And wait a week?"

"That's up to you."

"I've got as much right to go to Khe Sanh as anybody else."

"Right," said the lieutenant. "What was the name of that magazine again?"

Kendall suppressed a sigh and told him. "*Rocky Road.*"

The lieutenant shook his head. "Never heard of it," he said. "What the hell is it, an ice cream magazine?"

Kendall was getting tired of this. He had been explaining himself to brass and PIOs and other correspondents ever since he got off the Pan Am plane in Saigon a week ago. He was tired of defending his legitimacy. He was a real reporter for a real magazine.

"It's not about ice cream," Kendall began, trying very hard not to let his own sarcasm match that of the lieutenant. "And it's not about road paving, geology, or Rocky the Flying Squirrel. It's a rock music magazine."

"And you're going to report on the big Beatles concert at Khe Sanh?"

"I'm going to report on the men who are fighting this war. In case you haven't noticed, most of them are eighteen years old and they listen to rock music. It's their war, and I've got as much right to tell their story as any of your big name hotshots from AP and the *Times*."

"Sure you do, kid," the lieutenant said soothingly. Kendall was twenty-three, young enough so that being called "kid" was inevitable, and old enough to hate it, especially when it came from some smartass lieutenant who was probably only a year or two older than he was.

"I showed you my MACV card. I'm fully certified and accredited and—"

"Save it," the lieutenant cut in sharply. "I know you got your card. Everyone here has a card. They give them away with bubble gum in Saigon. If you want to go to Khe Sanh, sign the list." The lieutenant shoved the clipboard across the desk. A stubby yellow pencil was tied to it with a short length of dirty string. Kendall surveyed the heavyweight names and affiliations already listed.

"It'll take at least a week."

"Look, kid. I give you my personal guarantee that the war won't end before next Thursday. You gonna sign or not?"

There didn't seem to be any alternative. Kendall reached for the pencil and tried to sign, but the string was too short; the pencil wouldn't reach all the way to the bottom of the list. Kendall signed the list with his own ballpoint, then turned and walked quickly out of the press center. He thought he heard some snickering behind him, but it was drowned out by the bone-shaking sound effects of Vietnam. Over on the airstrip a flight of Phantoms was taking off, afterburners roaring like the final chords of a Who concert.

Kendall took out his pen and his number two notebook and wrote that one down. "Phantoms—Who concert." Kendall kept two notebooks, one for serious reportage and one for random inspirations. When it came time to write his story, he'd squeeze the mots and metaphors from the second notebook between the grim facts from the first, producing, he hoped, a serious but stylish piece of work.

Hanging around the press center was depressing him. It was like waiting for a bus in Cleveland. He was going to write that one down, but thought better of it. Da Nang was not Cleveland. Saigon was not Manhattan, and Vietnam, despite the best efforts of half a million men, was not America. For one thing, Da Nang, unlike Cleveland, was filled with Vietnamese.

Kendall didn't know what to think of the Vietnamese, so he tried not to think of them at all. After a week in the country he knew that they were not the oppressed, heroic freedom fighters eulogized by his friends at home. Nor were they sly, treacherous, inscrutable back-stabbers, or subhuman mud farmers. He didn't know what the hell they were.

Mostly, they were in the way. They cluttered up the war, a nation of loiterers and innocent bystanders. They were as out of place as a gang of Oriental extras from Central Casting, wandering onto the wrong sound stage in the midst of a Busby Berkeley production number, making a shambles of the intricate choreography of modern warfare.

Kendall wrote that one down: "Viets—B. Berkeley—choreog." It was a little unwieldy, but he might be able to hone it into something usable. That is, if he even remembered what the note was supposed to mean. The number two notebook already contained cryptic fragments that were a mystery to him.

Another flight of Phantoms boomed off the runway. Kendall supposed that he would get used to the noise sooner or later, but in truth, the Phantoms were a hell of a lot louder than a Who concert. They were louder than anything he had ever heard before. And the noise never really went away. Already, a big C-141 was angling in from the South China Sea for a landing at Da Nang, advertised as the busiest airport in the world. Then there were the choppers, everywhere all the time, loud, angry Hueys and louder, awesome Chinooks. And there was also the random distant explosion to punctuate the proceedings. Kendall figured that Vietnam, on the basis of decibels per square kilometer, was probably the loudest place on earth.

The press center was partially soundproofed, a provision that did nothing to make up for the drabness of the place. It was a collection of low whitewash-and-tile buildings that had once been a French hotel, back in the days when people still thought of Southeast Asia as romantic and exotic. Now, the compound called to mind the worst features of a VFW bar and a European youth hostel.

Kendall had been here two days and was already sick of it. There was a certain fascination in hanging around and listening to the veteran correspondents swapping war stories, but more often they simply bitched about how the morons in the home office had mangled their copy. As yet, Kendall had little to contribute to such conversations; he kept to the edge of things and tried to look as if he belonged.

But he didn't. He knew it and he was sure that everyone else knew it. No one had ever heard of him or his magazine, and there was always the unspoken suspicion that he had somehow managed to worm his way into the action without a shred of legitimacy. There were correspondents, and then there were the tourists, and Kendall had no doubts about which group people thought he belonged in.

He had come to cover the war, but he hadn't been able to find it yet. After his arrival in Saigon, after the MACV (Military Assistance Command Vietnam) orientation sessions and the obligatory night on the town, he had signed up for the Saigon Sound and Light Show: War on the Modified American Plan, a tourist excursion to local points of interest, complete with colorful maps and an unctuous tour guide. Together with three other new arrivals and four PIOs—one per customer—Kendall choppered off into the boonies to see the war. Forty miles from downtown Saigon they landed at a base camp and were loaded onto jeeps for a ride to the front. The front turned out to be a low ridge in the distance, four or five miles off, where Vietcong snipers were thought to be active. Kendall sat in the jeep and watched the war. A squadron of Phantoms appeared as if on cue and proceeded to plaster the ridge with napalm. When the roiling orange fireballs faded, a squadron of South Vietnamese jets ("Real gung-ho pilots," said a PIO, "and quick learners.") came in and raked the ridge with rockets. Then the rumbling echoes faded, the fires subsided, the jets flew away, and everyone went home. Kendall was back in Saigon in time for lunch.

This just wasn't the way Ernie Pyle would have done it. You were supposed to trudge through the mud with the grunts, hunker down in the foxhole and share your C rations. ("Where you from, soldier?" "Brooklyn. You hear the Dodgers' score?") You were supposed to get *involved* in the damn thing. ("If I don't make it, you gotta tell Becky Sue I was thinking of her." "Sure, kid.") You were supposed to record the experience of war in spare, manly prose, preserving the earthy wisdom of smooth-cheeked privates and grizzled topkicks.

But William Bendix was nowhere to be found. Mauldin's Joe and Willie had been rotated home, replaced by stylish PR men from *New Yorker* cartoons. And where the hell was John Wayne?

Kendall's faith in his own preconceptions had never been strong, but the gap between image and reality in this place was unnerving. He had sensed the same shuddering incongruity on his first visit to the Grand Canyon; standing alone on the rim, the stark statistical dimensions of that twisted scar in the earth had mutated into a tangible space through which one might fall. Rock bottom was never as near as you thought.

Nor was Khe Sanh. Kendall moved across the compound toward the transients' building, where he and thirty other correspondents stored their gear and fought over the twenty beds and cots. Inside, the main room was dark and smelled of marijuana. The ceiling fan pushed the languid air around in lazy circles, squeaking persistently.

Kendall paused inside the door and waited for his eyes to adjust to the gloom. He made out five forms sprawled on the beds. Four of them seemed to be awake, passing around a joint.

"Have a hit?" someone asked. It was an Australian correspondent Kendall had seen around the compound.

"Uh, not right now," said Kendall. "Thanks."

"You're a disgrace to your uniform," the Aussie told him. Kendall managed a short laugh, then began searching for his gear. His uniform consisted of faded blue jeans, khaki surplus jacket, and a Fabulous Furry Freak Brothers T-shirt. With his shoulder-length brown hair and the wiry frame of a speed freak, Kendall presented an idealized image of roadside American youth, hitching to Berkeley. Kendall suspected that he might be taken more seriously as a war correspondent if he cut the hair and picked up some black market gentleman-adventurer togs, but he just couldn't see himself in one of those multipocketed Abercrombie and Fitch Jungle Jim outfits. And cutting his hair was simply out of the question.

Kendall found his rucksack under a bed. He sat down and opened the pack, making a quick check of the contents. He didn't have anything worth stealing, but in Vietnam you never knew. His first night in Saigon someone had ripped off his toothbrush and an extra pair of shoelaces.

"Leaving us?" asked the Aussie.

"I guess. I thought I'd go over to the field and find a ride up to Quangtri."

"Quangtri sucks," said one of the dope smokers, a wire service stringer.

"Indeed," agreed the Aussie. "But Quangtri is just a hop, skip, and a jump from exciting Khe Sanh. Trying the back door, are you?"

"Well," Kendall admitted, "I thought I might get lucky."

"Forget it," said the stringer. "Nobody in I Corps is gonna help you get to Khe Sanh. Some captain told me he

26

was gonna cut orders for an air strike on the next correspondent who used the words 'Khe Sanh' and 'Din Bin Phu' in the same sentence."

"Take my advice," said the Australian. "Sit down and get stoned with the rest of us. Nothing's going to happen during the holidays, anyway. Go up to Khe Sanh next week. That's when the screaming yellow hordes will descend on the plucky, outnumbered Yanks. General Giap himself is up there, you know. The Lion of Din Bin Phu is personally arranging the fall of Khe Sanh."

"Careful," said the stringer. "I think that captain was serious."

The Aussie passed the joint to Kendall, who hesitated for all of a second before taking a hit. He handed it to the stranger and exhaled slowly. Amazing dope. One toke and he felt it.

Another toke and he'd stay for a week. Kendall got up and slung the rucksack over his shoulder.

"Thanks. I'll catch you guys later."

"We'll be here," said the Aussie.

Kendall caught the Navy minibus shuttle to the airfield. Why the Navy was operating the Da Nang mass transit system was one of the many minor mysteries that Kendall preferred not to dwell on. Like so many things in Vietnam, there was no explanation for it; it just *was*.

His own presence in Vietnam was one such mystery. At odd moments the reality of it would hit him and he would look around, astonished by the profusion of military hardware and the swarms of little brown men named Nguyen. Vietnam was no longer *there*, but *here*.

A year ago he had been struggling to avoid this place. His student deferment was about to vanish and something very like panic had consumed his life. The universe began to shrink, a general collapse of matter and energy, focused on the fragile mind and body of Joe Kendall. Continents and oceans slipped into extinction, and soon nothing remained but Canada, Leavenworth, and Vietnam. A strange, warped geography to inhabit, Kendall waited there for what seemed a long time.

Medical science saved him. At his preinduction physical, a bored, sallow-faced doctor discovered a heart murmur, an unsuspected syncopation in the Kendall rhythms. They didn't need murmuring hearts, not when there were so many others with a better sense of timing and discipline. Kendall's heart wasn't good enough for this man's army. They stamped it "IV-F" and sent him home.

He had escaped the draft, but the shadow of it still fell across the skewed and tilted landscape. The universe did not snap back into its proper shape. The effect would endure long after the cause was forgotten. Kendall began to realize that he would have to live in this new land instead of merely confronting it.

But within this shrunken raisin of a world, he was suddenly free to explore, to map its contours and scale its peaks. Motion was restored and any move seemed possible; the wrong move would no longer cost him his life or his freedom.

His first move was to the beach. Following graduation, he and three friends (two were trying for conscientious objector status, the other had already burned his draft card) fled to a North Carolina coastal town for a week or a month of intense dissipation. They would return to the real world when their money ran out.

One night, stoned and sunburned, they were playing pinball in a seamy arcade when two young marines walked in. Kendall, absorbed in the flashing lights and hollow sound effects, glanced at the marines and then returned his fragile attention to the game. The next time he noticed them they were screaming obscenities at each other and trading hard, angry, open-handed shoves. They could have been no older than eighteen, if that, iron kids with jackhammer muscles and reflexes sharp as meat cleavers. Kendall had seen fights before, but never one with such awesome potential.

The manager of the arcade reached into the cashbox and withdrew a heavy, menacing pistol, a .45 service automatic. He clunked it down on the counter top. "You boys best get out of here," he said to the marines. "I won't have that shit in here."

The marines turned to stare at the manager and the gun. Their eyes were wide and confused, as if they had been slapped awake from a tenacious nightmare. One of the marines lurched awkwardly forward but halted abruptly when the manager's hand moved closer to the gun. They froze there for an expanded instant. Then the marine retreated, crablike, raging profanely at the manager. He moved on out into the neon night, his curses fading like the sound of a locomotive howling past a small town.

The second young marine seemed dazed. His eyes darted and bobbed wildly, as if there were nothing in the world that was completely safe to look at. Finally, he stumbled out the nearest exit and was gone. Kendall and his friends looked at each other and said nothing.

Half an hour later the second marine returned. Kendall and his friends were still battling the same pinball machine. The marine shyly edged toward them, trying to be unobtrusive even though there was no one else in the arcade. He watched the game over their shoulders and finally ventured a "Nice shot," after someone nailed a bonus target with a deft flip.

Kendall turned to look at the young leatherneck. He was a kid, a child, really, with the face of a thirteen-year-old pasted to the body of a middleweight prizefighter. Before boot camp he had probably been a towheaded blond; his eyes were blue and shallow, everything was right there on the surface. Kendall said hello.

Later, Kendall realized that his reluctant, casual greeting may have been the first kind word the boy had heard in months. In any case, it seemed to have been enough to unlock something inside the kid. Now that he had been granted entry into the realm of civilian conversation, the words poured out of him like Mississippi mud streaming over a levee. He didn't stop talking for an hour, and no one was about to tell him to shut up. His words were a oil-and-water blend of inarticulate adolescence and slang-ridden military argot. Kendall and his friends listened, bored and awed at the same time, conscious every second of the fact that this boy had just completed basic training in the United States Marine Corps. Presumably, he could kill all four of them without a weapon or a second thought.

His name was Larry Frost and he was from northern Minnesota and he had just turned eighteen; he'd joined up at seventeen because the judge didn't give him much of a choice and anyway, after he quit high school, there wasn't really much to do in that small town except raise hell and get into trouble, which was why he was before the judge. He'd put in for cooks school but didn't think he'd get it because he had trouble calculating how much of every-thing to use in cooking for large numbers of men, al-though he knew precisely how many days he had left in the service, four hundred eighty-nine, unless he went AWOL, which he'd been thinking about a lot lately. This was his first leave since boot camp and he needed a place to crash for the night.

Kendall felt he had no choice but to invite the kid to share floor space in their motel room. If someone needed a place to crash, you did what you could because you never knew when you'd have to ask the same of some other total stranger. It was one of the obligations of being part of the Youth Culture, the crash pad community.

So Kendall spent the night smoking dope, drinking beer, and listening to the stream of consciousness monologue of Larry Frost. Frost's main concern was sex, but he had no money and therefore no luck. He was depressed by the bad "dude to chick ratio" in this town, but there really wasn't anywhere else to go in eastern Carolina. "Dudes" and "chicks" peppered his conversation like prepositions; "boys and girls" were obsolete terms now that he was a marine, but "men and women" seemed to be beyond him, as if saying the words would be presumptuous for some-one of his age. Frost was obviously nervous about being in the company of college graduates, and Kendall and his friends were nervous about being in the company of an inarticulate trained killer. It was an odd night.

Somewhere in the midst of it all, Kendall realized that he had found something in Larry Frost: a story, waiting to be told. Kendall had written for his college paper, and now, freed of the draft, he was considering journalism as one of the vague possibilities for his future. He just didn't know how to get started. But here suddenly was Larry Frost, a story without a by-line, a Cassady waiting for his Kerouac.

When Frost departed the next morning, in search of the buddy he nearly fought in the arcade, Kendall bought a notebook and a pen and spent the day on the beach, getting it all down on paper. After eight hours in his company Kendall was confident that he knew all there was to know about Larry Frost.

"If people were bred like French poodles," Kendall wrote, "then Larry Frost would take Best of Show in the Cannon Fodder Division." He described the tense encounter in the arcade, explaining that the emotions of the young marines had boiled over from the pressure cooker of basic training: "The Marines spent six months training them to kill, making them want to kill—and then wouldn't let them kill anyone." When Larry Frost got to Vietnam, "all the officers would have to do is point him in the right direction."

Kendall thought it was a good story. So did the editors of *Rocky Road*, who bought it a month later. As a biweekly newsprint fold-over, *Rocky Road* hovered on the fringe of print journalism, fueled by record-album advertisements and the collective energy and paranoia of its young staff. It was a magazine of rock music and radical politics, two suddenly important subjects that had been orphaned by the established media. Its pages seethed with rage and rebellion and served as the only real forum for novice journalists who had more anger than skill. It was vaudeville, a place to be loud and bad. But *Rocky Road* was also a place where a true talent might suddenly blossom; it happened often enough to keep the dream alive and the circulation figures rising. Kendall caught the wave as it was breaking. After four more articles and several months of hustling, Joe Kendall became *Rocky Road*'s Southeast Asia bureau chief. He was given a press card, a ticket to Saigon, and a promise of a return ticket if the magazine didn't fold in the meantime.

The minibus deposited Kendall at the military terminal of the Da Nang airport. He waved his press badge at a bored corporal and went into the Air Ops office. Fifteen or twenty people were already there, and all of them were talking. Whenever a plane landed or took off, which happened about once a minute, everyone raised their voices to a controlled shout; when the thunder of aircraft subsided, the voices did not. Kendall paused inside the doorway and tried to make sense of the scene.

A woman in combat fatigues was standing in front of the main desk, sounding shrill and formidable. "If this film isn't in Saigon by two o'clock," she threatened, "you'll be on your way to the Delta by three." The sergeant behind the desk was not impressed. "Stuff it, lady," he told her.

Variations on that theme were being played out wall to wall. Everyone wanted to be somewhere else in a hurry and the Air Ops staffers, who weren't going anywhere, simply ducked their heads and let the waves of vitriol wash over them. To them, any place in Nam was about as bad as any other place in Nam, so it didn't make much difference if you were here or there. Either way, it was still Nam.

Kendall spotted a soldier with a clipboard, threading his way through the crowd. Clipboards, Kendall had already learned, were of fundamental importance. Nothing happened in the realm of MACV without first being registered on a printed form that was attached to somebody's clipboard. Power lay in knowing how to find the right clipboard.

Kendall slipped through a gap in the throng and snagged the soldier's elbow. "Anything to Quangtri?"

"Chopper fourteen hundred," said the soldier. "Stick around and I'll get you on it."

Kendall checked the soldier's name tag. "Thanks, Danelli," he said. Danelli nodded, then disappeared into an adjoining office. Kendall found a chair and sat down to wait.

The woman with the film stormed out of the office, elbowing bodies aside on her way to the door. Leaving, she collided with two men coming in. One of them, a captain, gave her a casual salute as she swept past. The other, a civilian, didn't seem to notice her. He was a young man of medium height and stocky build, dressed in a white shirt, tan jungle-jacket, khaki trousers sharply creased, and polished wing tip shoes.

The shoes caught Kendall's attention. Nobody in Vietnam had polished shoes, except for Green Beret colonels and Saigon press officers—and they didn't wear wing tips. These shoes were new to Vietnam.

Kendall watched the captain and the civilian make their way to a desk in the corner of the office nearest him. The civilian looked angry, but the captain bore the same I've-heard-it-all-before expression that was so common here. He sat down behind the desk and stared passively at the civilian.

From where he was sitting, a dozen feet away, Kendall could barely hear every third word. Among the words he heard were "Khe Sanh." Kendall took out his number two notebook and pretended to study it while keeping his left ear tuned to the conversation. After filtering out the roar from the runway and the angry voices in the office, Kendall was left with the impression that the civilian was in one hell of a hurry to get to Khe Sanh. The captain didn't seem to care if he got there or not.

During a momentary lull in the rumble from outside, Kendall heard the civilian insist, "You *cannot* leave it here overnight!"

"We'll have to," said the captain. "The plane we had scheduled for this took a hit on its last run. It won't be repaired until morning."

33

"Then find another one!" the civilian demanded. The thunder of an incoming jet drowned out the rest of it, but the civilian seemed to be making reference to the ranks of idle aircraft out on the runway apron. The captain, patient and cool, responded with a lengthy explanation of the mechanics of aircraft allocation. Kendall began to lose interest. He sympathized with the civilian, but he knew the inevitable verdict on flights to Khe Sanh: you can't get there from here.

The civilian pulled a white envelope out of his jacket. He opened it, unfolded a letter, and held it in front of the captain's face. When the captain reached for it, the civilian abruptly pulled it away. He clearly did not want the letter to leave his hand. The captain gave the civilian a sour look, then examined the letter while the civilian dangled it in front of him. The captain's eyes suddenly opened wide. His mouth sagged a little. He reached for the letter again, but the civilian, almost defiantly, folded it up and put it back in his pocket.

Kendall watched them out of the corner of his eye. The captain had been transformed; whatever was in that letter was potent stuff. The captain was suddenly respectful, obedient, and eager to please. Kendall heard the word "sir" three times in ten seconds. The captain got to his feet, moved swiftly around the desk, and tried to open a path to the door for the civilian. As they passed him, Kendall heard the captain say, "You'll be on your way in an hour, Mr. Poole."

The captain and Mr. Poole left the Air Ops office. Kendall looked around to see if anyone else had noticed them, but apparently he was the only one. Kendall put his notebook away and casually walked toward the door.

Wing tip shoes and a high-voltage letter. Something was going on. Kendall decided that a good war correspondent would investigate, a story was in the air. He would get to the bottom of it.

The story, whatever it might be, was a secondary consideration. The important point was that there was going to be an unscheduled flight to Khe Sanh. With a little luck and imagination Kendall might find a way to get aboard. He had to get to Khe Sanh, and he had to do it soon.

Larry Frost was at Khe Sanh. Marines were dying there every day, and Kendall was haunted by the thought that Larry Frost could be one of them. Larry Frost's death would be a tragedy if it happened before Kendall could get there to cover it.

Chapter Three

Turner Poole was having the time of his life. Vietnam was turning out to be more fun than he'd have thought possible.

Poole knew he had a streak of natural perversity in him; he frequently found his fun in unexpected places. He always enjoyed his trips into the Mexican slums of Houston and Beaumont where Breeze Woodward owned vast tracts of property. Those trips, often in the company of a deputy sheriff, were a source of weird exhilaration. One would think there was no particular thrill in kicking entire jabbering families into the street—not that they'd stay there long—but the act itself carried a palpable electric charge for him. To pound on the door and announce to those dark faces in the musty hallways that he, Turner Poole, was about to initiate a profound change in their lives, to be the agent of upheaval and shock, to rattle the comfortable cages of the unsuspecting and ignorant was, for Poole, a species of fun.

Breeze called it *juice*. "When you got the juice, you got the goose," Breeze said frequently, the goose being the one that laid the golden eggs. For Breeze it was always the end product that mattered, gold or guano. But Poole found the juice in the process itself. Breeze knew it and was happy to let Poole handle the details of the Pershing Patrol, which was Breeze's name for the Mexican eviction proceedings. Breeze had gone along on the original Pershing Patrol with Black Jack himself, chasing Villa all over northern Mexico in 1916. Breeze talked about it a lot, but always insisted that they should have stayed long enough to chomp off a chunk of Mexican meat and swallow it whole, chili beans, hot peppers, and all. That image didn't do much for Poole one way or another, but he thought it would have been fun just to *go*.

And it *was* fun. He'd received VIP treatment all the way across the Pacific, even though no one knew who he was or why he was so important. Each day hundreds, even thousands, of people arrived in Vietnam, but on this day only Turner Poole carried a letter from Lyndon B. Johnson in his pocket. He didn't show it to anyone, but he knew it was there, and somehow other people seemed to sense its presence. It added to his dimensions, made him taller, like a pair of cowboy boots.

He changed planes at Guam, boarding the C-141 that would take him to Da Nang. The crew treated him with respect that was truly impressive. They knew he was somehow connected to the two metal canisters that had been loaded aboard in the dead of night on a far corner of the runway. They looked at Poole and they looked at the canisters, and they asked no questions.

Poole casually inspected the canisters and nodded thoughtfully, as if ticking off points on a mental checklist. The canisters were dull gray, six feet long, and about nine inches in diameter. No one but Poole knew what was in them.

After landing at Da Nang, he finally met someone else who seemed to know about the canisters. The C-141 shuddered to a halt on the runway apron, the whine of the engines died, and the crew quickly departed, leaving Poole alone in the cavernous tail section. A few moments later a tall, leather-faced officer boarded. He stared wordlessly at Poole, then walked past him, toward the spot where the canisters lay. They were packed in open-gridwork metal frames that looked as if they had been constructed from a piece of chain-link fence. The officer cautiously tapped a boot against one of the frames.

"Strange way to ship them."

"They're supposed to be kept cool," Poole informed him.

The officer didn't seem interested in this. He kicked one of the frames lightly, then turned back to Poole. No introductions had been made, but the man's name tag read, Kleinsdorf. He wore no insignia on his olive drab fatigues, but Poole supposed that he was at least a colonel, possibly a brigadier.

"You have instructions?" Kleinsdorf asked him.

"I was told someone would meet me at Da Nang. I assume that's you . . . General?"

Kleinsdorf acknowledged the identification and rank with a quick twitch of his jaw muscles. His eyes seemed to be focusing on a point about two feet behind Poole's head.

"I don't like this," he said.

Poole had already decided not to be impressed by generals or anyone else. If Kleinsdorf didn't like it, that was his problem. Turner Poole and Lyndon Johnson didn't care whether Kleinsdorf liked it or not.

"I don't like it at all," Kleinsdorf repeated.

Poole waited.

"Suppose this plane had crashed."

"It didn't," Poole said simply.

"This is Vietnam, mister. Planes crash all the time. They get shot down. They get mortared on the runways. Hangars and warehouses get rocketed. This isn't some goddamn test range in Utah. It's Nam."

"I noticed that."

"I'll just bet you did. In country all of ten minutes, haven't even gotten off the goddamn plane, and already you're an expert on Southeast Asia. We've seen your kind before, mister. Pentagon paper-pushers, with your charts and graphs and computer printouts. You know all about it, don't you? You've got it all down on paper, right down to the last pint of blood. You know . . . blood? That's the red stuff that—"

"Spare me the crap, General. Let's just get on with it, shall we?"

Poole stared him down. It was easy. The letter in his pocket gave him powers, a big red S under his Clark Kent clothing. Juice.

Kleinsdorf wilted, shrank, and looked away. He stared at the canisters for another moment.

"I absolutely do not like this shit."

"Like it or not, it's yours now, General."

Kleinsdorf pivoted sharply and pointed a long, bony finger at Poole. "Get it straight, mister. It's yours. My orders were to make preparations at this end and give you all necessary assistance. How I carry out those orders is up to my discretion. You don't tell me what to do."

The general withdrew the accusing finger. The steam had gone out of him. Poole knew what was coming next. Impotent rage was always followed by grudging compliance. This general, twice his age, was no different from the wetback tenants he routinely evicted. Poole, the mover and shaker, was in his element.

"I won't have this shit here," Kleinsdorf said in a more subdued tone. "One mortar round in the wrong spot and . . . Jesus. I get sick just thinking about it. I'm not about to store that stuff near so many of my people."

"Where you keep it is up to you, General."

"Damn straight, it is. If they want to use this stuff to save Khe Sanh, then that's where it's going. Khe Sanh. I've arranged for a plane. See Captain Reynolds at Air Ops."

Kleinsdorf started to leave, but Poole grabbed his elbow. "Khe Sanh? Are you serious?"

Kleinsdorf briskly disengaged himself from Poole's grasp. "You'll find that general officers in a war zone are almost invariably serious. I suggest you remember that, mister."

"But Khe Sanh? Will it be safe there?"

"It'll be as safe as those men at Khe Sanh."

"And how safe is that?"

Kleinsdorf smiled bitterly. "That's the sixty-four-dollar question, isn't it?"

The general strode toward the exit.

"Wait a minute," Poole called. "Is that it? Don't I sign anything?"

"You must be joking."

"Well, what happens at Khe Sanh?"

"You'll be met."

Kleinsdorf paused at the doorway. He looked back at Poole and fixed him with a cold, even stare.

"You never saw me, mister. I wasn't here. We've never met. Got it?"

Kleinsdorf didn't wait for an answer. He disappeared into the dazzling sunlight outside the plane. Poole stood in the shadows, alone with his cargo.

He hadn't counted on this. Johnson had said nothing about going to Khe Sanh. But that would be just like him, Poole figured. The President had got half a million men into Vietnam deviously, and he would hardly change the pattern for one more.

Still, it might be interesting. Khe Sanh was surrounded, but it wasn't Corregidor, it wasn't—Johnson to the contrary—the Alamo. Five thousand marines held Khe Sanh, and they weren't all going to get killed in one afternoon. The odds were with him.

Kleinsdorf, now that he was gone, was amusing. Poole wished that the confrontation had lasted longer, or that the general had a little more spine. Poole would have enjoyed showing him the letter. Having the juice was fine, but the real kick came from using it. The use of the juice. He'd have to try that one on Breeze.

Captain Reynolds was no problem. Kleinsdorf hadn't told him anything except that he should schedule a special flight into Khe Sanh. The plane Reynolds had reserved was peppered by shrapnel on its last trip out of Khe Sanh, and Reynolds automatically postponed the next flight. Poole let the argument run for a while, savoring the moment when he would haul out his heavy artillery. When it came, Reynolds was knocked flat. It was total, unconditional surrender to a superior force. Reynolds would have given Poole a B-52 if he'd asked for one.

Poole settled for a prop-jet transport. Reynolds found a plane and a crew to fly it in less than ten minutes. Poole wondered how long it would have taken without the letter.

Poole thought about that while he stood on the baking concrete outside the hangar where his plane was being readied. Without the letter with LBJ's signature, he would be just another civilian wandering around in the middle of a war. He would command no attention, no respect.

Turner Poole was not an imposing figure, and he knew it. At twenty-eight, his fine, sand-colored hair was already getting thin on top, a fact that made him grateful that long hair was becoming fashionable, even for people who weren't hippies. He could comb what he had over the places where his naked scalp was exposed. His face, however, he could do nothing about. It was a face that belonged to an accountant or a bank teller. It was a face that resolved to maximum definition at a distance of about ten feet; getting closer added nothing of interest to the picture. His voice was flat and slightly nasal, limited in range. He lacked the deeper resonances that gave a voice authority. His body was a standard model, medium-size bones covered with medium-thick flesh.

The real Turner Poole looked nothing like the one the world saw. Inside, there was a bristly, swaggering, rawboned Turner Poole who could kick ass with the best of them. That was the Turner Poole at the controls, the one who turned on the juice.

Except . . . it was borrowed juice. It was Breeze Woodward's money or Lyndon Johnson's power, on temporary loan to young Turner Poole. He was a conduit, not a dynamo. It was probably more fun being the instrument of all that juice than being the owner, but Poole's access to it could be cut off at any moment. One minor screwup, and Poole could be back on the pavement, a pawn instead of a knight.

The shadow of that dark possibility never entirely left him. Like a superstitious atheist, Poole was never quite sure that his fate was in his own hands. He felt like the moon, shining reflected light from a distant source, living in dread of an eclipse.

Poole stood by himself, leaning against the corrugated metal wall of the hangar. He stared at the distant green horizon and, for a moment, allowed himself to be frightened by this place. A narrow trail of black smoke curled upward from the green, marking the spot where someone had probably just died.

Here, the juice was no abstraction. It was a tangible, indispensable secretion, and people died from the lack of it. You couldn't borrow it, and the medics didn't keep supplies of it in their kits, along with their bottles of plasma and whole blood. Poole knew that there were men here who thrived on the juice, were addicted to it. The lurps, the long-range recon patrols, those were the guys who knew about the juice and couldn't get enough of it. They spent weeks in the boonies, and when pulled out of combat, they prowled the streets of Saigon and Da Nang like restless wraiths, impatient to return to their netherworld. They had fallen in love with life on the edge, where the juice flowed like blood and blood flowed like rainwater.

How would it be, Poole wondered, to feel that way all the time?

And how would it be not to feel that way at all?

Poole tugged at the collar of his shirt, peeling the fabric away from his sweaty skin. The day was hot and close and reminded him of Houston.

He watched a group of a half-dozen ground crewmen approaching the hangar. They moved at a tropical pace, loose and unhurried. When they reached the hangar door, one of the group split off and walked directly toward Poole. He wasn't part of the ground crew, Poole realized. He wore blue jeans, a fatigue jacket, long hair, and a canvas rucksack: a civilian. He stopped a few feet away from Poole and grinned shyly.

"Hi," said the civilian.

"Hi, yourself," said Poole.

"I'm Joe Kendall." The young man offered a hand for Poole to shake.

Poole accepted the stranger's hand, mainly because he couldn't think of a good reason not to. "I'm Turner Poole," he said.

"Headed for Khe Sanh, huh?"

Poole released Kendall's hand and eyed him warily. "What makes you think so?"

Kendall grinned again. He had a boyish, aw-shucks manner about him that seemed terribly out of context here.

"I was in the Air Ops office," Kendall explained. "I'm sorry, I couldn't help overhearing a little. You seemed to be in kind of a hurry to get to Khe Sanh. I noticed because I'm trying to get there myself."

Poole examined Kendall's civilian clothes again. Partially hidden by the fatigue jacket, a Fabulous Furry Freak Brothers T-shirt adorned the kid's chest. Long brown hair lapped over his collar.

"What the hell are you doing here?"

"Here? Well, I . . . oh, you mean Vietnam? I'm sorry, I should have said something. I'm a correspondent for a magazine in the States. Here, I'll show you my press card."

"Don't bother," said Poole. "A correspondent, huh? Who for?"

Poole thought he heard Kendall sigh. "*Rocky Road*," Kendall told him. "It's a rock music magazine."

"Sure. I've seen it. That's the newsprint job with the psychedelic lettering, right?"

"I'll be damned! You must be the only person in Nam who's even heard of it. Just get in?"

"About an hour ago."

"First trip?"

Poole nodded. He was beginning to feel a little uncomfortable about talking with this kid. Kendall seemed to be leading up to something. The last thing Poole needed was an inquisitive journalist dogging his steps. On the other hand, Kendall was obviously no Scotty Reston. He wasn't even a Halberstam.

"*Rocky Road*, huh?"

"Yeah. It's basically a music mag, but we try to write about other things that affect our readers."

"Sounds reasonable. So you're here to expose the whole sordid truth about the war?"

"Not really. I just write about the guys who are fighting it, you know? That's why I'm going to Khe Sanh. There's a marine there that I did a piece on a few months ago, and I just want to sort of keep tabs on him. I leave the big geopolitical stuff to the wire services."

"Stephen Crane instead of Tolstoi."

"Well, I didn't really think of it in those terms."

"Why not? Nothing wrong with a little ambition."

"Right now, my only ambition is to get to Khe Sanh."

"That about sums up my plans at the moment, too. Have you been there before?"

"Not lately," said Kendall.

"I hear the planes don't even stop. They just unload them on the run."

"They're pretty good at it, though."

"They'd have to be, I guess."

Poole stuffed his hands into his pockets and scuffed his shoe against the concrete. He wasn't sure how to play it with Kendall. So far, the conversation had been casual, but journalists could be devious. Did the kid already know something? Poole didn't see how that could be possible; if LBJ kept his own generals in the dark, how could some hippie reporter find out anything? Kendall didn't even seem particularly interested in what Poole was doing here.

There was a faint whiff of the juice in this, Poole realized. Danger, in whatever form, was readily available here. If Johnson could see him chatting amiably with a reporter, he'd probably castrate him with a rusty coat hanger. But Johnson wasn't likely to find out, and Poole felt an illicit thrill in the act of putting one over on the President. He skimmed a little from Breeze now and then; maybe he could play the same kind of games with Lyndon Johnson.

In fact, it was the kind of game that Johnson himself would play. Cultivate the young people, the President had said. Well, here was a certified young person, ripe for cul-

44

tivating. It wouldn't hurt to begin building bridges in other directions. If this operation went badly wrong, Poole might need a sympathetic ear in the press corps, even an ear that was hidden under Beatle-length hair. In the meantime, Kendall seemed harmless.

"Is there something I can do for you, Joe?" Poole asked.

"Well, as a matter of fact, I was looking for a ride over to Khe Sanh. I was on a morning flight, but we never got off the runway. One of the engines was overheating, so we turned back. When I heard you were going there, I thought . . . well, I hoped maybe I could hitch a lift."

"Is that the way it works here?" It seemed pretty casual to Poole.

"Oh, yeah," Kendall said quickly. "Correspondents get space available all over the country. Sometimes you get lucky, sometimes you don't. The networks and big papers can pretty well write their own ticket, but I—"

"Depend on the kindness of strangers?"

"That's about right." Kendall laughed.

"Well, hell, I've been there myself. As long as you were going there anyway, I guess it'll be all right."

"Thanks. I really appreciate it."

"There's just one rule."

"What's that?"

"No questions."

Poole didn't wait for Kendall to respond. He walked into the hangar toward the waiting plane, listening to Kendall's footsteps a couple of yards behind him. He'd got the hook in. Kendall now knew that Turner Poole was a man of some importance and no little mystery. It suited Poole's image of himself.

Khe Sanh sat astride the knobby spine of Vietnam, less than an hour's flight from Da Nang. Poole and Kendall saw little of the intervening territory; the land was cloaked with low, gray clouds that seemed to stick together like clots of sooty cotton.

Poole sat with his back to the wall, disdaining the uninspiring view that was available through the small, scratched window behind him. Kendall sat opposite him, leafing through a notebook with studied nonchalance. The drone of the engines made conversation difficult, so little was said.

The two cargo handlers, enlisted men, kept to themselves near the rear of the plane. Poole watched them and noticed that they casually ignored the two canisters that comprised the only cargo. The canisters were strapped to wooden pallets that could be shoved out of the plane in only a few seconds. All cargo bound for Khe Sanh received the same treatment, and if the enlisted men suspected that this shipment was a very special delivery, they gave no sign of it.

Kendall also ignored the canisters. Poole doubted that his admonition about asking questions was responsible. Kendall seemed to have a lot on his mind, and the mysterious mission of Turner Poole probably didn't have a very high priority. Poole felt his importance shrinking in direct proportion to their increasing distance from Da Nang. And Washington. The letter from Lyndon Johnson was turning light and brittle in his pocket. Paper does not stop bullets.

Poole smiled to himself. How did it go, again? Paper covers rock, scissors cut paper, and . . . what did rocks do? They broke scissors, he thought. Kids' games. A circular, self-devouring ecology. There were strengths and weaknesses in whatever choice you made, so the only defense was the right choice. The wrong one brought a sharp-knuckled jab in the fleshy part of the upper arm. Some kids spent their entire childhood sporting ugly purple bruises. Poole wasn't one of them. He knew how to play the game.

A young lieutenant came back from the flight deck and interrupted Poole's thoughts. He was holding a pair of helmets and two khaki flak jackets.

"Excuse me, sir," he said. "You'll be needing these when we hit Khe Sanh. In fact, I'd suggest you put them on right now. We're getting close."

The lieutenant handed Poole a helmet. It was a classic

GI steel pot, heavier than it looked. Poole thought it would look ridiculous on his head, so he put it down on his lap.

"A lot of guys put 'em there," said the lieutenant, cracking a knowing smile. "But considering that we're up here and Charlie's down there, you might be better off sitting on it, if you know what I mean."

Poole knew what he meant and was annoyed. He grabbed the helmet, plopped it down on his skull, and glared angrily at the boy officer. The lieutenant's smile disappeared. He offered Poole a flak jacket.

Poole started to take it, but stopped when he noticed that someone had scribbled obscene slogans all over it with a ball-point pen. "I'll take the other one," he said. The lieutenant shrugged and handed him the other jacket. This one was inscribed, Born to Be Wild.

"Where did these come from?"

"You don't want to know, sir." The lieutenant turned, tossed the remaining helmet and jacket to Kendall, then went back to the cockpit.

Poole put the flak jacket on and felt no safer for it. As he watched Kendall fumbling with his own jacket he wondered, for the first time, just what the hell he was doing here.

The plane banked sharply to the left, and Poole was nearly thrown out of his seat. He recovered, only to be thrown the other way as the plane maneuvered again. He grabbed at the webbing of his seat belt and buckled it tightly.

Outside the window Khe Sanh materialized from the gray clouds. A grubby little citadel surrounded by squat, hulking mountains, the place looked like a condemned construction site. Clusters of sandbag walls and corrugated huts dotted the rough landscape. Directly below the plane a maze of earthen trenches snaked toward the runway.

"I thought trenches went out with World War One," Poole said loudly, so Kendall could hear him.

"I don't think those are ours," Kendall said.

MARK WASHBURN

Poole quickly turned and looked again. He could see people in those trenches.

"I'll be damned. Vietcong."

"NVA regulars, more likely," said Kendall.

"I didn't think I'd actually *see* them. Have you? I mean, have you seen them before?"

"Not alive," Kendall told him.

Poole stared at Kendall for a moment. Maybe there was more to this hippie than he thought. Or maybe this was simply what war did: it created categories. Those who had seen the enemy and those who hadn't, those who had been fired on and those who hadn't, those who had been hit . . . and Turner Poole, smug and unsullied.

He felt the juice again, with a heart-skipping rush. It was remarkable how much it could sometimes resemble fear.

Poole crossed his arms and kneaded his left bicep with his knuckles. He smiled. Two for flinching, he thought.

The plane plunged toward the runway in a steep, shrieking dive, flared at the last possible moment, and returned to the earth in a jarring series of bounces. The enemy gunners let it land unmolested, knowing they would have a better shot at it a few minutes later when it lumbered back into the sky. In the meantime, a well-placed or lucky mortar round might dispose of the plane while it was still on the ground. The charred debris of an earlier victim lay in a twisted pile by one side of the runway.

The rear cargo bay doors opened while the plane was still rolling. Poole unfastened his seat belt and made his way back to the canisters. The enlisted men were already loosening the straps that anchored the mesh frames of the shipping cartons.

"Are we going to stop?" Poole asked them.

"Have to," one of them said sullenly. He looked at Poole accusingly.

"You'll wait for me, right? This shouldn't take more than a couple of minutes."

"A lot can happen around here in a couple of minutes."

48

The airman turned his head and spat out the back of the plane, as if to show what he thought of Khe Sanh or, perhaps, Poole.

The plane taxied briskly for a few more seconds, then executed a sharp pivot to the left, rolled another twenty yards, and came to a halt. The airmen instantly threw out a metal ramp, secured it, and began manhandling the two wooden pallets.

The young lieutenant had come back from the flight deck. He bent down to get a better angle of view at the ramshackle base and the threatening hills around it.

"Lieutenant," said Poole, "I want you to wait until I get things straightened out here. Someone is supposed to be meeting me."

"Then why don't you get the hell down there and meet him?" The officer fixed Poole with an angry, impatient stare. The courtesy and subservience he had encountered at every stop from Washington to Da Nang had vanished. Entirely different rules seemed to apply here.

Kendall approached the ramp and paused next to Poole. He turned to the lieutenant to thank him, but the officer wasn't interested in gratitude.

"What the hell are you waiting for? Move your ass, damn it!"

The correspondent nodded, then moved cautiously down the ramp, following the canisters. Poole thought about lacing into the lieutenant for his rudeness, but realized that it would only be interpreted as another needless delay.

"Wait right here," Poole told him. Without waiting for a reply, he strode down the ramp.

Four unkempt marines were already wrestling the pallet onto the tines of a forklift. The airmen scrambled back up the ramp and into the plane, like mice racing to the nearest hole. The plane's four engines were still turning, loud and angry. The pilot seemed to be revving up each of them in turn, like a driver pressing down on the accelerator while waiting for a light to change.

Twenty yards to the right a camouflage-mottled helicopter sat, rotors whirring. Someone in full combat gear, M-

16 slung over his shoulder, emerged and began trotting toward Poole.

Poole tried to take in the scene. He did a slow three-sixty and gazed at the dark mountains beyond the warren of bunkers and sandbags. He felt as if he were standing in the bottom of a huge bowl. He was no military expert, but he didn't need to be one to see that this would be a god-awful place to try to defend against a determined attacker. There was no place to hide here, nowhere to run.

He had heard it said that the hills around Khe Sanh displayed seven distinct shades of green foliage, but on this gray day it all looked as if the Marines had spray-painted the world a standard olive drab. Wispy tongues of clouds cleaved off some of the mountaintops, giving the impression of an unfinished canvas, the work of some gargantuan artist who had quit in disgust, appalled by the ugliness of his creation.

And it was cold here. Fiftyish, with an aimless breeze bringing languid drops of rain that plopped silently into the metal links of the runway.

Kendall stood next to him, adjusting his helmet, looking lost.

The soldier from the helicopter reached him. He wore captain's bars and a three-day growth of beard. His flak jacket was festooned with hand grenades and extra clips for his M-16.

"Mr. Poole? I'm Captain Bascomb. The chopper's waiting."

"For what?"

"For you, sir. Colonel Weiss is up at Hill Six fifty-one."

"Where's that?"

Bascomb pointed toward the horizon. "About ten klicks. He wants you to meet him there."

"Why can't he meet me here?"

The corners of Bascomb's mouth turned down slightly. "Orders, sir."

"Whose orders?"

"His."

Poole thought he saw a look of contempt flicker across

50

Bascomb's face. Was it directed at him, or was it just standard Marine arrogance? Well, if Bascomb needed orders, then by God, he would show him some orders that would make his eyes pop. Poole reached for the letter in his pocket.

A loud, reverberating *thump* pierced the drone of the airplane's engines. The runway shook beneath Poole's feet. A hundred yards beyond the helicopter, a column of black smoke and uprooted earth was rising into the air.

Bascomb whirled around like a startled gopher. He readjusted his helmet and turned back to Poole.

"Shit, this plane has been sitting here for ninety seconds. What the hell do they think they're doing?" Bascomb stuck two fingers in his mouth and whistled like a traffic cop. He raised his right arm and rotated it in tight, quick circles.

The lieutenant on the plane waved in affirmation, then darted toward the cockpit. The ramp had already been retracted. Seconds later the plane began to roll.

"Wait a minute!" Poole protested. "I told them to—"

"*You* told them? Who the fuck do you think you are? I think you'd better get on that chopper. I think you'd better do it right now, mister. We're going to Hill Six fifty-one."

Kendall suddenly intruded. "Hill Six fifty-one? That's where I'm headed."

Bascomb looked at him incredulously. "And who the hell are *you?*"

Kendall fumbled for his press card. "I'm Joe Kendall. I'm a correspondent and—"

"Christ! Is the circus in town? Is he with you?"

"Not exactly," said Poole.

Kendall turned to Poole. "How about it? I really need to get there. Can I hitch a lift?"

Poole didn't know what to say. Things were happening too fast for him to figure all the angles. All he knew for sure was that his plane was already roaring down the runway without him. He felt naked.

Bascomb grabbed Poole by the flak jacket and started him moving toward the helicopter. "Colonel Weiss is waiting."

"What about him?"

"You can take your white-haired old grandmother if you want. Just get on the goddamn chopper . . . *sir*."

There didn't seem to be much point in fighting it. Poole had the feeling that irredeemable mistakes had already been made, and this was not the time and place to try to unravel it all. He doubted that even the letter from Lyndon Johnson would help. Bascomb looked like a Republican.

Chapter Four

Joe Kendall felt his gut heave alarmingly as the chopper sprang into the air, tilted its nose down, and shot forward. He didn't like roller coasters and he was beginning to hate helicopters.

He sat on the aft-facing metal bench, balanced on his tailbone, cheeks as tight as a clenched fist. The sliding doors of the chopper were wide open, giving Kendall a partial view of what he was leaving behind. The horizon lurched to crazy angles as the Huey bobbed and weaved out of the bowl of Khe Sanh. Bascomb was perched on the bench opposite him, M-16 cradled in his lap. A young black enlisted man covered the door to the left, his eyes roving over the passing terrain. Between them Turner Poole was hanging onto some webbing; every few seconds he licked his lips and inhaled deeply. The floor space separating the benches was taken by the two gray canisters, nesting silently in their mesh cages.

The black marine brought his left hand up to the stock of his weapon and fired a long burst, spraying bullets like a fireman hosing down the last embers of a stubborn blaze. Kendall looked down, but could see nothing moving in the brown blur below them. Poole seemed startled by the sudden chattering of the M-16.

"Keeps them honest," Bascomb shouted. He fired a short burst of his own.

Kendall's nerves were clawing at him. Just to be doing something, he took out his notebook and pen.

"Where are you from?" he yelled to Bascomb.

The marine slowly brought his gaze back from the open doorway and fixed it on Kendall. Bascomb was about thirty and had brown eyes. He didn't blink very often.

"Roanoke, Virginia," Bascomb said, just loudly enough to be heard. Kendall tried to write it down, but the pen skipped wildly over the paper.

"Family?"

"Yeah," he said slowly. "I got a family."

"How long have you been here?"

Bascomb had already lost interest. He turned once again to the outside. Kendall couldn't bring himself to look in that direction, so he turned to Poole.

Poole, his timing bad, was propping one foot against the framework of one of the cages. Kendall followed the movement, then looked up at Poole's face. Somehow, that inadvertent motion had raised the question of the canisters.

After lying his way onto the plane at Da Nang, Kendall had been reluctant to push his luck by asking about the canisters. The situation was too awkward to stand much probing. Kendall was where he shouldn't have been, and so, he suspected, was Poole.

Whatever Poole was up to, he seemed to have provoked the resentment of a lot of people.

Kendall's main job now, he realized, was to avoid making waves. Encounters with authority were to be avoided. If the brass discovered him in Khe Sanh, the eleventh man in a ten-man game, they might pull his MACV card and boot him out of the country altogether.

On the other hand, he was pleased to have got this far. Back in the Da Nang press center, correspondents took endless delight in telling each other how they had one-upped the military, pulling off journalistic coups under the very noses of officers who would have ordered summary

54

executions if they had only known what was really going on. Reputations—even legends—grew from such feats. Kendall imagined himself strolling casually into the press center. Where have I been? Oh, I was up at Khe Sanh for a few days. How did I get there? Sorry, trade secret.

The ultimate standard, though, was not where you went, but what you brought back. The story. A day in the life of Larry Frost, marine grunt. If he was still here, if he was still alive. Even in his most dedicated fantasies Kendall couldn't quite mold Larry Frost into Pulitzer material.

But Turner Poole might be the genuine article. Poole seemed to be a catalyst for all sorts of unusual behavior. The man himself was ordinary enough, but his luggage was not run-of-the-mill American Tourister.

Hell, he thought, they might just be tanks of acetylene. Or nitrous oxide, maybe. Now *that* would be a story for *Rocky Road*. Laughing gas for the marines to keep that devil-may-care smile on their faces as they confronted certain death. The Japanese used to get blasted on rice wine before banzai charges; the Afghans and Kazaks and the wild folk of central Asia went into battle stoked to the gills on hashish. But for the American soldier in Vietnam, a technological high, better dying through chemistry.

Kendall was almost willing to believe it. At the very least, he could use it as a joke, an opening wedge to the forbidden subject of the canisters.

But the thunder of the whirling rotors made conversation, much less an interview, all but impossible. Poole didn't look as if he wanted to talk, anyway. His face was gray and sagging. He was either very scared or very airsick, possibly both.

The helicopter dived suddenly. Bascomb fired another burst out the door. The ground outside got very close, then receded again as the chopper angled upward, following the contour of what had to be Hill 651. Kendall started to slide off the bench and had to brace his feet against the canister containers. Poole gave him a quick, sharp glance.

The chopper tilted up, almost to a stall, then straightened out and descended to a feather-soft landing.

55

Bascomb and the enlisted man hopped out immediately, leaving Poole and Kendall staring blankly at each other, wondering what they should do next. Kendall figured it out quickly. The helicopter was a fat, sitting target for anyone within range; that was why the marines had exited so hastily.

Kendall stepped around the canisters and jumped out onto the muddy soil of Hill 651. Poole emerged a moment later, ducking his head against the possibility of having it cleaved off by the rotor blades. It was an instinctive move, but it wasn't really necessary. Kendall walked briskly away from the helicopter and Poole followed close behind.

Hill 651 wasn't much to look at. There was a central cluster of sandbags, outlining what was apparently the command bunker; radio antennas sprouted from its corrugated roof. Scattered around the sprawling dome of the hill were smaller concentrations of sandbags and corrugated huts, some of them connected by shallow trenches.

They had landed on what Kendall judged to be the southeast side of the summit. The slope here was steep, falling away from the graded helicopter pad. The crest of the hill was more like a ridge, running in an S curve to the northwest. The command bunker was positioned at the first turn in the S; beyond it the ridge narrowed to a causeway a few meters wide. The top of the S blended into the peak of another, slightly higher hill. Kendall saw the barrels of cannon poking through camouflage netting that was strung around most of the visible perimeter of the other hilltop.

Halfway down the slopes a meandering line of concertina wire marked the edge of American turf. Below it dense green vegetation blanketed the hillside, extending down into the mist-shrouded valleys. Above, the protean gray clouds hovered barely a hundred feet over Kendall's head.

He turned slowly, taking it all in. He stopped when Poole reentered his field of view. Poole was making his own survey, which ended when he turned around to face

Kendall again. They exchanged awkward, embarrassed grins.

"A real vacation paradise," Poole declared.

"Lavish. Lush."

"Where the hell is everybody?"

"Keeping their heads down, I guess." Very few marines were in evidence. Bascomb already had a squad busy transferring the canisters to the back of a jeep, but Kendall and Poole seemed to be the only people standing idly in the open. Kendall realized there was probably a very good reason for this, and began looking for someplace to hide. But Poole started moving toward the jeep, and Kendall decided he might as well follow.

"So what's in them?" he asked abruptly. "Laughing gas to keep the troops happy?"

Poole paused and turned toward Kendall. His lips began to form a word, but a hoarse shout from Bascomb cut him short.

"Incoming!"

Kendall heard a shrill, whistling sound that was many octaves higher than the insistent beat of the helicopter's blades. He dropped to the mud and tried to make himself flat. His helmet bounced away, and as he scrambled to retrieve it, he saw a pair of wing tip shoes standing next to him an inch deep in the mud. Kendall grabbed Poole's ankles and pulled. Poole and the mortar shell hit the ground at the same instant.

The concussion bounced Kendall's head out of the mud and back into it. His right cheekbone hit something hard. Warm pebbles and mud-clots rained down on him, banging rhythmically on the helmet that should have been covering his head. The drizzle faded away, and Kendall realized he was still clutching Poole's ankles.

Kendall released his grip and pushed himself up to hands and knees. Poole was still flat on his back, arms crossed tightly over his face. By the time he brought them away, a worried Bascomb was kneeling over him.

"You okay, Mr. Poole?"

Poole didn't seem to know. He took inventory of his

57

arms and legs and concluded that nothing was missing. Propping himself up to sitting position, he looked around warily. A small, smoking pothole had blossomed about ten yards away.

Bascomb looked at Kendall briefly, then turned back to Poole, helping him get to his feet.

"You can be glad you brought this guy along," said Bascomb.

Kendall felt a warm flush creeping into his cheeks. From someone like Bascomb, the comment was the closest thing to praise he was likely to hear.

Poole still seemed a little dazed. He busied himself brushing dirt from his clothes.

"You'd better get in the jeep, Mr. Poole," said Bascomb. "I'm supposed to deliver you to Colonel Weiss in one piece."

"Where are we going?"

Bascomb pointed to the hill at the far end of the causeway. "The colonel's up in the French bunker. Grenoble, we call it. Let's move it, Mr. Poole."

Poole let Bascomb take him by the elbow and lead him to the jeep. Poole shakily sat down on the right while Bascomb got behind the wheel.

Before Bascomb could put the jeep in gear, Poole looked back at Kendall, standing alone on the hilltop.

"Joe," he called, "if you ever get to Houston, dinner's on me." Poole gave a waving salute as the jeep sped away.

Kendall watched the jeep for a few moments. "People come and go so quickly here," he mumbled.

Poole and the story, whatever it was, had got away from him. Hotshot journalist that he was, he had learned exactly nothing about the mysterious canisters. A week from now, or a year, he would probably read all the answers in a *New York Times* story.

He remembered that he was still standing in the open. It was time to get moving, time to find Larry Frost.

Kendall walked to the nearest bunker, a hootch dug into a hollow. The low, corrugated metal roof was propped up on the sandbagged entrance. A stenciled wooden sign above the open door read, Holiday Inn. As he ducked under the sign, the odor of marijuana hit him. Christ, he thought, it's everywhere.

The interior of the hut was square, perhaps twenty feet on a side, and was illuminated by a single unfrosted light bulb. It reminded him a little of the transients' quarters at Da Nang, except that the ceiling was barely six feet high. A dozen marines were sitting on cots or the bare earth floor. In the sharp shadows cast by the light bulb, they all looked like elderly Chinese huddling in an opium den.

The marines stared at him in silence. Kendall stared back, shifting from face to face in search of Larry Frost or, at least, some marginally human reaction. But the marines just stared, the way the Philippine natives might have stared at Magellan before they ate him.

"Any of you guys know Larry Frost?"

There was no reaction.

"He was supposed to be here. I mean, the last I heard he was at Hill Six fifty-one. That's here, right?"

The unchanging silence gave Kendall a sudden chill down his spine.

"He didn't . . . he's not . . . not . . ." Kendall trailed off, not knowing how to phrase the question. The etiquette of death was precise and unforgiving.

One of the marines stirred. From his spot on the ground, back against the rear wall of the hootch, he straightened a little and lifted his rifle. He propped it against his right knee, the barrel angled toward the low ceiling in the general direction of Kendall's head.

"You wipe your feet, man?"

Kendall looked at him uncomprehendingly. The marine shifted the M-16 more toward Kendall.

"We're very neat here, man."

"I can see," Kendall responded cautiously.

"Fuckin' A, man. House rule," said another marine. "Charlie wants to come in here, he's gotta wipe his fuckin' feet first. We ain't pigs."

Kendall tried a smile. "I'm not Charlie," he said. "I'm Joe Kendall. I'm a correspondent for *Rocky Road*."

"Looks like Charlie to me," said a third marine.

"And I bet he didn't wipe his fuckin' feet, either," added another voice.

"Oh, I did," Kendall assured him. "Twice."

"Fuckin' liar," said the second marine. "Look at him. Mud all over. Looks like a fuckin' pig."

"Fuckin' VC pig."

"Grease the fucker."

"But make him wipe his fuckin' feet first."

Kendall felt hysterical laughter welling up inside him. It was like one of those weird dreams where you find yourself standing naked on the fifty yard line of the Rose Bowl. It was all a joke, but it sparkled with serious insanity.

"Hey, really, I wiped them. No VC. Scout's honor."

"Fuckin' boy scout."

"All VC are liars," said the first marine. "You say you're not VC. Therefore, you must be VC because all VC are liars."

Kendall stared at him. The sudden burst of Greek logic surprised him. He remembered the reference. "No," he said, "I'm not VC. I'm Cretan."

"A fuckin' cretin!"

"No," said the first marine. "Cretan. From Crete. In the Aegean Sea. But all Cretans are liars, right?"

"Wrong," Kendall replied quickly.

"That proves it. The man's a Communist Cretan liar who doesn't wipe his feet."

"Grease the fucker."

"No, we'll test him first. Who plays first base for the New York Yankees?"

Kendall knew, but he was damned if he was going to give them the satisfaction. "Bart Starr," he said.

"Correct!" yelled a new voice. "Now do you want to go for the washer-dryer or go back to Crete with the fuckin' toaster oven? Don Pardo, tell us about it!"

"Well, Art," said a marine with a surprisingly deep, mellow voice, "Charlie has won the exciting new BS— twenty-four hundred bolt action, repeating, air-cooled toaster oven. With locking vent and the unique Rapid Roast Rotissery for barbecueing tender baby gooks in just twelve seconds from paddy to plate. Napalm not included. The latest in home warfare technology from Lockheed. Back to you, Art!"

"Thank you, Don Pardo! What's it gonna be, asshole?"

"Oh, I'll go for the washer-dryer," said Kendall. "I know how much you guys value neatness."

"He's going for it, ladies and gentlemen! How about that!"

The marines cheered and whistled. Kendall bowed.

"Now for your question," intoned the marine who was playing cmcee. "Think carefully, 'cause if you get it wrong, we're gonna blow your fuckin' head off. Your question is, why did the chicken cross the DMZ? You have ten seconds."

On cue the marines began dah-de-dahing the theme jingle from *Jeopardy*. Their pitch was perfect, and Kendall felt another draft of spookiness as the marines' soft voices filled the bunker. When the jingle ended, someone fired a single shot into the roof. Kendall jumped, but managed to keep his cool.

"Time's up. The answer, please. Why did the chicken cross the DMZ?"

"To resist the imperialist aggressors and cleanse the land of the foreign devils?"

The emcee got to his feet and looked Kendall in the eyes. "That," he said, "is . . . *correct*! Give the man a cigar!"

Another marine leaped up and stuck a joint into Kendall's mouth. It was about the size of a big cigar. Kendall toked deeply, amid applause and cheers.

While Kendall coughed, the first marine got up and inspected the Furry Freak Brothers T-shirt.

"*Rocky Road*, huh?"

"That's right," Kendall gasped. He handed the cigar to the marine. He took a quick drag and passed it on to someone else.

"Well," said the marine. "You've come to the right place.

The roads just don't get any rockier. Anybody know where Frost is?"

"Over at the Ramada," someone said.

The marine took Kendall's elbow and led him, still coughing, toward the exit. "C'mon, Hemingway. I'll be your native guide."

Outside, in the diffuse light that filtered through the low clouds, Kendall got a good look at the marine. He was a little older than the others he'd seen, maybe twenty-three or twenty-four. Kendall's age. He was dark and grubby-looking, rather short but powerfully built. His sleeves were rolled up to the biceps, revealing hairy, muscular arms. His name tag read, Vitaglia.

"Well, Vitaglia, are you a student of the classics?"

Vitaglia grinned. "Surprised you, huh? Hell, some of us can even read and write. Some, not all."

"What about you?"

"Philosophy major. Columbia, 'sixty-seven."

Vitaglia pointed out their direction. The Ramada seemed to be another hootch halfway up the S of the hill-top, at the base of the narrow causeway that led to Greno-ble. They walked at an unhurried pace, but Kendall noticed that Vitaglia's eyes never stopped moving. He wanted to see whatever there was to be seen.

"So what are you doing here?"

"Real life, man. You spend four years reading abstract bullshit and you begin to wonder if anything is real. Any-way, what the hell can you do with a philosophy degree? When I got my draft notice, I decided I might as well make the whole experience as meaningful as possible. So I went down to the post office and joined the Marines."

"Has it been meaningful?"

Vitaglia stopped and looked at him. "You won't believe this," he said, "but it's the best damn thing that's ever hap-pened to me. I might even re-up, if I last that long."

"But why be a grunt? You could get a commission, if you like it that much."

"Maybe someday. Right now, I'd rather take orders than give them. It's the whole moral responsibility thing. I don't think I could order somebody into a situation where he might get killed, but I could take such an order, even if it comes from some redneck jerk-off who doesn't know the difference between shit and Spinoza. Does that make any sense?"

"I don't know," Kendall admitted. "I didn't major in philosophy."

They started walking again. Kendall had to detour around a shell hole.

"But you're here," said Vitaglia. "Neither one of us had to be, but here we are. You just couldn't miss it, could you?"

"As someone once said, it's the only war we've got."

"And a pisspoor one at that. But that makes it more interesting. I'm not sure I could have waded ashore at Tarawa or climbed Surabatchi, or any of that John Wayne bullshit we marines are so proud of. It was too clear-cut. It lacked ambiguity. Ambiguity is what makes life so fascinating. If all the choices were obvious, we'd be no better than robots. We're human because we have to make choices without understanding the consequences. You know why I majored in philosophy?"

"I'd be interested to know."

"Davy Crockett."

"What?"

"Davy Crockett. Or Fess Parker, really. Or Walt Disney's script department, if you want to get right down to it. You remember what Davy Crockett always said?"

Kendall smiled at the memory. "Be sure you're right, and then go ahead."

"Beautiful. God, I loved that. But the problem is, how can you be sure you're right? And if you're not sure, can you still go ahead? Or anywhere? Or do you fall into Zeno's paradox and stop moving altogether? So what it comes down to is that in a world where certainty is impossible, you have to go ahead *without* being sure you're right. So, anyway, I majored in philosophy in search of certainties, and now I'm on a hilltop five miles from the DMZ, pursuing ambiguities. So what are you here for?"

"A story."

"Don't be facile. You obviously didn't get drafted, but you managed to get to Nam, anyway. It couldn't have been easy. You must have wanted it pretty bad. So why are you here?"

"I suppose it's some sort of test," Kendall said. The answer seemed to come from the top of his head; he had never really spent much time pondering his deeper motivations. Except . . . just once, he had plunged into the inner Kendall. He had never told anyone about it.

"I dropped acid once," Kendall said suddenly.

Vitaglia laughed. "Only once?"

"It was a weird experience."

"It's supposed to be."

"Not like that. I saw all the Peter Max designs and all that crap, but then . . . I don't know how to describe it. I had this . . . *vision*."

Kendall waited for Vitaglia to make a joke, but he didn't.

"It was like I was seeing into myself. I was seeing what was really inside of me. And I saw this incredible wooden box, with beautiful carvings on it and all kinds of gold and ivory inlays. It was really a beautiful thing to see."

"Sounds like a good thing to have inside you."

"Yeah, but it was just a box, you know? It was the package. I wanted to know what was inside it. And what was inside it was another box, just like the first one. And inside that box there was another one, then another one. But I finally came to what I knew was the last box. Inside it, I knew I was going to find the real me, the absolute core of my existence. And you know what was in that box?"

Vitaglia looked at him as if he knew what the answer was going to be, but he remained silent.

"Nothing," said Kendall. "Not a damn thing. A perfect void. That was what I found at the center of myself."

Vitaglia nodded. "So welcome to Hill Six fifty-one."

Chapter Five

Larry Frost was glad to see Kendall. The visit gave him a certain amount of status—a correspondent coming all the way to Hill 651 just to see him. Frost's bunker mates in the Ramada were friendly but reserved, not entirely sure what to make of the hippie war correspondent.

They hunkered down in a corner of the Ramada, a twin to the Holiday Inn, and passed the inevitable joint. Vitaglia decided to hang around and see how Kendall did his job. Kendall, stoned and dazed by all the things that had been happening to him in the last few hours, was not really sure what to do. He took out his number one notebook, but managed to record only graceless doodles.

"I read that thing you wrote about me, man," said Frost. "I don't see why you changed my name. I'd of been famous, man."

"Not very," said Kendall. "Anyway, I was afraid it might get you in trouble." Kendall had been more afraid that he would get himself in trouble by using Frost's name. He didn't want to start his journalistic career with a libel suit. The article had made Frost look like what he was—an inarticulate, half-bright adolescent who was utterly lost in the world of the marines. He was a little apprehensive about seeing Frost again, but evidently the kid didn't mind Kendall's judgments.

"Yeah," said Frost, "maybe you're right. The officers, man, they get on your ass about things you wouldn't believe. Beaucoup chickenshit. Nam is even worse than Lejune, you know? We got a fuckin' lieutenant here who says we gotta fuckin' spit shine our boots before we go back to Khe Sanh. Can you believe that shit, man?"

"What about all the dope?" Kendall asked as he passed the joint to Vitaglia.

Someone laughed. "Fuckin' officers know better than to fuck with our dope, man. Some asshole lieutenant over at Four-sixty-seven got his legs blown off a couple weeks ago. And it wasn't Charlie, you'd best believe that."

Kendall looked at the man who had spoken. He was a runty little guy with a wild look in his eyes.

"Would you frag someone?" Kendall asked him.

"Fuckin' A, I would! These assholes know it, too."

Kendall turned to Vitaglia, hoping for some sign of sanity from the philosophy major. Vitaglia simply shrugged.

The marines continued their bitching about life in the Corps and life in Nam. Kendall had heard much the same sort of talk in Da Nang, but there it was more like complaints about a skin rash; here, the talk was of cancer. These men shared some gruesome secret about the world.

Kendall wasn't too stoned to realize that much of the tough talk about fragging was for his benefit. They wanted him to know that even if the war against the Communists was going badly, they were winning the war that counted, the one against the men who had led them to this horrible place. Kendall wondered if the officers realized how deeply they were hated. They must, he thought, and they must be scared shitless all the time.

"What about the VC?" he asked.

"Fuck the VC," said a black marine. "And fuck the NVA. Chickenshit little fuckers. Gooks ain't got no more guts than they got brains."

"But they have you surrounded here," Kendall pointed out.

"Big fuckin' deal," said the runty marine with the wayward look. "They're hidin' out there, man. They just lob in some mortar rounds to make it look like they ain't afraid to fight. But man, they don't have the guts to try and take this fuckin' hill. They know, man. They know what they'd get."

"We'd hand 'em their fuckin' heads, man," said Frost.

Kendall suddenly believed it. These crazy, dope-addled kids were genuinely frightening. All the hand-wringing editorials about how American youth had gone soft were tragically wrong. Beneath the overindulged, pampered surface lurked a searing flame of incredible heat. Kendall wondered where it had come from. Vietnam and Camp Lejune together could not account for such hatred and ferocity.

Maybe it explained the war, he thought. Maybe someone high up had recognized the volcanic force that was building in his generation . . . maybe they had intentionally stoked the fires. And the war was just an excuse to tap that energy and direct it outward, before the volcano erupted under the feet of those who lived on its slopes. Plots and awesome conspiracies pinwheeled through Kendall's mind, an unfolding canvas of limitless paranoia that encompassed godlike cabals capable of twisting reality to whatever shape fit their evil designs.

Kendall struggled to his feet. He had to get out of this dense, dope-laden atmosphere before he started believing his own ravings. Outside the bunker he breathed deeply in the damp, fading daylight. He found Vitaglia standing next to him, looking at him with concern.

"You okay?"

"Yeah, I think so. Jesus."

"I know," said Vitaglia. "I could see it hit you. Sometimes it just rolls over you. You just suddenly realize that you're on some godforsaken hilltop ten thousand miles from home, and everyone around you has a gun and is completely crazy."

"No, that wasn't it. Not exactly. It was . . ."

"Another vision?" Vitaglia smiled.

"Sort of. Not really. Hell, I don't know. I just had this weird glimpse of the Big Picture, or something. Too much dope, I guess. Vitaglia, how the hell do you stay sane here? How does anyone?"

Vitaglia grinned knowingly. "What makes you think we do?"

"Someone must."

Vitaglia turned to look at the dark valleys spreading toward the north. "Charlie does," he said, "Charlie knows why he's here and what he wants to do. That's why he'll win in the end."

"You really think so?"

"Shit, yes. Read your Kipling, man."

A jeep roared past them, bouncing down the causeway from Grenoble. Bascomb and Poole. Kendall watched them as they rolled past the command bunker.

"Somebody thinks we're going to win," he said. "That guy in the jeep does."

"The civilian? Who is he?"

"Damned if I know, but he's more important than he looks. He just delivered something to the hill, and whatever it is makes a lot of people very nervous."

"What? A-bombs, maybe?"

Kendall stared at Vitaglia. Did he know something? For the last week there had been wild rumors floating around Da Nang that nuclear weapons were about to be introduced along the DMZ. No one really believed it, but the story persisted. Could those two unpretentious canisters have been atomic bombs?

He still couldn't believe it. No one in MACV was stupid enough to store atomic bombs in a place like Hill 651. It made no sense. Anyway, Kendall didn't think atomic bombs looked like that.

Vitaglia saw that he was considering the possibility. "You don't really believe that, do you?"

"I guess not."

"You hear all sorts of rumors up here. Latest one is that the North Vietnamese have got a couple of Russian bombers stashed at an air base just north of the DMZ. Some night they're gonna fly down here and bomb the shit out of us."

Kendall had heard that one, too. "I don't think I can swallow that, either."

"Maybe not. But here's one that's no rumor. They've got tanks."

"Tanks? Guerrillas with tanks?"

"Not guerrillas," said Vitaglia. "NVA regulars. And they've got 'em all right. Sometimes at night, you can hear them moving around out there. You want a good story, there it is. It'll change the whole nature of the war."

"No doubt." Kendall still wasn't sure he believed it. Anyway, he suddenly had an abundance of good stories to pursue. And one of them was getting away. A helicopter was lifting noisily into the sky, carrying Turner Poole back to wherever he had come from. Kendall felt a pang of guilt. He should have pressed Poole for answers while he had a chance. Instead, he had meekly settled for The Larry Frost Story.

"It's getting cold," said Kendall.

"It does that here."

"Yeah." Kendall watched Poole's helicopter disappear behind another hill.

"Well," said Vitaglia, "I gotta get back. Things get more interesting around here at night."

"Thanks for the tour."

"No sweat. Stop in and say hello before you leave."

"I'll do that."

Vitaglia shifted his M-16, tilted his helmet down, and began trudging slowly down the hill. Kendall watched him until he was out of sight, then turned and went back into the Ramada.

"I pulled LP duty tonight, man," said Frost. "You oughta come along, there's room."

"LP duty?"

"Listening post, man." Frost pointed to what looked like a low shed, dug into the side of the hill about two hundred yards below the crest of 651. Kendall could just make it out in the gathering darkness. It didn't look like a particularly safe location.

"It's cool, man," Frost assured him. "Smack and me have

a righteous time down there. Fuckin' lieutenant's too tight-assed to fuck with the LP's, man."

"Who's Smack?"

"You rang?" Kendall turned and saw the runty marine with the craziness in his eyes. He was a head shorter than Kendall and couldn't have weighed more than a hundred twenty pounds. He had a dark, patchy growth of beard and he smelled terrible.

"You gonna do LP with us?" Smack asked hopefully.

"I guess."

"Fan-fucking-tastic! You're gonna dig this, no shit."

Kendall glanced toward the LP. It looked dangerously far away.

"Why do you guys act like it's so much fun down there?"

"You'll see, man," said Smack, "you'll see."

Kendall doubted that he would, but he had already backed away from one story today. If Frost was going to spend the night in the listening post, then so would Kendall. It sounded as if the officers stayed away from the LP, which suited Kendall's needs. He was increasingly paranoid about what would happen if someone finally realized that he wasn't supposed to be here at all.

Five minutes later night descended with the finality of a curtain closing. The blackness was so complete that Kendall could barely see men standing next to him. He felt a tug at his sleeve.

"Just stay close, man," Frost told him.

Kendall stumbled down the hillside, trying to maintain physical contact with the two marines. He reminded himself that darkness was a soldier's friend. If he couldn't see Frost, then it was unlikely that a VC sniper could see him. Unless they had infrared sniperscopes. Kendall didn't think they did; tanks and bombers, maybe, but no sniperscopes. Invisible wavelengths of light were the exclusive property of Americans.

They reached the LP without being fired upon. The LP was little more than a dugout. A corrugated metal roof angled into the hillside; sandbags propped up the front. Inside, a tarpaulin covered the bare earth and a few more sandbags provided something to lean on. The three of them just fit, as long as no one needed to straighten his legs. As Kendall's eyes adjusted to the dark, he could make out a field telephone tied to a sandbag and what seemed to be a Playmate of the Month taped to the corrugated ceiling. Kendall tried to make himself comfortable at the rear of the hut while the marines secured their gear and positioned their rifles in the cracks between the sandbags.

"All the comforts of home," Kendall observed.

Smack cackled wildly. "You ain't seen nothin' yet, man!"

"What's the point of all this? I mean, why do they need people down here at night?"

"To listen," said Frost.

"Yeah, man," added Smack, "why do you think they call it a listening post?" He laughed some more and Kendall began to have serious doubts about the man's stability.

"What do you listen to?"

"We listen for Charlie," Frost told him. "If Charlie's comin' up the hill, we're supposed to hear him and call up the CP to let 'em know we got company. The things is, if Charlie really wants to come up the hill, he ain't gonna make no noise, anyhow. Fuckin' Charlie ain't no fool."

That wasn't what he had heard earlier in the Ramada. Kendall was beginning to understand that the marines had invested their enemy with mystical powers. Charlie could be anything, anywhere.

"If Charlie doesn't make any noise, what's the point of listening?"

"We don't," said Smack. "Least, we don't listen for Charlie. You wanna know what we really listen to?"

"What?"

A loud, angry blast of rock 'n' roll suddenly filled the bunker. Kendall jumped and banged his helmet on the metal roof. He couldn't believe it; The Jefferson Airplane.

"Jesus fucking Christ!" he shouted. "Are you guys crazy?"

71

The two marines laughed insanely, as if to answer him. Kendall wanted to get the hell out of there, but he couldn't get past the two giggling marines.

"Hey, man," said Frost, putting his hand on Kendall's knee, "don't freak out on us. It's cool, man. It's just Smack's tape deck."

"Got it in Bangkok," Smack said proudly. "Woulda cost five hundred in the States. I got it for a hundred. Great sound, huh?"

"Yeah," said Kendall. "Super."

"And this," said Smack above the wail of Gracie Slick, "is why we call it the listening post."

"They let you guys get away with this?"

"That's what's so great about this place," said Frost. "Fuckin' officers can't even hear it. It's, like, acoustics, you know? We test it, man. You can't fuckin' hear this thing a hundred feet up the hill. No way."

"What about the other direction?"

"That way?" asked Smack, pointing toward the valley in front of them. "Shit, they can probably hear it all the way to Hanoi. Charlie doesn't mind."

Kendall did. He had been in Vietnam long enough to know that the Communists were serious about this war, even if the marines weren't. This seemed like a very quick way to get to rock 'n' roll heaven.

"Hey, man," said Frost, "it's cool. I promise you, man. We've been doin' this for months. Shit, if we stopped doin' it, Charlie'd probably get pissed off. Charlie's out there doin' the same fuckin' thing we're doin', man. Groovin' on the music and gettin' loaded."

A match suddenly flared, casting flickering shadows as Frost lighted a joint. He passed it to Kendall, who didn't hesitate. He needed something for his nerves.

Maybe it wasn't so crazy, after all. He remembered countless World War II movies, in which one side or the other sang loud, hearty songs to show the enemy that they weren't afraid. Times changed, and now "Lili Marlene" had become "White Rabbit."

"Gonna be better than ever tonight," said Smack. "I got

72

a Care package today from my lady in San Francisco. You know what that sweet bitch sent me? Jujyfruits, man!"

Smack held up the box to prove it.

"No thanks," said Kendall. "They stick to my teeth."

"Hey, man, *these* will stick to your fuckin' *brain*!"

"Eeelectric Jujyfruits," said Frost.

"You mean . . . ?"

"Fuckin' A, man." Smack beamed. "She coated 'em with acid, man!" Smack popped a piece of candy into his mouth. Frost took the box and did the same.

The deed was done. Kendall was so appalled that his mind slipped out of gear and refused to function at all for a minute.

"Sure you don't want some?" asked Smack solicitously.

"Uh, I think I'll pass."

Smack shook his head disgustedly, as if Kendall had just confirmed all his notions about candyass civilian correspondents.

Kendall thought of his own experience with LSD. That one trip into the emptiness of his soul had been more than enough for him. Acid was a passport to exotic and frightening lands, but he was already in such a place. Five miles south of the DMZ, staring into the blackness of the enemy's stronghold, he had no wish to venture any closer to the edge.

It must be different for them, he thought, straining his eyes to see the enraptured expressions on the faces of the two marines. Maybe they had more to fear from the real world than from anything they might discover crouching in their ids. There was certainly no shortage of things to fear. Escape to the inner playgrounds might be the only thing that kept them functioning in the grim reality of Hill 651: mental R and R.

But I know too much, he thought. I'm educated and intelligent and I live on an entirely different plane from these filling station cowboys. They're too ignorant to be afraid of the things that frighten me.

Even as the thoughts came tumbling out, he knew he

was being an elitist, an arrogant intellectual snob. He didn't understand these people at all. He didn't understand how they survived the kind of life that had brought them here. Joe Kendall could not have made it in their world.

But here he was, *in* their world. And he was not doing so badly. He had outwitted the military authorities. And he had even acted quickly and bravely when the mortar shell came plummeting down out of the sky. He had saved the life of Turner Poole, and a man of the self-evident toughness of Captain Bascomb had acknowledged the fact. He was not a coward, or he would never have come here. He was simply afraid, and under the circumstances that was probably a sign of maturity. With only two tripped-out teen-agers standing between him and the North Vietnamese Army, fear was an entirely reasonable emotion.

Now that he had confronted the fear, it receded. Kendall smoked some more dope while the marines smoothed things out, and even the blaring music made him feel comfortable. The Grateful Dead, now, soothing the jangled nerves of one who was gratefully undead.

"Feel that, man?" Frost was shaking Kendall's knee.

"Feel what?"

Frost turned the volume down on the tape deck. Kendall listened and heard a low rumbling that sounded like a distant freight train. He felt it now, a subtle vibration that penetrated to his bones.

"Over there," said Smack, pointing to the left. Kendall looked and saw a faint glow, outlining the silhouette of the battered horizon.

"Rolling thunder," said Smack, his voice holding a measure of awe.

"B-52's," said Frost. "That's Laos over there, man. The gooks are gettin' bombed to shit."

Kendall stared at the display. "Jesus," he said, "can you imagine being under that?"

"Charlie gets it every night. Man, I'd be AWOL so fast a fuckin' roadrunner couldn't catch me."

The rumbling went on and on. Smack turned off the tape and the three of them watched in frightened silence.

Time slid by like honey oozing across a tabletop. Kendall wasn't sure it was passing at all. Nestled in the back of the LP with his head propped against a sandbag, helmet pulled low over his eyes, he was in retreat from the cold, the fatigue in his aching body, and the numbing fear that had clung to him ever since he boarded Turner Poole's airplane in the remote morning. The blaring music from Smack's tape deck dulled his senses and insulated him from everything that was not himself. Frost and Smack were far gone on their trips, withdrawn to another place, incommunicado. They were like triplets, he thought, sharing a metal and rock womb, safe in the glow of the pulsating red light.

"*Light my fire,*" the music insisted. Kendall thought of a warm, red fire, dancing in time with the sinuous organ solo, sparks leaping into the black sky, flashing on and off like a stoplight.

The red light was real, he suddenly realized. From the opposite corner of the LP, it kept a steady rhythm, on and off, on and off. He raised his eyelids a little and tried to focus, to find the source. It was a box, another goddamn box. But this one wasn't like the delicate, empty Chinese boxes; no gold and ivory, just the tiny round light, beating on, then off, on, then off.

It was the field telephone. Kendall roused himself to a level of consciousness that permitted movement. He pushed upward and scraped the metal roof with the top of his helmet. His hand extended and closed around the receiver of the phone. He kicked Frost lightly and thrust the receiver toward him. Frost stared at it a moment before accepting the offering.

"Yeah," he said to the phone.

The reply crackled through the earpiece, cutting through the music, loud enough for Kendall to hear. The voice was frantic, furious:

"*Don't you see what's happening?*"

Frost dropped the receiver and looked outward. Kendall and Smack did the same. Outside the tiny hut the night was ablaze. Streaking tracers crisscrossed the sky; a chunk of the metal roof was missing, ripped away in a great, jagged splotch. Chaotic, rippling explosions shook the earth.

"*Jesus!*" Smack screamed.

The marines clawed for their weapons. Frost ripped a hand grenade from his flak jacket and slung it sidearm into the night. He hadn't pulled the pin.

They began firing their M-16's, sweeping the ground ahead of them in fearful arcs, shooting holes into the body of the dark. Brilliant flashes illuminated their taut faces in strobelike pulses, their wide, swollen eyes reflecting the glare like alien moons trapped in the maelstrom of an exploding star.

Kendall watched, openmouthed, afraid to understand what he was seeing. It was simply part of the music—"*try to set the night on fi-yuh!*" Jesusgod, they had! Blazing, booming, coming straight at him in all his innocence. Their cozy womb was being ripped apart. This must be what an abortion feels like, he thought, from the inside. He wasn't ready for this, he would never be ready for it.

Smack tore an empty clip from his rifle and fought to get another one in. He couldn't make the connection and sobbed in frustration, breathing in great, jerking spasms. It finally clicked into place and he turned back to the night, screaming madly. Frost was throwing another grenade, pulling the pin this time. He loosed one more before the first had exploded. Kendall had already forgotten it by the time it went off, and the second rocking detonation startled him as much as the first.

There was nothing out there, he thought. Nothing but night and fire. A great, flaming emptiness.

The void was suddenly filled with a scream and a lunging human form. Frost and Smack buckled under the weight of it, flailing, grappling awkwardly with the flapping limbs. Kendall pushed himself back into the hill and held his arms out to shield his face. A dark hand clawed at his chest, ripping fabric. Fingernails scraped across his skin, raking his flesh in parallel furrows. The hideous weight pressed down on him, warm and desperate, jerked spasmodically, and was still.

Kendall lowered his arms. A face hovered in front of his own. The mouth was stretched wide, two rows of twisted, stubby teeth guarding a dark, endless hole. The eyes were black and frozen, fixed forever on Kendall. The only motion was of blood, flowing cold and dark from the smashed, gargoyle nose.

He stared into the dead face of Charlie. The two marines were already firing back into the night, ignoring the legs protruding from the space between them. But Kendall was transfixed by the dead man who still clutched the ripped cloth of the frivolous T-shirt. The ruined face wore no expression except the final determination of a man who was not yet ready to die. But he had. He had spewed the last of his life in one racking sigh, right into Kendall's face. Kendall knew he was breathing in the poisoned vapors of a dead man's last, awful exhalation.

He had to get out. This was another man's grave, an open, yawning wound in the earth waiting to be filled. The noise, the light, fire and night—there had to be some place where none of this was happening.

Kendall pushed the dead man away and launched himself out of the dark corner, past the screaming marines and onto the hard, open hillside. Flares, floating lazily down from the empty darkness, lighted the way for him. At the top of the hill men were running, firing angry tattoos into the swarming night. Kendall ran toward them, yelling, "No!" so they would know he was one of them. He was not like the others.

Stumbling on the steep ground, he forced himself to keep moving upward, away from the corrugated tomb behind him. Around him there were flashes and quakes. Ahead, to the right, a rock exploded, spraying a shower of stinging pebbles. He kept going, focusing on each frantic step, the crunch of boot on dirt.

Hands grabbed at him. He swatted them away.

"You fucking asshole! Get down!"

Kendall wasn't going to get down. He had to get to the

top of the hill. Something heavy knocked him off balance and pulled him to the ground. He scrambled to get out from under, but the weight pressed down harder. He struggled against it until he knew he had made it. He was at the top and he could stop struggling.

"It's that fucking correspondent!" someone shouted. Kendall found himself being rolled over. Another face floated above him, but this one was alive and angry.

"Where are Frost and Smack?"

Kendall discovered he couldn't talk. He could only suck at the cold air and gasp. He managed to point toward the way he had come.

"They're still firing," a voice called.

The marine above him let go. "You crazy fucker," he said. "Are you okay?"

Kendall really didn't know. The marine looked him over. Except for the bleeding scratches on his chest, he seemed to be unharmed.

"Relax," said the marine. "You'll live. If any of us do."

Another marine appeared. "Who the hell is this man?" he demanded.

"Some correspondent. Showed up this afternoon, sir."

"Mary, Jesus, and Joseph! Get him the hell out of here, Peterson. Take him down to the aid station. And then get your ass back here."

"Yessir," said the marine. He looked at Kendall. "What about it, Mr. Rocky Road? Can you get up?"

Kendall still hadn't caught his breath, but he understood that he was being removed from this place. He nodded and tried to push himself up. Peterson hooked him under the armpits and got him to his feet.

They made their way to the aid station, back at the command bunker. Kendall was able to walk unassisted by the time they reached it. Peterson turned him over to a black corpsman who had blood all over his uniform.

"He hit?" asked the corpsman.

"No," said Peterson, "he just got himself a dose of the Fear. Take care of him, man, and see that he doesn't go running wild again, okay?" Peterson gave Kendall an admonishing stare, then turned and trotted away, keeping his head low.

Kendall looked around, trying to get oriented again. He was standing outside the sandbag walls of the command bunker, at the lower end of the hilltop. He gradually became aware of the battle that was still raging around the perimeter of the base. Shells were hitting barely a hundred yards from where he stood, but it all seemed amazingly remote now. The corpsman was staring at him.

"You're that correspondent dude, right?"

"Yeah," said Kendall. The single syllable sounded strange coming from his own mouth.

"You shoulda been a sportswriter, man. Cover the Knicks." The corpsman did a quick, phantom jump-shot. "You coulda written about me, man. I was some kinda hot shit, you know what I'm sayin'?"

Kendall wasn't sure if he did. Basketball?

"What the hell is going on?"

The corpsman grinned cynically. "What's goin' on is fuckin' judgment day, man. Been listenin' to the radio in there. It's rainin' shit all over Nam tonight. Gooks in Da Nang, gooks in downtown Saigon, man. Charlie's pissed somethin' fierce, I tell you. He wants it back, man, he wants it all back. Come mornin', ain't gonna be a white man left alive in Nam. No black men, neither. Just gooks. You want some iodine for that chest?"

Kendall looked down at the bleeding grooves on his torso. He couldn't tell if they hurt or not.

A helicopter suddenly materialized out of the blackness, settling unsteadily to the ground a hundred feet from where Kendall was standing. He looked around, but the corpsman had disappeared. An instant later four marines lugging a stretcher bulled past him, trotting clumsily toward the chopper. Four more emerged from the bunker with another litter. The first squad was already running back to the aid station for another stretcher.

The world suddenly went white. Before he could react, Kendall was knocked flat by a tremendous, shattering explosion.

Was that it, he thought. Am I dead now?

He wasn't. Dazed, he picked himself up again and stared at the source of the astonishing brilliant flash. Up the hill the bunker they called Grenoble had vanished in a roiling, seething column of fire.

"They got the fucking ammo," someone yelled.

Kendall watched. Secondary explosions shook the hilltop as Grenoble blasted itself to dust. Long, graceful arcs of fire streamed outward in all directions, and a violent orange dawn settled over the surrounding hills. The whole world was on fire.

He had to get out. Again and again, till he was safe at last, he had to get out.

Kendall ran toward the waiting helicopter. Marines struggling with heavy litters ignored him as he fled past them, toward the open door of the chopper. There, a sullen, scowling black man stood in his way.

"I gotta get on that chopper," Kendall pleaded.

The marine looked him over. "You ain't wounded," he said.

"No, I'm a correspondent. I gotta get out of here."

"We got wounded men here. You just wait your turn, mister."

"But I have to get out of here!"

"I told you, we ain't got room for no correspondent."

"Yes we do," said a man on the helicopter. "We just lost this guy. Help me get him off, he can wait."

Kendall watched breathlessly as the two marines lifted a stretcher and brought it out of the chopper. They gently lowered it to the ground.

The black looked up at Kendall. "You can get on now," he said flatly.

"Thanks. Thanks, I really appreciate this. I really have to get out of here. I've got a deadline."

The marine regarded him in silence for a moment.

"I've got a deadline," Kendall repeated.

"You sure do, man," said the marine. "You sure do."

Kendall climbed into the helicopter and clutched tightly at the webbing. He couldn't look at the marine, so as the

Chapter Six

Domingo was terrified by the crowds. As far as he could see, up and down the long, baking street, there were swarms of people. They hustled and shoved past one another, collected in fitful clusters at corners, charged unheeding into the lurching traffic. Storefronts siphoned some from the flow and squirted more back into it. The chaotic motion never stopped.

Red, white, and blue were everywhere, hanging from streetlights and signposts, draped over billboards, splattered across the sides of snorting buses, wrapped around the people themselves. The random dots of other colors, green or yellow, seemed like an intrusion, an invading bacterium engulfed in a multihued bloodstream.

So many people, he thought. So many fat, confident Anglo faces, streaming along the street from here to forever. And tomorrow, the Great Day, the whole surging throng would be multiplied by some incalculable number. Tomorrow, it would be worse.

Sanchez nudged him, elbow to the ribs. "Tomorrow, Domingo. Tomorrow, eh?"

Domingo stared at Sanchez's narrow, pocked face. Had Sanchez been reading his thoughts again? Could such a thing truly be possible? Here in the great machine of the Anglo city were mystical powers permitted?

"Tomorrow they will not walk. Tomorrow they will run."

Sanchez spoke softly in Spanish, but Domingo was afraid, anyway. A million ears surrounded them, and many of them must understand Spanish. In this inconceivable city they spoke a hundred languages. Sanchez's Spanish words were no safer from them than were Domingo's own thoughts safe from Sanchez.

"You must not be afraid, Domingo. *They* are the ones who should be afraid. We have nothing to fear."

It seemed to Domingo that he had everything to fear. A mounted policeman, blue, helmeted, self-assured, moved slowly past them on a great black horse. Even here, he thought, even in the city of Philadelphia, they were like the cowboys in the Hollywood movies. Tall and proud in the saddle, pistol on the hip, cool, alert, and vengeful. In the movies they gunned down Indians and Mexicans by the score, as if they were no more than flies. Would a Puerto Rican receive more courteous treatment? Would this mounted lawman, with his badge and his gun, stop and inquire if they were not worthless Mexicans, but Puerto Ricans, American citizens like himself?

No, he would not. None of them would. And that was the point of it all, of course. The Anglo machine made no such distinctions. Brown skin, red skin, black skin, yellow skin—it was all the same to those with white skin. That was why they were here. That was why tomorrow was necessary.

"This way, Domingo," said Sanchez, pulling at his sleeve. "I want to see it one more time."

"Again?" moaned Domingo, but Sanchez had already plunged back into the crowd. Domingo hurried to stay with him. He did not want to become separated in this endless crowd. He was not sure that he could find his way back to the hotel alone.

Sanchez walked too fast. Domingo had to push past rich businessmen and white-haired ladies to keep up. Surely, they must be calling attention to themselves by walking so fast. Domingo looked warily at the eyes of the people he

encountered in his path, but they seemed to take no particular heed of him. They met his gaze with the same bland
suspicion that was on their faces always.

They passed again through the courtyard of the huge,
ugly building with the statue on top of it. Sanchez had
told him that the statue was of a man named William
Penn, and the Anglos honored him because he had stolen
all this land from the Indians. The Americans always
killed the little thieves and put up great monuments to the
big ones.

Finally, they came to the broad plaza that faced the old
brick building called Independence Hall. A big wooden
platform in front of it, decorated all over in red, white,
and blue, was the center of attention. People were staring
at it and taking pictures of it, even though nothing much
was happening there. The platform was crowded with
workmen and policemen and silent, watchful men in dark
suits.

Sanchez stopped in front of a bench, a hundred feet
from the center of the platform. Domingo had been to this
particular spot before, and he felt uneasy being here again.
He didn't want anyone to see him lingering here. Perhaps
those men in the dark suits would remember when they
saw him here again tomorrow.

"You will be here," said Sanchez, "and I will be there."
He nodded toward another bench, closer to the platform.

"I know where we will be," Domingo said impatiently.
"We have been over it a thousand times. I don't like
standing here, Sanchez."

"You are an old woman, Domingo."

"What if they see us here?"

"They have already seen us here. Just as they have seen
ten thousand others. And tomorrow, there will be so many
people here that they couldn't see us even if they were
looking for us. Which they are not."

Domingo didn't like contemplating such a crowd. There
were so many today, and tomorrow it would be awesome.
Sanchez said they would be safe because there were so
many people, but Domingo thought he would never feel

safe until he was alone, far away from this place. What if all those people should turn on him? What if they *knew,* the way Sanchez always seemed to know exactly what he was thinking?

"The trash can is full," said Sanchez, flexing his fingers over the rim of the metal container. "They will empty it out tonight, but tomorrow it will be full again. They will never notice when you put one more paper bag into it."

"What if someone does notice? What if someone makes me open the bag?"

Sanchez laughed contemptuously. "It will not happen," he insisted. "No one will be interested in the contents of one brown paper bag carried by some nameless Puerto Rican. And what would they find in that bag, anyway? They would find a string of firecrackers! Firecrackers on the Fourth of July! Believe me, Domingo, nothing could be more innocent."

"But when they go off . . ."

"You should be far away. You light the cigarette, then you place it in the bag, into the metal clip, and you put the bag in the trash can, and by the time the firecrackers go off, you will be gone."

"But there will be so many people. You said so yourself. How will I get through them?"

"They are people, Domingo, not a brick wall. They will be crowding toward the platform, and they will be glad to make room for someone who wants to get away from the platform because that will let them get a little closer."

Sanchez always made it sound like the easiest thing in the world. And Sanchez would be even deeper in the crowd, and he would not be carrying firecrackers. If Sanchez could feel such confidence, why couldn't he?

Because he wasn't Sanchez. Sanchez was a real man of the world, sophisticated beyond belief. He spoke of places he had visited as naturally as if he were speaking of his last visit to the neighborhood cantina. Sanchez had been to Cuba, a place Domingo could at least conceive of, but he had also been to places like Libya and Albania, which seemed more alien to Domingo than even the planet Mars, where the Americans were trying to land one of their robots. Domingo thought he knew more about Mars than about Albania. He had at least spoken with some of the people who worked at the great radio telescope in Arecibo, near his home; they talked, sometimes, about Mars, but he had never met anyone who talked about Albania. Except Sanchez.

From the first, Domingo had lived in awe of his cousin. When Sanchez had arrived in the tiny rural village, his family had taken him in without question. It was not unusual. The young men went off to San Juan or even America, and sometimes they returned, in trouble. Trouble seemed so easy to come by in the big world outside. No one asked questions when the young men returned, scared and haunted.

But Sanchez was different. He disappeared for months at a time, but he always returned, his confidence undiminished. If anything, it seemed to grow.

He had confided in Domingo, it seemed, simply because he was bursting to tell someone about his adventures. At first Domingo had refused to believe him, but when Sanchez came back, one time, with a shiny black pistol manufactured in Czechoslovakia, he knew it was all true.

Sanchez educated him. Domingo's village was less interested in politics than baseball and cockfighting, and if it hadn't been for Sanchez, he would have known nothing of the cruelty and injustice inflicted by the Americans. Again, Domingo had been slow to accept the truth of Sanchez's words. His own brother, Alfredo, was in the American army; true, he had been drafted, but the last time he saw him, Alfredo seemed hugely proud of the uniform he wore. But Alfredo never returned. He was missing in action in Vietnam, and Domingo knew he would never see him again, not even dead. To be missing was somehow even worse than being dead. It was as if the Americans had misplaced Alfredo and didn't care enough to try to find his body. Sanchez had been right about the Americans.

Domingo began to long for independence. His father

thought statehood would be good, but his father was an ignorant shopkeeper who had never been anywhere. He didn't even care that it was the Americans who had killed Alfredo. Only Sanchez seemed to understand what must be done. Puerto Rico must be free, and freedom could only be achieved in the same way the Americans themselves had become free from England.

So it was natural and logical and necessary that they should be here, now, on the two hundredth anniversary of American independence. Tomorrow, Puerto Rico would declare its independence. Tomorrow, before the eyes of the world, they would throw off their shackles and begin the struggle for freedom.

Domingo knew that what was to be done was right and just. And yet he could not stop wondering if this were truly the only way. Sanchez assured him that it was, and Sanchez knew a great deal more than he ever would. Domingo supposed that his doubts and fears were born of ignorance. Sanchez, the wise and wordly, had no such ignorance. And so tomorrow, for the cause of freedom and independence, Sanchez was going to kill the President of the United States. And Domingo was going to help him do it.

At last, they returned to the hotel. The lobby made Domingo think of a train station, with so many people milling around in impatient confusion. Except for the bellboys, they were all rich Anglos. Domingo was amazed that Sanchez had managed to reserve a room in such a grand hotel on such an auspicious occasion. It must have required a great deal of money. Sanchez never said where his money came from, but he seemed to have an inexhaustible supply of it.

In their room on the eighth floor André was waiting. Domingo felt some nameless fear whenever he saw André. If he still believed in God, he would think that André was sent by the devil himself.

André was brown-skinned, like Domingo and Sanchez, but he was not Puerto Rican or Latin. He didn't quite look like an Arab, either, although Domingo wasn't entirely sure what real Arabs looked like. André spoke Spanish with some terrible, unidentifiable accent, although his English was much better than Domingo's. Perhaps André was Albanian.

"You should not be wandering around," André told them when they had closed the door.

"And you should not be here," said Sanchez.

"No one noticed me."

"And no one noticed *us*."

"Then there is no problem," said André.

Sanchez flopped down on one of the two huge beds in the room. He rolled over onto his back and laughed at the ceiling. André was sitting in a big armchair facing the beds. He wore dark sunglasses, and Domingo wondered how he could see anything.

"It will be easy," laughed Sanchez. "Years from now the historians will marvel at it, because it was so easy."

André seemed displeased by Sanchez's laughter. "You would do well," he said, "to think more about your own task and let the historians handle their own work. And if it is easy, it is because it was planned well. And because I have given you the equipment!"

"Ah," said Sanchez, "the equipment!"

He reached under the bed and after a moment's fumbling brought up a flat, round can. It was seven or eight inches in diameter and about two inches thick and it looked like a can for storing film or tape. It was made of dark metal, and at the center of it there were three small holes that looked like the sockets in a stereo where headphone jacks could be plugged in.

"Such sophisticated equipment!" laughed Sanchez.

"Stop acting like an amateur," snapped André. "Sometimes I think you are no better than your cousin, who has the brains of a fish and the heart of a mouse."

Domingo stood in the center of the room and said nothing. Sanchez turned his eyes toward the dark sunglasses.

"Domingo is my cousin," said Sanchez, "and he will do well tomorrow. Do I have to remind you that you, yourself, approved him for this operation?"

"I work with what is available."

"I have yet to see you work at all, my friend. I only see you sitting there like some fat-assed banker, telling people what to do and calling them names because they have the courage to do what you are afraid to do. Who is it that will be standing in Independence Mall tomorrow when President Ford arrives? Who is it that will detonate your marvelous equipment in front of the eyes of the world? Is it Sanchez, the amateur? Is it Domingo, the mouse-hearted? Or is it the great and terrible André, scourge of four continents?"

Domingo felt proud of his cousin. He took no shit from this haughty Albanian.

"You are nervous, Sanchez," said André coolly. "That must be the reason you are talking nonsense. Each of us has his job to do. While you are doing yours, I will be doing mine. The difference is, I could do your job if necessary, as I have many times before. But could you do my job, Sanchez? Could your brave young cousin? You take my job, Sanchez, and we will all spend the rest of our lives in Philadelphia."

Sanchez laughed again. "You have made your point, my friend! You are absolutely essential! Please do not get run over by a bus before tomorrow."

Sanchez lay back against the pillow and flipped the can into the air. It came back down, spinning, and Sanchez clapped it between his hands.

"Please don't do that," André said quickly. Sanchez looked at him, grinning mischievously.

"This frightens you, does it?" Sanchez tossed the can again and caught it one-handed.

"You might drop it," said André.

"And of course, it will explode if it should fall on this hard bed, eh? Even though the detonator is not attached and you, yourself, have assured me that it is perfectly harmless without the detonator?"

"You could drop it on the floor. You could damage the mechanism."

"You offend me, André." Sanchez flipped the can again,

higher this time. "I have hands of gold, my friend. We Puerto Ricans are great baseball players, André. You have heard of Clemente? Cepeda? It is in our blood!"

"Baseball! The game of a child, a child like you, Sanchez."

Sanchez tossed the can so high it nearly hit the ceiling. "The game of a child, eh? Did you know that Fidel once played baseball? He once tried out for the Chicago White Sox, did you know that, André? He was a pitcher. Just think, André, if Fidel only had a better curve ball, history would be completely different!"

"History does not depend on individuals, Sanchez. And stop doing that!"

Sanchez grinned at André and spun the can upward, one more time, toward the ceiling. When the can reached the top of its arc, it exploded.

Sanchez screamed and threw his hands in front of his face. André dived to the floor. And Domingo stood rooted to the floor, amazed that he was still alive.

The explosion was neither large nor loud. It was a muffled *wumpf*, not as loud as the clang of the twisted can as it hit the floor. But the air was filled with a fine, gray dust that drifted slowly toward the floor and clung to whatever it touched.

Domingo ran to Sanchez. Blood was oozing from between his fingers and he rolled from side to side, moaning. Domingo grabbed his cousin's wrists and pried his hands apart. What he saw filled him with relief. Sanchez had many tiny cuts on his forehead and cheeks, but he did not seem to have been badly hurt.

"It's all right, Sanchez," he said soothingly. "You can open your eyes. It is not bad."

André had got back to his feet. His sunglasses had gone askew. He straightened them and looked down at Sanchez. Domingo turned on him.

"Your great bomb has exploded, Señor André!" he mocked. "See the results? You may thank God that you gave us junk!"

"Idiot!" André shoved Domingo aside and leaned over Sanchez.

Sanchez opened his eyes and stared accusingly at André. "Without the detonator, you said, it wouldn't—"

"I didn't expect you to play games with it! Now listen to me. You must clean this room completely, you understand? It must look as if nothing happened here. And then you must leave immediately. Do you understand me, Sanchez?"

Sanchez nodded.

"I will be at my hotel. Come to my room, you have the key. I will leave money and tickets for you."

"And you, André?" asked Sanchez. "Where will you be?"

"Just do as I say! And do it quickly." André seemed pale and frightened as he looked around the room at the settling gray dust. He pointed a finger at Domingo.

"Clean it," he ordered. "Every speck!" André walked quickly to the door and left without looking back.

Domingo looked at Sanchez. His cousin seemed to be recovering from the shock. He looked terrible, as if he had gone headfirst through a glass door, but the wounds did not seem serious.

"What do I do, Sanchez?" Domingo asked.

Sanchez looked at the night table next to the bed. He ran a finger over the surface, through the film of gray dust that had already accumulated. He stared at his dirty fingertip.

"What do I do?" Domingo repeated.

"Do as André said. Help me to the bathroom and I will try to stop this bleeding. You take towels and toilet paper and clean this room. Every bit of it."

This sudden obsession with cleanliness mystified Domingo. The whole thing seemed completely ridiculous to him.

While Sanchez leaned over the bathroom sink, Domingo went to work with the towels, blotting up the strange dust from tables and lampshades and walls. He wondered what the stuff was. It had no identifiable odor and its consistency was very fine.

"Sanchez," he called, "explain this to me. This great bomb of André's, it was nothing but junk! Did he expect us to kill President Ford with this?"

"Keep cleaning," said Sanchez. "And do it quickly. There is no time for questions."

So Domingo cleaned and saved his questions for later. He had a great many of them. But the one question he kept asking himself was, why, when all was said and done, why should it be he, the young and ignorant Puerto Rican, who had to do the cleaning? His people were always left to clean up someone else's mess. He began to believe that the great struggle for independence would make no difference at all. In the end, he would be doing what he was doing now, cleaning up for others—Albanians, maybe, instead of Yankees, but it seemed that it would always be the same.

Sanchez showered and changed his clothes. Then he made Domingo do the same. Domingo didn't try to understand it. His cousin looked peculiar, and it was strangely frightening to see the cool and confident Sanchez acting as dumb and frightened as Domingo himself.

After all, the bomb had been a dud, junk. They were in no danger now. Perhaps Sanchez was simply afraid of what would happen to him because the mission was a failure. André would probably blame it all on him, even though his great equipment was junk. Maybe Sanchez had had his fill of his globe-trotting adventures. Maybe it would be enough for him to come back to the village in Puerto Rico and forget about all this political bullshit. It would certainly be enough for Domingo. He was damned if he was going to fight some stupid revolution just for the privilege of cleaning up after Albanians.

They threw their dirty clothes and the filthy towels down a laundry chute in the hallway outside the room. Sanchez had complained that the room wasn't clean enough, but he didn't want to stay and finish the job himself. That was typical, thought Domingo. Sanchez was a great talker, but he never did anything that involved real work. Domingo didn't care. He figured the hotel maids would clean up the rest. Puerto Rican maids, no doubt.

Sanchez, with cuts all over his face, seemed terribly conspicuous in the crowded lobby. But no one seemed to notice. A Puerto Rican could bleed to death here and no one would care, as long as he didn't get the carpet dirty. As they pushed through the doors and reached the street, Domingo took a deep breath. The city air stank, but the air in the hotel had given him a headache. He was more glad than he could say to be out of the rich, stinking Yankee hotel. Let the fat cat Anglos stay in such places. Domingo would never go near it again.

On the sidewalk he turned and looked up at the sign above the door.

"*Adiós*," he said bitterly. "*Adiós*, Bellevue-Strafford."

Together, Domingo and his cousin plunged into the angry streets of Philadelphia.

1980

Chapter Seven

The ribbon needed to be changed. The pages he had written last week were obviously darker and sharper than anything he was typing today. The *e*'s and *a*'s were also getting a little blurry; it was probably about time to clean the machine. And the shift key was still slow in returning. More often than not, a lower-case letter following a capital would wind up half a line high. Maybe he should take the typewriter into the shop for a tune-up. That would effectively kill a week—more, if he was lucky.

"How the hell can I write anything on this piece of junk?" Kendall flicked the On-Off switch to the down position and leaned back in the padded leather chair. He dug a cigarette out of the pack next to the typewriter and tried to light it, but his lighter refused to operate. He was developing a tough, thick callus on his right thumb from too many cigarettes, a condition the surgeon general had yet to study in depth. The lighter finally managed a low, blue flame that was enough to get the cigarette going.

Kendall looked at his wristwatch. Eleven fifty-three, minus the two minutes the watch had gained. That was the trouble with digital watches—too much trouble to reset. Technology run amok.

He thought again of a word processor. Now there was technology a man could use. He knew exactly what he wanted: a little Apple II with Magic Pencil programming, a good display screen, and a hookup with an IBM Selectric. A man could write *War and Peace* with equipment like that. Or play *Star Trek*, at least.

Eleven fifty-eight, now, minus two. He had promised himself that he would make the Texas calls at noon, eleven their time. Everyone would be awake and available out there. Kendall felt a sudden, acidic message from his stomach, telling him it was time for lunch or another antacid tablet, or both. Texas would have to wait. Of course, that would mean it would be lunchtime in Texas by the time he was ready to call. He would have to wait until late afternoon to make sure they were back from lunch. He didn't intend to waste a long-distance call, deductible though it may have been, chatting with secretaries. But by late afternoon he would have put in his hours at the typewriter and would be in no mood for phone calls. He could make the calls tomorrow.

It had been a productive morning. He had written five sentences and invented an adequate excuse for not calling Texas.

Kendall picked up a rubber band and shot it at the ceiling. He tried to remember if the Sox were on the tube tonight. Torrez was scheduled, which meant lots of three-two counts, many hits, a three-and-a-half-hour game, and almost assuredly, a Boston defeat. Unless Rice finally came out of his slump. The man ought to hit fifty homers every year, but—

The telephone rang. Kendall flinched in surprise. Whenever he was busy writing, the phone sounded as loud as an air raid alarm. No wonder he never got any work done.

He let it ring a couple of times, then picked up the receiver.

"Hi, Joe." It was Sara. "How's it coming?"

"What are you doing, checking to make sure I'm working?"

"Joe!" Sara sounded hurt. It was one of her skills.

"Sorry," he said automatically. "It's coming along. Slow, but steady." There was a moment of silence on the line.

100

The silence of disapproval. Like a talented musician, Sara could make the rests as meaningful as the notes.

"Are you free for lunch?" he asked. Lunch downtown could take care of a good two hours.

"I can't, Joe. We've had a crazy morning around here and I'm just going to eat at my desk and try to get things straightened out."

"Then why did you call?"

"Do I have to have a reason?" Now it was Kendall's turn to let the silence speak. He was learning to beat her at her own game. If they stayed together for another year, it might never be necessary to speak at all.

"Okay, okay," she said. "I wanted to find out how it went with whatshisname—Poole. Will he see you? Did he say anything?"

"Not yet," Kendall admitted. "I haven't called yet. The time difference and everything."

"Oh, come on, Joe! It's eleven o'clock in Houston. You're just making more excuses."

"Look, why don't *you* write this goddamn book? You seem to be the big expert around here on writing. You're the one who got me into this thing in the first place."

"Nobody held a gun at your head," Sara replied coldly. "If you didn't want to do it, all you had to do was say so. And who was the one who did all that talking about the great Vietnam book he was going to write? *I'm* not the one with all the fascinating little war stories. I'm not the one who's got the big hangup about the sixties. And I'm not the one who got the big advance to write the stupid book."

"Big fucking advance. Six thousand."

"Are we going to play Little Orphan Joe again?"

"Give me a break, Sara."

They let the silence speak for a while. Kendall lighted another cigarette. His relationship with Sara was becoming more and more like his relationship with the book. There were too many blank pages.

"Joe?" said Sara. The sharp edge was gone from her voice. "Should I come over tonight? I could fix dinner."

"I don't have anything in the house."

"Then we could go out."

"Sox are on the tube."

"Oh," she said. "Then maybe I'll see you in October, after the World Series."

It was beginning to get away from him. He tried to soften it. "September should be okay," he said. "The Sox will be eliminated by Labor Day."

Sara seemed to feel the same need to back away from whatever edge they had been approaching. "Well, that's different," she said lightly. "Does that mean I should start rooting for the Yankees?"

"Not if you value your health, lady."

"I see."

Kendall didn't see. He had no idea where this was going or why he was being such a prick.

"Sara? Call me this afternoon, okay?"

"Okay," she said after a pause. "This afternoon. Love ya."

"Me, too," said Kendall. He cradled the receiver and stared at the wall for a while.

Turner Poole had problems. He was well accustomed to problems. Sometimes he even enjoyed his problems because he was so good at solving them. He had a chess master's knack for keeping track of all the pieces on the board, appreciating the strengths and weaknesses of each, and figuring out which moves must be made. But the board was getting horribly crowded these days, and the right moves were less than obvious.

Poole got out from behind his desk and prowled restlessly around the office. His eyes came to rest, momentarily, on the liquor cabinet. Temptation flickered invitingly, but it wasn't even noon yet. He shifted his gaze to the mirror on the wall above the liquor.

Perhaps it was a mistake hanging the mirror in such close proximity to the liquor cabinet. Each seemed to lead him to the other. Lately, when he wasn't staring at his reflection on the wall, he was seeing it, warped and distorted, in the bottom of shot glasses. The contrasting images were equally accurate.

He ran a hand across his scalp, rearranging the few remaining wisps of hair. He thought about a toupée again, but he was afraid of how it might look. A man in his sort of work could not afford to look phony. Poole didn't even like to look Texan. The urban cowboy fad struck him as ridiculous. He preferred well-tailored eastern suits and shoes, not boots. In a world of good old boys, shitkickers, and transplanted preppies, it paid to appear solid and unpretentious.

He may have been looking a little too solid around the waist. A prosperous man of forty really ought to have a little extra bulk there, a bit of a corporation, but Poole didn't want to end up as a bloated parody of Breeze Woodward.

It was disturbing how often Breeze Woodward came into his thoughts of late. Breeze had been in his grave for five years, and Poole doubted that he had heard so much as a mention of the old bastard's name in at least two or three years. Houston, a city built on a swamp, had roots that extended outward, grasping new possibilities; there was little that was buried in the shallow ooze that anyone considered worth hanging onto, certainly not the life and lowly legend of a man like Breeze Woodward.

Still, if there were such things as ghosts, Breeze was the type who would volunteer for duty. He stretched every joke just as far as it would go, because the last laugh was the one that counted. Poole wondered if Breeze wasn't doing a little chuckling along about now.

Breeze wasn't laughing, eight years ago, when Poole made his move. He should have seen it coming but he didn't, and that was probably what hurt the most. When he figured out what had happened, he stormed and raged and promised merciless vengeance, but Poole was unimpressed. Breeze had lost his touch—which had never been very nimble to begin with. Something inside Breeze seemed to wilt after that, while the rest of him puffed up in compensation. Gout and a bad liver finally ended the work that Poole's maneuver had begun.

It had been simple and obvious. Poole frequently acted as the bagman when Breeze found it necessary to make payoffs to local politicians. One day in 1972 Poole was delegated to deliver a suitcase containing $200,000 in cash to an ambitious but not very bright state senator. The money was earmarked for the Nixon campaign chest, various slush funds, and the senator's savings account—everybody, it seemed, would get a cut. Poole decided to take his cut off the top. He deposited all $200,000 in his own bank account, then met with the senator. Instead of cash, he brought a tape recorder and played for the politician a carefully edited selection of their previous conversations. Poole made it clear that if the senator kept his mouth shut about the money, the tape would remain in a safety deposit box, its existence unknown to anyone else. The senator quickly agreed, and the next day Poole resigned from Breeze's operation and founded his own company, Turner Poole Enterprises. By the time Breeze figured out what had happened, it was too late to do anything about it.

Poole was on his way. Turner Poole Enterprises sprouted wings and flapped all over the Texas landscape. Dealing and double-dealing, Poole soon became a bona fide millionaire, and if the basis of his fortune was a blatant theft, then he was in good company.

Poole's acquisitions—including two wives—gave him satisfaction, but the getting was still more fun than the having. He disposed of his holdings—including the two wives—almost as fast as he accumulated them. It was a high-grade, distilled blend of the juice that fueled Turner Poole Enterprises, and its fumes made the atmosphere heady and exciting.

He wasn't sure when or how it began to go wrong, but it undeniably had. Staring into the mirror now, he searched his own eyes for an answer. Had he plunged into too many unknown waters, reached too far for a prize he couldn't see? How, for instance, had he managed to lose half a million dollars in an Egyptian cotton deal? He had never been to Egypt and he knew diddly about cotton, of which there was one hell of a lot right there in Texas if he absolutely had to get into the cotton business, which he didn't. And what insane impulse ever made him think he could sell chicken-fried steak franchises in New England? Breeze would have laughed loud and long at that one. Poole didn't even *like* chicken-fried steak.

Maybe he would have that drink, after all. It was well past noon in Egypt.

Poole's secretary buzzed him. Reluctantly, he turned away from the liquor cabinet and went back to his desk.

He picked up the phone. "Yes, Bonnie?"

"Mr. Poole, you've got a call from someone named Joe Kendall."

Poole thought he recognized the name from somewhere, but it meant nothing to him. "What does he want?"

"He didn't say, but he's calling from Boston."

"Boston, huh? Okay, Bonnie, put him through." Poole had nothing on the fire in Boston, but maybe in a few minutes he would. It happened that way, sometimes.

"Turner Poole here."

"Mr. Poole? Hi, this is Joe Kendall. I don't know whether you remember me or not. You gave me a ride to Khe Sanh a long time ago."

Poole sat up straight. "Jesus, yes! I thought I recognized the name. That really was a long time ago, wasn't it? How've you been, Joe?"

"Oh, not bad," said Kendall. "And you?"

"I've been just fine, Joe. You still writing for that rock 'n' roll magazine?"

Kendall laughed. To Poole it did not sound like a very happy laugh. "Not lately," Kendall answered. "They went disco."

"Yeah," said Poole, "I know what you mean. Sometimes I think the whole world's gone disco. So what are you doing these days?"

"I'm writing a book. That's the reason I called."

"Oh?"

"It's going to be about Vietnam, and everything that happened the day the Tet Offensive began."

"That was quite a day," said Poole.

"A lot happened. I'm trying to write sort of a Jim Bishop, *The Day Lincoln Was Shot*, kind of thing, with a bit of the Cornelius Ryan-John Toland-Bruce Catton grand-sweep-of-history perspective. That sort of thing."

"Sounds like a tall order. You've raised your sights a bit since the last time I saw you. What was it you were writing, something about some marine? You ever find him?"

"Yeah," said Kendall. "I found him."

"How'd that come out?"

Kendall paused. "Not very well," he said after a moment. "Look, I'm spending the summer doing interviews for the book. I'm going to be in Houston in two weeks. There's an ex-colonel I want to talk to, and as long as I'm going to be there, I wondered if you would mind doing an interview. Remember, you said that if I ever make it to Houston, dinner is on you."

Poole was hoping Kendall wouldn't bring that up. Kendall had saved his life, more or less. It was something he didn't like to remember.

"I did say that, didn't I? Well, sure, dinner is on me. But I don't know how much help I'll be for that book. I wasn't in Vietnam very long."

"You were there that day. That's all I'm after."

"I'll give you all the help I can, Joe. Give me a call when you get to town, and we'll set something up."

"Great," said Kendall. "See you in a couple of weeks."

Poole hung up the phone. He drummed his fingers on the desk for a minute, then got up and walked to the liquor cabinet.

Arnold Ginsburg had problems, too. Some of his men seemed to think that the Bureau's budget was a science fiction novel. They were awesomely efficient when it came to examining other people's bank statements, but it apparently never occurred to them that their own ledgers were subject to the same meticulous scrutiny—by

Ginsburg. He knew he had a reputation as a paper clip counter, but damn it, *somebody* had to count them. If Ginsburg didn't, his superiors would.

It was a bad year to be running over budget. There was always more to do in an election year; the psychos and freaks emerged from the garbage like a swarm of four-year locusts. And with a Kennedy running, there was the possibility that a big investigation might be required at any moment.

As the deputy assistant director of the Special Investigations Branch, Ginsburg had problems not faced by his opposite numbers in other branches. Some of them simply looked at their budgets and announced, "Okay, men, we can afford to catch three hundred bad guys this year." If they caught more than their quota, they were praised for their efficient use of the taxpayers' dollars. In the end, the Bureau—composed largely of lawyers and accountants—had the same bottom line mentality as a bank.

At SIB, though, predictions and quotas had about as much to do with reality as the astrology column in the *National Enquirer*. It was a guessing game, and nobody's guess was really worth very much. Major investigations could cost millions and produce exactly nothing; meanwhile, ten-year fugitives casually walked in off the street as if they had an appointment.

Ginsburg's budget predictions might just as well *be* science fiction novels. That thought had struck him so often over the years that now, on the sly, Ginsburg was actually writing such a novel.

He shoved the budget figures to one side of his desk and unlocked the bottom drawer. After a surreptitious glance through the windows at the outer office, Ginsburg removed a sheaf of yellow notebook pages. He stared sadly at the ball-point scrawl and wished that he had the time to type it all. It would look more professional that way, and he would have a better idea of how much he had actually written. If only there were a secretary he could trust. He knew that if word ever got out that he was writing a science fiction tale, his life at the Bureau would become

107

MARK WASHBURN

unrelieved torture. People would call him Flash. They
would file reports on flying saucer landings and green-
skinned spies. No one would ever take him seriously again.

He hadn't even told his wife about the novel. There was
always the danger that *she* wouldn't take him seriously, either. She seemed to regard his job as a kind of make-believe—grown-up men playing cops and robbers. Writing a
science fiction novel would, in her eyes, reduce him to the
level of their ten-year-old son, who spent most of his time
reading comic books and most of his allowance playing
Space Invaders.

Ginsburg wondered if his son would understand. How
would little Jimmy react to the news that his father let his
mind ramble in the same fantastic fields where the kids
played? Several times he had come close to telling him,
but he always stopped short. Jimmy might tell him, "Come
on, Pop, grow up!" Ginsburg didn't think he could take
that.

He skimmed through the familiar pages. Some of it
seemed, well . . . rough. But there were some good parts,
too, and he reread them frequently. For a paragraph or a
page his characters came alive, and the universe they in-
habited was bright and hard. His hero, Ace King, looked
him right in the eyes and breathed the same air he
breathed. Sooner or later, though, Ace would go back to
flying spaceships and Ginsburg would have to return to the
budget figures.

Someone knocked at his door. Ginsburg stuffed the papers back into the drawer and quickly closed it.

"Come in."

Vance Hodges entered. Hodges was a husky, ex-Big Ten
linebacker, and Ginsburg, a five-foot-six chess player, always felt uncomfortable in his presence. Ginsburg thought
he was reasonably well adjusted to the fate of being short,
but some people, like Hodges, seemed to make a fetish out
of being big. Hodges took a chair and sat down, stretching
his long legs in front of the desk.

"How've you been, Arn?"

"Busy," said Ginsburg. "What can I do for you?"

Ginsburg wasn't very good at small talk and liked to keep it to a minimum. He wasn't sure if it made people think he was serious, or merely stuffy.

"I'm not sure," Hodges said. "Maybe I can do something for you. Have you still got Nightwind?"

"Nightwind?" Ginsburg stared at Hodges. Very few people knew about Nightwind.

"That's right. Remember, I was on that for a while."

"Right, right, I do remember. Yes, Vance, I still have it. Don't tell me you've got something."

"I don't know if I do or not. It might be nothing, but the last I heard, Nightwind was stalled."

Ginsburg pursed his lips, annoyed. "Your information," he said, "is accurate. Now what have you got?"

"Well, it goes like this. Uh, do you mind if I smoke?" Hodges already had the cigarette poised at his lips.

"I'd prefer that you didn't," said Ginsburg.

Hodges smiled apologetically and returned the cigarette to his pocket. "Oh, that's right, the allergy thing. Sorry, Arn. It's been a while since we worked together."

"You were going to tell me something about Nightwind."

"Yeah, right. Except it might not have anything to do with Nightwind. I just thought I should tell you about it."

"So tell me."

"Okay. There's this operator named Poole, down in Houston. He's been involved in a lot of questionable activities, although his record is still clean. One of his activities is a fleet of shrimp boats in Corpus Christi. The DEA thinks some of those boats are offloading mother ships from Colombia. They asked us to track some of the money. We did, and lo and behold, some of it turns up in the account of a congressman we've been watching for years. This guy is a real sleaze. He makes the Abscam players look like class. But he's smart and so far we don't have anything we can take to court. So this guy Poole begins to look like a possible handle. Last month we got an order for a tap on Poole."

Ginsburg shifted his weight in the chair. "I assume that at some point this is going to connect with Nightwind?"

"I told you, Arn, I don't know. But let me go on."

"Please do."

"Yesterday, Poole took a call from a Joe Kendall in Boston. They seemed to be old acquaintances. During the conversation Kendall made a reference that seemed to imply that the last time they saw each other was in 1968 at Khe Sanh, Vietnam."

"So?"

"So according to everything we've been able to dig up about Poole, he was never in Vietnam."

Ginsburg began to get interested. But it was still a very, very long shot.

"You checked his military record?"

"Of course we did," Hodges answered sharply. "He hasn't got one. He was four-F in the early sixties. And according to the State Department he never had a visa for South Vietnam. On paper, he was never there."

"Could the Khe Sanh reference have been some sort of code between Poole and Kendall? Maybe Poole knows he's being tapped."

"That's possible. So we pulled Kendall's file. . . ."

"He has one?"

Hodges smiled cynically. "A beaut."

"Drugs?"

"Worse. He's a writer."

Ginsburg winced a little. "Could you be more specific?"

"Kendall was a campus lefty back in the late sixties. In 'sixty-seven he started writing for *Rocky Road*. He was their Vietnam bureau chief, and he was definitely in Nam for about five weeks at the beginning of 1968. That jibes with what was said in the conversation. Apparently he and Poole were together at Khe Sanh on the day the Tet Offensive began. So that puts Poole in Vietnam in late January of 1968."

Hodges sat back and waited for Ginsburg to react. Ginsburg was intrigued, but he didn't intend to get carried away.

"Vance, that's interesting. But there were half a million men in Vietnam in January of 1968."

"But Turner Poole wasn't supposed to be there. He was a civilian without a visa."

"Could he have been running dope? There was a hell of a lot of it in those days."

"That's possible, I suppose. In fact, that was our first reaction. That's why we checked it out. But here's where it gets interesting. In 1968 Poole was working for a good old boy by the name of Breeze Woodward. Woodward was your basic Texas wheeler-dealer, from the old school. He had his fingers in just about everything. And you'll never guess who Woodward's favorite good buddy politician was."

"Lyndon Baines Johnson."

"Bingo."

Bingo, indeed. Ginsburg ignored Hodges's triumphant grin. This suddenly had the smell of the real thing.

"Anything else?"

"Just bits and pieces. Poole has big tax problems, if that means anything. But when we turned up the Johnson connection, something clicked and I remembered Nightwind."

"Have you told anyone else about this?"

"You were the first, Arn."

"And the last. Okay, Vance, bring me the files on Poole and Kendall. Maybe you've got something here."

"If I do," said Hodges, "I want a piece of it."

"We'll see."

"Arn, you're going to need warm bodies. I'll bet you don't have a single agent on Nightwind."

"Okay, okay. If there's anything here, I'll bring you in."

Hodges stood up. "Is that it, Arn? Not even a thank-you?"

"Thank you, Vance," said Ginsburg.

"Oh, you're welcome. Any old time. You're one hell of a guy, Arn."

Ginsburg scarcely noticed when Hodges left. He was already retracing the intricate web of Nightwind.

Ginsburg had been with the Bureau for nineteen years,

nearly half his life. During his time in the field he had
conducted door-to-door searches in the Detroit ghetto,
photographed rioting SDSers, and negotiated with armed
hijackers. He had investigated the assassinations of the
Kennedy brothers. He had delved into the bottomless
muck of Watergate. He had seen his brother agents tried
for crimes committed at the behest of their superiors. In
nineteen years he had seen and done a lot.

And in all that time only one case ever led him to lie
awake all night. Only one case had ever made him afraid.

Nightwind.

Chapter Eight

Louisiana, from the air, looked unnervingly like Vietnam. No bomb craters were in evidence, but the place had the same sort of wet, green thickness about it, a soggy, dripping density. Kendall usually preferred the window seat, but on this trip he would have been happier sitting on the aisle. Nothing forced him to stare down at the green carpet below, but he found it difficult to look away.

He was already caught in the gravitational tug of Vietnam; he didn't need visual reminders. As soon as he had signed the contract for the book, he knew he was trapped, and that eventually the tidal forces of his own past would pull him back down to the bottom of it all. The book, in fact, was really no more than a formality, a legal and professional obligation, an excuse to make a controlled reentry into that flaming atmosphere. For twelve years his orbit had never been free from the insistent weight of Vietnam, and if there had been no book, he would nevertheless have been drawn back, fated to return, if not to Vietnam, then to Vietnam under another name.

The 727 flying him to Houston, like the thundering Huey that had borne him away from the blazing hilltop in the night, traversed no more than airspace, miles on a map. No known mode of transportation was capable of altering his mental distance from that hilltop. There had been no easy cartographic escape, no safe point on the compass. The night unerringly found him still in Vietnam.

At Khe Sanh they discovered that Kendall was where he was not supposed to be. The press officers angrily threatened him with expulsion; Kendall didn't mind. It was what he wanted. His sole desire was to be safely aboard an airplane, with Vietnam fading in the distance beyond the wing tips. If they threw him out, he could return home and tell his editors that he had tried, that he had done his best.

But the Tet Offensive permitted no easy solutions. No one had time to deal with the minor infractions of some overeager hippie journalist. They did send him back to Da Nang, when it was again possible to get a plane into Da Nang. His case, he was told, was pending.

Kendall haunted the bar in the Da Nang press center and explained to his colleagues that he was officially in limbo. It was best, for now, not to venture back into the field. Waves should not be made. He drank and smoked and waited to be sent home.

He wasn't. Incredibly, the military forgave him. His fellow journalists had gone to bat for him and saved his MACV card. He could stay in Vietnam. He had to stay. Now that he had the respect of the other correspondents, it would be impossible to tell them that all he wanted was to get the hell out of Nam. He couldn't explain to them that one night on a cold hilltop, he had lost his nerve. The game just wasn't played that way.

So Kendall went north again, to the ruined city of Hue, following the pack. He saw the bodies and heard the gunfire and took notes on it all. And one morning he woke up with a wasting fever and trembling limbs. They put him in a military hospital, dripped fluid into him, inspected the blood they took out of him, and finally, they sent him home.

He forced himself to write the articles that were expected of him. They didn't come very close to the reality, but that didn't seem to matter to anyone but Kendall. He won praise and some minor fame for his work, and spent the next years roaming the country for *Rocky Road,* writing gloomy stories about disintegration and decay. It was easy enough to find.

But after Nixon was gone, the magazine and, presumably, its readers wanted stories that Kendall was incapable of telling. He couldn't find the right verbs and adjectives, and the proper tone for the times eluded him. The Youth Culture had veered off onto some road Kendall could no longer follow.

Past thirty now, he tried free-lancing for grown-up magazines. It was a more difficult life than he had imagined, and somehow the checks never seemed to arrive until after the rent was due. Finally, he landed a job teaching journalism to night students at Boston University.

He had been there three years now, leading an undemanding life. He had never quite adjusted to the absolute strangeness of stability. With no deadlines to meet or planes to catch, Kendall wasn't sure what to do with his time. His department chairman suggested that, if he wanted tenure, Kendall ought to think about doing some sort of book. Kendall thought about it and played with proposals, but in the end, there was only one book he could write. The Vietnam book.

Thinking about it wasn't the same as actually writing it. Putting the words on paper, tapping the keys, demanded a direct, physical confrontation with his subject; blurry abstractions about the Meaning of It All would only fill the already polluted air with more smoke. To write facts, he first had to face them.

One sweaty night the noise from Hill 651 woke him again. Sara lay next to him, already awake.

"Sooner or later," she said, "you're going to have to tell someone about it. It might as well be me."

So Kendall told her. Sara was an attractive, thoughtful blonde, eight years younger than Kendall. She had just missed the sixties; while Kendall was under fire in Vietnam, she was living in a world of rock concerts and high school drug busts. For her those strange times were rooted in an adolescent fantasy world, and it was hard for her to accept the idea that anything that happened then really counted. She knew it was different for Kendall; his personal clock was somehow stuck in 1968, and the night could draw him back to that Zero Year. She wanted to understand him.

"You know," she said when he had finished his story, "it could have been worse. People were trying to kill you and it shook you up. If it didn't bother you, *that* would be something to worry about. At least you don't have memories of shooting babies or something as awful as that."

"You're missing the point," Kendall told her. "It's not so much what I did—it's what I didn't do. I was there to do a job, and I blew it. I cracked. And ever since then . . . I don't know, it's like I'm waiting for it to happen again."

"But it won't. It can't. Vietnam is over. It's history."

"History!" Kendall laughed. "Like the War of the Roses."

"Okay, it's *your* history. But it's still history. Let it go."

"That's not what you're supposed to do with history, Sara. You're supposed to study it and analyze it and make sense of it."

"Fine, then do that. Do anything. But do *something*. Don't just sit there and let it eat at you."

Kendall thought she might be right. For years he had been pondering a Vietnam book. He could go back, intellectually at least, and piece together all that had been shattered on that awful night. Like an FAA investigator rummaging through the debris of a plane crash, he couldn't erase the damage, but he might come to an understanding of it.

With his department chairman pushing and Sara pulling, Kendall at last approached the book. He sparred with it for months, looking for an opening. The story, he came to realize, went beyond the fiery perimeter of Hill 651. If what happened to him on that night was to have any meaning, it had to be fitted into the context of what happened to everyone on the same night. His experience need be no more than a slim chapter in a broad history. He

116

would interview generals and grunts, politicians and pundits, and find the ineluctable truth of that night.

"I don't think you should do it that way," Sara commented after she had read the outline. "I think you should write more about what happened to *you*."

"Look," he protested, "what am I doing here, anyway? Am I writing a book or conducting an exorcism?"

"You tell me."

He couldn't, because in the end, he didn't know. He suspected he was trying to do both, and unless he found some middle path, neither effort would be successful.

Kendall had never written a full-length nonfiction book before. Some of his articles had been anthologized between hard covers, and during his lean years he had cranked out some pseudonymous paperback mysteries, but the demands of a two-hundred-thousand-word tome were new to him. He found that concentration was essential; and concentration seemed to require solitude. He tried to explain this to Sara, but she took it as a personal rebuke—which, in a way, it was. He didn't want her to be looking over his shoulder while he uncrated his past; the empty boxes were still there, and too many of them were lying open and exposed.

The plane landed at Houston, and Kendall found himself in the midst of a shimmering heat wave. Texas was an oven this summer. Sealed in the long, black cocoon of the airport limo, Kendall stared at the passing scenery and remembered how much he disliked Texas, land of dead armadillos and plastic grass. Long ago he had covered a story about some unlucky kid from Waco who was sentenced to forty years for possession of an ounce of marijuana. The kid's father had applauded the sentence. Texans had no monopoly on injustice, but it bothered Kendall that they seemed to take so much pride in it.

Kendall checked into his hotel room, turned up the air conditioning, and stretched out on the bed. He wondered what the hell he was doing here.

He forced himself to concentrate on the job at hand. He

was here to collect information for a book, to conduct interviews. This was not simply a replay of his past, no matter how much his room resembled all the other rooms he had stayed in during his days as a roving correspondent. It was 1980 and he was thirty-five years old.

Kendall dug out his notebook, found the phone numbers, and placed a call to the colonel he was supposed to see the next day. Ex-colonel. Now the vice-president of a computer company. In 1968 the man had helped direct the street fighting around the American Embassy in Saigon. The ex-colonel was unavailable, but his secretary confirmed Kendall's appointment for the following morning.

He hung up and checked the book for Turner Poole's number. Kendall didn't want to talk to him, didn't want to see him. The ex-colonel was just an interview; it would be like extracting data from one of the man's computers. But Poole shared memories with him. Poole could make it real again.

"Hello, Joe," said Poole. "You in town?"

"I just got in. I was hoping we could get together tomorrow."

"Tomorrow? Well, sure, I suppose we can. I was going to buy you dinner, right?"

"I won't hold you to that, but I would like to talk to you."

"No, no. Dinner it is. But I'll tell you the truth, Joe, I don't think I'm going to have very much to say about Vietnam. I was only there for a day."

"But it was the day I'm interested in. And I've had some questions I've wanted to ask for a dozen years."

Poole gave a short, ironic laugh. "I don't doubt it," he said. "But I don't really think I can give you any answers."

"Why not?"

"If I told you why not, that would *be* an answer. I don't want to give you a hard time, Joe, I really don't. You come round to my office about six tomorrow afternoon. We'll have dinner and you can ask me all the questions you want. I'm just afraid that you made a long trip for nothing. There's not much I can tell you, Joe."

"Anything at all would be a help."

"Don't count on it," said Poole. "See you tomorrow."

Kendall wondered if Poole's reticence was connected with those strange canisters, or if it was simply a personal reaction. If their positions were switched, Kendall thought, he might be reluctant to talk about that day himself. He knew he wouldn't tell some nosy interviewer what had really happened on Hill 651. Maybe Poole's day had been as bad as his own.

Not wanting to think about it more than he had to, Kendall switched on the television set and leaned back against the pillows. A soap opera ended in unresolved crisis and was followed by a rerun of *Welcome Back, Kotter*. Kendall sympathized with the actress who played Kotter's wife. Her only line was "And then what did your uncle do, Gabe?" Kotter then delivered the punch line and for the rest of the show the action was elsewhere. That seemed to summarize Kendall's life as a journalist. He asked inane straight-line questions, got jokes for answers, and spent the rest of the time watching from offstage while other people's plots unfolded.

Bionic Woman was next up. Kendall stared lustfully at Lindsay Wagner for a while and decided that, without too much imagination, there was a slight resemblance to Sara. Of course, Sara couldn't jump over buildings and bend tire irons in her bare hands—which was probably just as well, all things considered.

Kendall was drifting off to sleep when he was roused by a sharp knock on the door. He switched off the TV and went to the door, feeling tired and heavy.

Two men were standing outside in the hall, one of them nearly a foot shorter than the other. The short one thrust a badge and ID card into Kendall's face.

"Mr. Kendall, we're with the FBI. I'm Special Agent Ginsburg and this is Special Agent Hodges. May we come in?"

Kendall looked from the ID card to the man's face.

Ginsburg stared back at him, bearing the flat, serious expression of a man who had come to disconnect the telephone. Kendall tried to clear the cobwebs from his brain; he had been watching *Bionic Woman*, not *The FBI*. Life seemed to have changed channels on him.

"What's going on?"

"We'd like to talk with you. May we come in?" he repeated politely.

Kendall couldn't think of a reason not to let them in, so he did. He closed the door behind them and tried to figure out what his attitude should be here.

"Make yourselves at home," he said, gesturing to the motel room furniture. Ginsburg sat down in one of the chairs, but Hodges remained standing, resting his rump against the screen of the television set. Kendall sat on the edge of the bed.

"Mr. Kendall," said Ginsburg, "we would like to ask you a few questions."

"Go ahead."

Ginsburg removed a notebook from his breast pocket and consulted it for a few moments. Kendall waited, growing more apprehensive by the second. He felt guilty already, and they hadn't even told him what he had done.

"We understand," said Ginsburg, "that you plan to conduct an interview tomorrow with a Mr. Turner Poole. Is that correct?"

"Yes, it is. What's this all about?"

Ginsburg ignored the question. "You are writing a book about the Vietnam War."

"Yes."

"And the interview is for that book."

"Right again."

"And you first met Mr. Poole in Vietnam in 1968."

"Yes. Look, what is this? You said you wanted to ask some questions, but you seem to know all about me already. You want to tell me what's going on?"

"What are you so uptight about, Kendall?" Hodges, the tall, beefy special agent, gave Kendall a thin, predatory smile. Kendall opened his mouth to deliver a blistering reply, but closed it again, the words unspoken. He knew from experience that FBI agents were not long on humor and tolerance.

"I just want to know what the hell is going on," he said evenly. "For starters, you can tell me how you know so much about me."

"That shouldn't be hard for a crack journalist to figure out," said Hodges.

"Let me handle this," Ginsburg said sharply. Hodges shrugged and repositioned his weight against the television set.

Ginsburg turned back to Kendall. "Mr. Kendall," he said with an air of forced patience, "we are conducting an investigation. Your name has come up in connection with that investigation. You are not under suspicion of anything. All we want is your cooperation."

"I'd like to know exactly what I'm cooperating with."

"I told you, an investigation."

"Of what? Turner Poole?"

"Naturally," said Ginsburg, "we can't reveal that information. Now, would you tell us what you intend to ask Mr. Poole tomorrow."

"Naturally," said Kendall, "I can't reveal that information." He folded his arms and stared defiantly at Ginsburg. The agent looked disappointed.

"Mr. Kendall," he said, "I'm sure you don't want to obstruct a federal investigation."

"Mr. Ginsburg," said Kendall, mimicking the agent's sorrowed tone, "I'm sure you don't want to violate my First Amendment rights." Kendall's paranoia was galloping. He was angry, but until he figured out what the hell was going on, his best move seemed to be to stonewall it.

"If you're worried about your rights, Kendall, we'll take you to see an attorney." Hodges offered another cold grin. "The federal attorney downtown. If you want to be difficult, we can take you in right now as a material witness."

"To what, for chrissakes?" Kendall shouted.

"We'll figure that out later," Hodges answered placidly.

Kendall looked quickly from one agent to the other. "What is this?" he demanded. "Good cop, bad cop? I'm supposed to be afraid of *you* and grateful to *you*, is that it? He's the muscle and you're the brains?"

Now Ginsburg smiled. "You watch too much television, Mr. Kendall."

"Well *somebody* around here sure as hell does." Kendall got to his feet and confronted Hodges, face to chin. Hodges had blue eyes and a nose that had been broken a few times. Kendall stared at him for a moment, then sat down again, not entirely sure why he had got up in the first place.

Ginsburg tried again. "Believe me, Mr. Kendall, we are aware of your First Amendment rights. But I would remind you that your status as a journalist does not give you unlimited privileges. Now, why don't you just cooperate and answer our questions? No one has asked you to violate a source."

"You asked me what I was going to ask Poole. Why don't you wait a day and ask *him*?"

"Don't tell us how to do our job," said Hodges.

"And don't tell me how to do mine, damn it. I don't know what you're after, but if you think I'm going to pump Turner Poole for you, you're sadly mistaken."

There was a moment of silence, and Kendall knew he'd hit it. The FBI wanted something from Poole and couldn't get it themselves. Suddenly, Kendall had some leverage. Now all he had to do was to figure out what to do with it.

Ginsburg looked faintly embarrassed. He glanced down at the notebook again. Hodges stared at Kendall with undisguised animosity.

"Let's forget about Mr. Poole for the moment," said Ginsburg. "You were in Vietnam in late January of 1968, is that right?"

Kendall nodded. He had a sudden premonition of where this was leading.

"Where, exactly, were you at that time?"

"Da Nang, mostly."

"Where else?"

"Here and there. A lot was happening."

"While you were in Da Nang, you met Turner Poole."

"I thought we were going to forget about Poole."

Ginsburg ignored the comment and briefly checked his notebook. "You then proceeded to Khe Sanh, in the company of Mr. Poole."

"How did you know that?"

Hodges snickered. "We never violate a source, Kendall."

"But you did go to Khe Sanh with Turner Poole," Ginsburg persisted.

"That's right."

"And how did you get there? What was your transportation?"

"We skied," Kendall answered, suddenly fed up with the cat-and-mouse nonsense. He knew what they were after. He just didn't know if he was going to give it to them or not.

"Don't try to be funny, Kendall," Hodges warned. "Nobody here is going to laugh."

Kendall stood up again. "Your name is Hodges? Special Agent Hodges? Well, listen up, Hodges. I spent half the day on an airplane, I'm tired and cranky, I'm jet-lagged, I don't like Houston, I don't like the weather, and I don't like you. I'm in no mood to listen to Eliot Ness impressions. So get your ass out of my room. Both of you."

Hodges and Kendall stared at each other. Kendall was just angry enough to be reckless. Ginsburg saw what was developing and quickly moved between the two men.

"Give us a moment, Mr. Kendall." Ginsburg tugged at Hodges's sleeve and started him moving toward the door. Hodges kept his unblinking eyes on Kendall as long as he could. Ginsburg herded him out the door and closed it.

Kendall lighted a cigarette and sat down on the edge of the bed to wait. Over the years he'd had occasion to cover stories that involved the FBI. He found them to be arrogant, humorless, and very impressed with the mystique they imagined attached itself to anyone who possessed an FBI badge. They were also tough, persistent, thorough, and sometimes intelligent. He knew that throwing them out of his room was not going to be the end of it; but it was the first trick, and Kendall had taken it.

After a minute Ginsburg came back into the room. "Hodges will wait outside," he said.

"I kicked both of you out, Ginsburg."

Ginsburg smiled apologetically. "But I'm sure you didn't really mean it."

"Don't bet on it." Kendall let Ginsburg remain standing by the door. The longer he stood there, the more he'd feel like a vacuum cleaner salesman.

"And don't you be fooled, either, Mr. Kendall," said Ginsburg. There was a hint of iron in his voice now. "Don't think that because I'm not as big and strong as Hodges, I'm any less determined than he is."

"Okay," said Kendall. "Give me a reason why we should continue this conversation."

"I think you know the reason as well as I do. Our business, yours and mine, is to ask questions. Both of us want answers to those questions. Tomorrow, you're going to ask Turner Poole some questions. But we both know that you're probably not going to get answers."

"How do we both know that, Mr. Ginsburg?"

Ginsburg waited for Kendall to figure it out, and he did.

"You've got him bugged!"

Ginsburg tilted his head slightly to one side. "You can assume whatever, you want, Mr. Kendall."

Kendall tried to remember everything that had been said in his two conversations with Poole. Damned little, actually. Except that Poole didn't want to talk about Vietnam.

"Have a seat, Mr. Ginsburg." Kendall gestured to the chair. Ginsburg went to it quickly, sat down, and looked at Kendall with the slightest hint of a smile on his lips.

"Now," said Ginsburg, as if they were starting all over again, "why don't you tell me what you intend to ask Poole?"

"Is there going to be a quo for my quid?"

"Possibly."

"Possibly isn't good enough." Kendall was on thin ice now, and he knew it. Dealing with cops and feds for information was a delicate game. A journalist could get burned badly, but he could also score a legitimate coup. The same rules applied to the cops.

Ginsburg made a steeple out of his fingers and tapped the tips together in sequence. "Joe," he said conspiratorially, "I think we're both after the same information. We both have pieces of the story. If we put our pieces together, we'll both know more than we did."

Tapping an ash from the cigarette, Kendall made up his mind. Ginsburg, with his largish nose and bald head, looked like a high school principal. He probably thought of himself as an honorable man, and that would be important to someone so unprepossessing. Ginsburg wouldn't be above shafting him, but he would probably feel badly about doing it. That was something, at least.

"Okay," said Kendall. "You first."

"The quo before the quid?"

"Come on, Ginsburg. You're holding better cards than I am and we both know it. You can afford to be generous."

Ginsburg thought about it and seemed to be in agreement with Kendall's assessment. "All right," he said, "I can tell you this much. We both want to know what Poole was doing in Vietnam."

"You'll have to do better than that."

"I can. I will. Joe, we think Poole may have been a kind of messenger. A delivery boy, perhaps. How's that?"

"Not bad," said Kendall. "It's consistent with what I know."

"Which is?"

"He was definitely delivering something."

"What?"

"You tell me."

"It's still your turn, Joe. Was it bigger than a breadbox?"

Kendall cracked up. The laughter surprised both of them, and soon Ginsburg was chuckling along with him. Kendall stubbed out his cigarette; the air was clear now.

"Yes, Miss Francis, it was bigger than a breadbox. That's one down and nine to go; to you, Mr. Cerf."

"Life as a game show," said Ginsburg reflectively. "What have we come to?"

"I don't know," said Kendall. "A while ago I was thinking it was more like a sitcom. All I want is to be sure it's not going to turn into *The Gong Show*."

"You're not going to get gonged," Ginsburg assured him.

"Is Poole?"

"Possibly, but not for this. You don't know much about him, do you?"

"Almost nothing," Kendall admitted.

"Well," said Ginsburg, "as it happens, we know quite a lot about him. Mr. Poole has been under investigation for some time by an entire flock of official bodies. Everyone from the FBI to the Corpus Christi Board of Health. He's in very deep water. But our present investigation isn't concerned with any criminal acts that we're aware of. We're not asking you to help us nail him for anything. What we need is information."

"Leading to what?"

"I can't tell you that."

"You're going to have to. Look, Ginsburg—"

"People call me Arnie. Or Arn."

Kendall paused and thought about the implications of being on a first-name basis with an FBI agent. It seemed to suggest a slightly deeper level of trust.

"Okay, Arn, I've just confirmed to you that Poole was delivering something large to Khe Sanh. You weren't sure of that before, were you?"

"We suspected it."

"But you didn't *know*, and now you do."

"Granted."

"And you already know what it was."

"We think so. We're not sure of that, either."

"Well, Arn, that's as far as it's going to go. I'm still in the dark here, and Poole isn't going to enlighten me. Unless I can throw some facts at him, he's not going to

126

give me anything. I need a wedge. I need to know what I'm after. Specifically."

"I don't know how specific I can be, Joe." Ginsburg sounded honestly regretful.

"Look, I'm a journalist. I can't write rumors and suspicions. I'll make you a deal, Arn. You tell me everything you can—and I mean everything—and I'll agree not to publish any of it until six months from now, or until you give me a go-ahead. I don't want to compromise your investigation. And I won't use your name or quote you without permission."

"I don't know if I can make that kind of deal, Joe."

"You'll have to. You can't get the answers you need directly from Poole or you'd already have done it. But I can, if you give me something to work with. Whatever it is, it's bound to come out sooner or later, anyway. This way, at least you have some control."

Ginsburg looked thoughtful. "Six months?"

"Or until I get your go-ahead, whichever comes first."

"Make it a year."

That was fine with Kendall; his book wasn't due to be published for nearly two years, anyway. "Okay," he said. "A year it is."

"Deal," said Ginsburg. He extended his right hand, and Kendall took it.

"One more thing," said Kendall, still shaking Ginsburg's hand. "If any part of this story comes out somewhere else in the meantime, all bets are off."

"I can't guarantee there won't be any leaks."

"Shit, Arn, this *is* a leak."

Ginsburg dropped Kendall's hand. "Yeah," he said, "I suppose it is."

The agent shifted his weight in the chair, but a look of deep discomfort remained on his face. Kendall wondered if he should feel sorry for the guy.

"Before we begin," said Ginsburg, "there's something else I'd like to ask you. This has nothing to do with the investigation. It's . . . it's personal."

"Sure. What?"

"Well, I suppose you must realize that we have a file on you at the Bureau."

"That doesn't surprise me. I thought about trying to get it under Freedom of Information, but it was too much of a hassle. I suppose you've read it."

Ginsburg nodded. He seemed to be hesitating for some reason, and that worried Kendall. What personal item in his file had attracted Ginsburg's curiosity?

"According to the information in the file, you published five novels under a pseudonym back in the mid-seventies."

"That's right," Kendall admitted. "Paperback mysteries. Strictly bargain basement. It's amazing, the things you wind up doing to pay the rent. So what do you want, Arn, an autographed copy?"

"No," said Ginsburg, "I'd like you to tell me how you did it."

"What?"

"I mean, how do you go about publishing a book under another name? You see"—Ginsburg smiled wanly—"I'm writing a novel. I was hoping you could give me some advice."

Kendall couldn't help himself. He laughed.

Chapter Nine

"It was called Nightwind," said Ginsburg.

The word felt strange on his lips. It was not a word he had spoken aloud very often, although it had been alive in his mind for years. Carrying the secret so long had made it a part of him. Telling Kendall about it now, he felt as if he were confessing to some deeply personal sin. He was also taking a terrible risk; if Kendall proved to be untrustworthy, Ginsburg would soon discover how it felt to be on the receiving end of the Bureau's wrath.

"It was started back in the mid-sixties. The defense budget was sky-high and nobody was asking very many questions. There were dozens of cloak-and-dagger projects like it, but most of them came to nothing. Nightwind was different. They got lucky."

Kendall was watching him in silence, sucking on another cigarette. Ginsburg wanted to tell him to put it out; a few more minutes and his allergy was going to assert itself. But he didn't want to be impolite to Kendall. He was going to need every ounce of Kendall's goodwill and confidence.

"They were looking for an effective, limited biochemical warfare agent. They didn't want plagues and doomsday viruses. All they wanted was something they could spread over a limited area that would make everyone in that area sick and immobile for a few weeks. And they found it.

"You have to remember, in those days the techniques were not as sophisticated as they are today. Recombinant DNA and gene splicing were still science fiction."

Ginsburg stopped as the words "science fiction" came out of his mouth. He hadn't told Kendall that his novel was science fiction, which somehow seemed even more disreputable than Kendall's mysteries. Kendall was already amused by the idea of an FBI agent writing a secret novel; if he knew it was science fiction, he might stop taking him seriously altogether. And it was vital that Kendall take Nightwind seriously.

"Basically," said Ginsburg, "they were using the same techniques as Gregor Mendel. Mendel was—"

"I know who Mendel was," said Kendall. "Fruit flies and all that."

"Right. Basic genetics. Mix and match and see what you get. The Nightwind scientists were doing that with bacteria and viruses. Since those organisms reproduce rapidly, they were able to produce many generations in a short time. They were looking for useful mutations, and to promote mutations they irradiated their samples."

"It sounds like a hit-or-miss operation," said Kendall.

"In a way, it was. But they weren't groping blindly. They knew what they were starting with, and they knew what they were looking for. They obviously had reason to believe that they could succeed. And they did. They came up with a new strain of bug that produced almost exactly what they were after. It made humans very ill but it wasn't necessarily fatal. And it didn't travel well. That was important, because if you use something like this in combat, you don't want to make your own troops sick. This particular bug didn't survive for very long outside the lab. Unless it found a sheltered, warm and wet environment, it tended to die out within a few weeks. Again, that's exactly what they wanted."

"Did they test this on people?" Kendall asked.

130

"Not at first. Mainly, they tested it on sheep, sometimes unintentionally."

Kendall sat up straight. "Dugway! All those sheep that got killed in Utah. Was that Nightwind?"

"And its successors." Ginsburg nodded. "They weren't as careful as they should have been. And that's one of the reasons the whole project was terminated in 1967."

" 'Sixty-seven?"

"I know," said Ginsburg. "This is where it gets complicated. From the time Nightwind was canceled, in July of 'sixty-seven, we're just not certain where the trail leads. I suppose that's one of the underlying results of Vietnam. When one part of the government starts lying to another part of the government, there's no telling what can happen."

"You're beginning to lose me," said Kendall. "Exactly who canceled Nightwind? And who was lying to whom?"

"The joint chiefs canceled it. They were never very enthusiastic about it to begin with, apparently. The military likes fancy new weapons, God knows, but they tend to be suspicious of anything that doesn't make a loud noise. When a Nightwind test killed some sheep that weren't supposed to be killed, that gave the chiefs the excuse they needed to cancel the project. That should have been the end of it."

"But it wasn't?" Kendall crushed out the cigarette and Ginsburg took a deep breath. He might as well get all the fresh air he could, because he figured that Kendall was going to need another cigarette very soon.

"In 1976," said Ginsburg, speaking slowly and choosing his words carefully, "the Nightwind bug reappeared."

"Reappeared how?"

"In the environment."

"In Utah?"

"No," said Ginsburg, "not in Utah."

"Where?"

Ginsburg told himself that he should have realized this would happen. Kendall was a good journalist and wasn't going to let him gloss over anything. There were questions that should not be answered, but if he tried to be cute, Kendall's cooperative attitude might evaporate.

"I'd rather not say, Joe. We're both walking a very thin line here, and I'd appreciate it if you didn't press."

Kendall considered it for a moment, then shook his head. "You're changing the ground rules, Arn. I'm not going to play blindman's buff."

"And I'm not going to play twenty questions. I'm sorry, but that's the way it has to be."

"You can't even tell me where the bug reappeared? Why is that such a hot question?"

"I can't even tell you that. Just accept the fact that the bug showed up again four years ago."

"In 1976."

"Yes."

Ginsburg could almost see the wheels turning inside Kendall's brain. He was going to get it. Ginsburg waited for the inevitable.

It didn't take long. Kendall's eyes widened suddenly.

"Jesus!" He stared at Ginsburg's eyes, and Ginsburg wasn't enough of a poker player to get away with it. Kendall knew.

"It reappears in 1976," said Kendall urgently. "It's a bug that likes warm, wet places. It makes people very sick but doesn't necessarily kill them. God damn it, Ginsburg! It was Philadelphia, wasn't it? At the Bellevue-Strafford Hotel. The Nightwind bug is Legionnaire's disease, isn't it?"

Ginsburg could only nod. Kendall reached for a cigarette.

"Jesus Christ, Arn!" Kendall took a deep drag on the cigarette and exhaled slowly.

"You figured it out for yourself," said Ginsburg. "I didn't tell you. Remember that. I didn't tell you."

"My God! This is . . ." Kendall groped for words.

"It's appalling," Ginsburg offered.

"It's a hell of a lot more than that! You mean all those people died because of some half-assed James Bond project that was canceled in 1967?" Kendall got to his feet and stomped angrily around the room. He looked as if he wanted to hit something. Ginsburg knew the feeling.

"How?" Kendall demanded. "How the fucking hell could it happen?"

"That," said Ginsburg, "is what we are trying to find out. That, and how to keep it from happening again."

"And all this is tied to Turner Poole? Vietnam in 1968? Is that what Poole was delivering?"

"It begins to look that way. We weren't even sure Poole was connected at all, until you told us that he was making a delivery. And it's still just a guess. We don't *know* that he was delivering the Nightwind bug. That's why your cooperation is so important, Joe. We've got to find out exactly what Poole was up to. We need details."

Still agitated, Kendall sat down again and nervously tapped the cigarette against the ashtray. "It doesn't make any sense," he said. "Assuming Poole was delivering Nightwind, how the hell does it jump from Vietnam in 1968 to the Bellevue-Strafford Hotel in 1976? What's the connection? For that matter, how did it even get to Vietnam? I thought you said the whole thing was canceled?"

"This is where the lying comes into play," said Ginsburg. "The investigation requires a great leap across the Lyndon Baines Johnson Memorial Credibility Gap. By 1968 LBJ felt he was under siege, not just from the media and the students, but from people in his own administration. He thought they were all out to get him, one way or another. You know, I can almost sympathize with him. He was in a hell of a spot."

"If he was, he put himself there."

Ginsburg raised his hand, palm outward, like a traffic cop or, more to the point, like Dave Garroway's signaling "peace" on the old *Today* show. It was the original source of Ginsburg's gesture, a vestige of the decade that had shaped Ginsburg as surely and completely as the sixties had sculpted Kendall.

"Let's not argue politics," Ginsburg said. "Back in the days when you were writing sympathetic articles about radicals, I was busy trying to put them in jail. If we get

133

hung up on the right and wrong of it, we'll never get anywhere."

"No," Kendall said, "right and wrong was at the center of it. We've refused to come to grips with it, and until we do, we're never going to understand what happened to us then. We'll never find out who we really are."

"Is that why you're writing the book?"

"Partly."

They regarded each other in silence for a moment, like Robin Hood and Little John standing on opposite banks of a swiftly flowing stream.

"Good luck with it," Ginsburg said at last. "I hope you find some answers."

"What difference does it make?" Kendall asked, accepting the impossibility of what he was trying to do. "You wouldn't agree with my answers, anyway."

"Probably not," Ginsburg said.

"LBJ," prompted Kendall.

"Yes," said Ginsburg, "LBJ. There is reason to believe that sometime after the joint chiefs canceled Nightwind, Johnson reactivated it. If he did, it was outside of normal channels. There are absolutely no records."

"Then how do you know he did anything?"

"Somebody did, and Johnson was the only man who had the power. After the project was canceled, all the Nightwind bug that had been produced was stored in a security warehouse in Utah. Everybody who had been involved more or less forgot about it.

"When the Legionnaire's flap hit in 'seventy-six, one of the epidemiologists working on the case happened to be a man who had worked on Nightwind. He recognized the bug when he saw it again and was smart enough to call the FBI instead of the newspapers. We began our own investigation and discovered that two canisters of the Nightwind agent were missing from the warehouse. When we checked back through the old inventory records, it turned out that they had been missing ever since 1968. Nobody noticed because almost nobody knew about Nightwind in the first place."

"Nice," said Kendall.

"Oh, that's just the tip of the iceberg," Ginsburg assured him. "If LBJ did reactivate the project, he took care to cover his tracks, which wouldn't have been too difficult for him to do. We know that Johnson liked the Nightwind concept because it seemed to be a way to quarantine South Vietnam. The original plan envisioned an operation to spread the bug across the DMZ and the Ho Chi Minh Trail in Laos, effectively sealing the country. That, theoretically, would limit the scope of the war and reduce the need for bombing in the north, which always made Johnson nervous.

"We know that by the beginning of 1968 Johnson was looking for some kind of quick fix. He had reliable intelligence that the Communists were planning a big offensive, and he may have seen Nightwind as a way of preventing it. But if Poole was delivering the bug on the day Tet began, then he was too late. After that, I would guess that things just happened too fast. Right after Tet came the New Hampshire primary, then Bobby Kennedy's entry into the race. Johnson realized that he wasn't going to win—the election or the war—so he bowed out of the election and called for a bombing halt and peace talks."

Kendall nodded. "So that leaves us with Nightwind in Vietnam and LBJ on the way out."

"Right," said Ginsburg, "and that's the key to it. If he managed to get Nightwind into Vietnam surreptitiously, he'd have to get it out the same way. But Johnson still had hopes of ending the war before he left office, so maybe he wanted to keep the bug in place. Or maybe he just forgot about it; God knows, he had enough to think about that year. Anyway, 1968 ends, Johnson goes out, and Nixon comes in. Since almost nobody in the Johnson administration knew about Nightwind, it's entirely possible that the Nixon people were never told about it."

"Jesus," said Kendall suddenly. "I think I see where this is leading. If nobody knows about Nightwind, then . . ."

"Then it just sits there, somewhere in Vietnam, and the

Americans pull out and leave it behind when Saigon collapses in 1975."

Kendall leaned back on the bed and stared at the ceiling. He closed his eyes for a few seconds, then straightened up and looked at Ginsburg.

"Okay, Arn. I'll give you a little more quid for all that quo. Poole was delivering two long metal canisters. I saw them. They looked kind of like acetylene tanks. Nightwind?"

Ginsburg sighed. "Nightwind."

"Christ," said Kendall, "I was on the same plane with them."

"So he took them to Khe Sanh?"

"Not exactly. Khe Sanh was more than just the one big base. There were a series of camps all over the surrounding hills. We landed at Khe Sanh and about two minutes later we took off in a chopper, with the canisters."

"Where did you go?"

"A delightful little place called Hill Six fifty-one. Poole delivered the canisters to someone named Colonel Weiss."

Ginsburg began writing rapidly in his notebook. He had trouble keeping it legible. It was almost like buck fever, he thought, when the deer suddenly appears in your sights after a long hunt. He felt light-headed and giddy.

He put the notebook back in his pocket and smiled at Kendall. "Joe," he said warmly, "you've been more help than you realize. In the last two minutes you moved this investigation ahead farther than we've gone in two years. You just gave me the information we were hoping to get from Poole. Now all we have to do is track down this Colonel Weiss and we'll find out exactly what became of those canisters."

"Don't count on it."

"Why not?"

"I already tracked him down," said Kendall. "For the book. Colonel Weiss was killed in action that same night. So was his second-in-command, Captain Bascomb. And from what I saw, I don't think anyone else knew about Nightwind."

136

"Shit," said Ginsburg. He rarely used rough language, but this news seemed to demand it. "Now we're going to have to try to find every man who was anywhere near Hill Six fifty-one."

"I can help a little. I've got some names and addresses I can give you, but they were all grunts."

"Well, maybe they saw something or heard something. We've got to establish whether or not the canisters were left behind."

"I'm still confused here," said Kendall. "If they were left behind, how do they get to Philadelphia?"

Ginsburg got to his feet. "It's a long tale," he said. "I think I'm going to need a glass of water first. And Joe, could you not smoke? I'm allergic."

"Sorry," said Kendall.

In truth, Ginsburg could have used something much stronger than water. This was the part of the case where the facts were few but frightening. The spaces between the facts had to be filled by speculation which, inevitably, was even more frightening.

Returning to his chair with a plastic glass, sanitized for his protection, Ginsburg decided that he might as well tell Kendall everything. The more Kendall knew about Nightwind, the more careful he would become. He might even be scared away from the story entirely.

So Ginsburg laid it out for him. Kendall listened intently and asked few questions. The lines in Kendall's face deepened as the sunlight leaking in through the drawn curtains moved slowly away from him. By the time Ginsburg finished, Kendall looked as if he had aged by a decade; Ginsburg didn't believe it could all be attributed to the changing shadows.

The scientists investigating Legionnaire's disease had been thorough. They compiled a list of possible undiagnosed victims of the disease in the hope of finding some common element among those who were stricken. When the FBI entered the case, they ran the additional names through a computer, looking for a direct link to Nightwind or Vietnam or even Lyndon Johnson. They found no such link. But they did find the name of Sanchez Raposo.

On the night of July 3, 1976, weeks before the outbreak of the disease, Sanchez Raposo and his cousin Domingo Raposo were removed from a New York-bound train at Metuchen, New Jersey. Both men were violently ill; food poisoning was suspected. In addition to his other symptoms Sanchez had many small cuts and contusions. Treatment was administered at a local hospital, but by morning Sanchez was dead. Domingo fell into a coma and died the following night. When a routine autopsy revealed that there had been no food poisoning, the deaths were ascribed to lethal doses of some contaminated drug. No further investigation was attempted.

The FBI computer, however, recognized the name of Sanchez Raposo. There was a thick file on him. Raposo was known to be associated with a group of radical Puerto Rican separatists. The group was already infiltrated by FBI agents, and further information on Raposo was collected. In September the Bureau staged a raid on a tenement building in Brooklyn. The agents found one old woman who knew nothing. They also found, secreted within the walls, twenty-three explosive devices containing the Nightwind vector.

The Nightwind project was concerned not just with the development of the bug but with its delivery system. The long, cylindrical canisters that Poole had delivered to Vietnam each contained twenty-four devices, six inches in diameter and two and a half inches thick; because of their shape the Nightwind scientists referred to the devices as hockey pucks.

As originally planned, the cylinders were to have been slung beneath specially adapted helicopters. The copters would fly over the drop zone while the cylinders ejected one hockey puck every fifteen seconds. The pucks contained centrifugal trigger mechanisms that were activated by the spinning motion created by ejection. After a predetermined number of revolutions the pucks would explode, spraying the Nightwind agent over the Indochinese countryside below. The operation was to have been conducted at night and would have been dependent on the wind conditions: thus, the name.

The pucks contained a gray, cakelike culture medium, providing an agreeable environment for the Nightwind bug. When the puck exploded, the cake disintegrated into millions of dust particles that were supposed to descend on the land like a thin, deadly blanket. Anyone living in or passing through the affected area would be certain to come in contact with the dust; the Ho Chi Minh Trail would become a highway of disease and death. Eventually, removed from its protective culture, the Nightwind bug would dwindle and die. Four months after the operation the target area would again be safe for travelers—this time headed north.

Instead, Nightwind found its way to the Bellevue-Strafford Hotel. The FBI pursued the Puerto Rican groups and eventually pieced together part of the story. The Raposos had gone to Philadelphia to assassinate President Ford when he made his Bicentennial address at Independence Hall; their weapon, evidently, was a single Nightwind puck. Something went wrong and the puck exploded inside the hotel, fatally infecting the two cousins.

The remaining twenty-three pucks had been designated for other targets around the nation during that jubilee year: the Republican and Democratic conventions, the World Series, college football games. A wave of biological terrorism was to have been unleashed, culminating (or so went the plan) in the independence of Puerto Rico. But the botched Philadelphia mission ended the offensive before it properly began. Sanchez Raposo seemed to be the only person who knew where the Nightwind weapon had come from, and he was dead. No one else was eager to follow in his footsteps.

Raposo himself had led an intriguing life. He had spent considerable time abroad, and the CIA reported that he was known to have contacts among European and Middle Eastern terrorist groups. But the trail also led in another direction. Another of Sanchez's cousins, Domingo's older brother, had been reported missing in action in Vietnam. Alfredo Raposo had simply disappeared from his unit in the Da Nang area; he may have been killed, he may have been taken prisoner, or he may have deserted. In any event, there was a definite link between Sanchez Raposo and Vietnam.

The scanty trail soon disappeared entirely, leaving investigators with no more than flimsy theories. The two Nightwind canisters could have followed any number of paths from Vietnam to Philadelphia. American troops may have brought them back, as secretly as they had been delivered, only to lose them in some manner once they had been returned to the States. Or the canisters may have been left behind in Vietnam. If that was the case, then perhaps a turncoat Alfredo Raposo had somehow obtained them and found a way to bring them home for use by the separatists. Alternatively, the Vietnamese may have found them and subsequently sold them to a terrorist organization, which eventually turned them over to Sanchez Raposo.

There were many problems with each theory. The most troubling problem, by far, was the fact that only one of the canisters had been accounted for. The other one could be anywhere.

"We want to find that second canister," Ginsburg told Kendall, "and we want to find it quick. The Puerto Ricans wanted to hit the political conventions in 'seventy-six, but they missed. They'll have two more chances this summer."

"Assuming they have the second canister," Kendall pointed out.

"Whoever has it, the conventions would be logical targets. The entire power structure will be gathered in a few hotels and two big auditoriums. A few of those pucks planted in the right spots could chop off the nation's head."

Kendall looked subdued, reflective. "I keep thinking of Iranians," he said.

"So do we," Ginsburg said. "What could be more appropriate than striking at the Great Satan with his own infernal weapon? But it doesn't have to be Iran. It could be

140

anyone at all. Unless we can get some kind of lead on the second canister, we won't even know which way to look."

"There's something I still don't understand," said Kendall. "Why didn't people start getting sick in Philadelphia on July third? Why the delayed reaction?"

"That's a good question. The prevailing theory is that the Raposos accidentally set off the puck in a room at the Bellevue-Strafford. If they did it on July third, it could have taken several weeks for the bug to establish itself in the hotel's air conditioning system and reach a great enough concentration to be dangerous. It apparently reached critical mass by the time the Legionnaires had their convention."

"I've got another question. As I recall, the victims seldom recovered. There was a very high mortality rate."

"True," said Ginsburg. He waited for Kendall to ask the next question, the one he had been hoping he wouldn't have to answer. But the question was inescapable.

"Why," asked Kendall, "did they die? I thought the bug was only supposed to make people sick?"

Ginsburg stared at the journalist for a long moment. Kendall may have had a right to know, but once he had the knowledge, he might find himself longing for the bliss of ignorance. Ginsburg sometimes did.

"Joe, the bug that caused the Legionnaire's outbreak was not the same as the bug invented by the Nightwind scientists."

Kendall looked blank. "I don't get it," he said.

"It mutated," said Ginsburg. "Remember, I told you that they produced the original bug by radiation-induced mutations. In 1967 the bug they had was the bug they wanted. But by 1976 it had become something else—call it Nightwind B. Not all of the effects of radiation are immediately evident. Sometimes the effects may not show up for generations. In the case of the puck that went off in Philly, the original bug had mutated into a much more deadly bug while it sat inside the culture cake for nine years."

"I see," said Kendall. "So the second canister is full of Nightwind B."

"No," said Ginsburg, "you don't see. Each puck is a

141

self-contained unit, Joe. What happens in one has no effect on what happens in the others. When the other twenty-three pucks from the first canister were recovered and examined, they found that some of them contained the original bug, a few had Nightwind B, and a few had completely different bugs. We're up to Nightwind G. Not all of the strains are deadly. Some are completely harmless. And at least one is twice as lethal as Nightwind B. If that one—Nightwind D—had gone off, it would have killed half the population of Philadelphia."

Kendall looked up at the ceiling and said nothing. Ginsburg let him absorb the implications.

"How long?" Kendall asked. "How long can that stuff stay alive inside the pucks?"

"Twenty years is the best guess. No one is really very sure."

"Thirteen years," said Kendall. "It's still alive. Christ, what if that second canister is full of Nightwind D?"

"It's had four more years since Philadelphia, Joe. By now, it may have become Nightwind Q or Nightwind Z. Nobody knows. Nobody can even make an intelligent guess. The Nightwind scientists weren't trying to make a doomsday bug—but by now, they may have one. We have to find that second canister, Joe. It could kill everyone ...*everyone*."

Chapter Ten

The sight of Joe Kendall made Turner Poole feel strangely uncomfortable. Sitting across the table from him in the dimly lit corner booth of the restaurant, Kendall looked both young and old. He still had all his hair, Poole noted sadly, but it no longer fell to his shoulders, and the side-burns had more than a little gray in them. Kendall was heavier and his face had a few more lines around the eyes and mouth, but he was recognizably the same person as the awkward kid who had hitched a ride to Khe Sanh a dozen years ago. But the present version of Kendall was more sober and impressive, a professor of journalism at a major university, a successful writer, and the author of what would probably become an important book about Vietnam. Kendall had obviously spent the last twelve years doing more than making deals and money.

Poole was afraid that for him, the reverse was true. The man he saw in his office mirror each day appeared to bear no relationship to the Turner Poole of 1968. Yet inside, he was still the same grasping hustler who had run sleazy errands for Breeze Woodward. He had accomplished nothing that would endure, nothing of value. Kendall, the hippie journalist, had somehow acquired dignity and substance, while Poole had acquired nothing but cash and a deserved reputation as a fast operator. When all accounts were settled, Kendall would still have that solid inner core and Turner Poole would have nothing at all.

And the accounts, Poole reflected morosely, might be settled very soon. Perhaps he could acquire dignity and substance while doing the laundry at Leavenworth.

Poole took a healthy slug of bourbon. It went well with the steak and potatoes. These days, it went well with everything.

"I've got to say, Joe, it's kind of strange to see you. You know what I mean?"

Kendall looked at him for a second and nodded.

"I mean," Poole continued, "it's kind of like a high school reunion or something. You bump into people you never really knew very well and you think, boy has *he* changed. You ever go to a high school reunion?"

"My tenth," said Kendall. "One was enough. My old girl friend was heavily into natural childbirth and breast feeding. That didn't leave us a whole lot to talk about."

"Yeah," said Poole, "I know what you mean. I went to my twentieth a couple of years ago. I guess I was sort of a wimp in high school, and I wanted to impress everybody with all the money I'd made and how successful I was. Self-made millionaire and all that. And you know something? I don't think it made any difference at all. I think they still thought I was a wimp."

"But a rich one," said Kendall. "They were probably green with envy. Down deep, everyone thinks he's still seventeen. Or ten. Everyone else has grown up, but we stay the same."

"That's almost profound, Joe."

Kendall smiled. "That's my business," he said. "As a writer, I deal in semiprofundities the same way you deal in . . . what is it, oil?"

"A bit. And cotton. And chicken-fried steak."

"And marijuana?"

"Where," Poole asked carefully, "did you get an idea like that?"

"I've been doing some research on you, Turner."

"Really?" Poole sipped at his bourbon and waited. He hadn't expected anything like this from Kendall.

"Don't worry," said Kendall. "I'm not going to put that in the book. And I probably won't say anything about your little navy of Vietnamese refugee shrimp boats, although that does have a nice touch of irony."

"What the hell are you after, Kendall?"

"Answers. I want to find out how a guy who becomes a dope importer and real estate sharpie could have gone to Vietnam in 1968 with a letter from Lyndon Johnson in his pocket."

Poole leaned back against the leather padding of the booth. This was all he needed; first the feds and now the press. If he didn't watch it, he was going to wind up on the cover of *People* magazine.

"Where'd you get a crazy idea like that, Joe? What would I be doing with a letter from the President?"

"Come on, Poole. Nobody here but us chickens. I was *there*, remember? I saw you whip out that letter in the Da Nang Air Ops office."

"And you think that letter was from LBJ?"

"I know it was. You were his delivery boy."

"Was I?"

"Yes, you were." Kendall said it so flatly and with such confidence that Poole knew it was useless to try to deny it. Kendall obviously had found himself a reliable source.

"You're a real digger, aren't you? How the hell did you find out about that?"

"That's not important." Kendall paused to take a sip of his own drink, a gin and tonic. "What is important is the fact that you were making a top secret and highly irregular delivery for Lyndon Johnson."

"Lyndon Baines Johnson," Poole said slowly, accenting the syllables of the name as if it were a private mantra. "That fucking asshole. He told me I'd be a goddamn hero someday. I'd walk in the front door of the White House. Shit, three years later I couldn't even get into the LBJ Ranch. The fucker double-crossed me. I nearly got my ass blown off for him and he pretended he never heard of me.

That long-eared jackass taught me an important lesson, Joe. Everyone's on the make, and politicians are just like everyone else except they're even sleazier. They'll sell out anything or anyone for a vote or a buck. And the surprising thing is how cheap they come. You know, I've got me a genuine U.S. congressman in my hip pocket."

Poole took another drink of bourbon and raised his hand to signal a passing waiter. He tapped the empty glass to indicate his needs.

"Yessir," said Poole, "you can buy anyone. Hell, boy, I could even buy you."

The waiter arrived with fresh drinks. Poole stared at his for a second and wondered why the more booze he drank, the more he sounded like Breeze Woodward. Kendall hadn't reacted yet to the suggestion that he could be bought, and Poole knew that the bourbon-and-swampwater approach probably wouldn't work with him. Kendall was no doubt a man of principle, or thought he was, which meant that he'd have to go through a few minutes of agonizing moral debate before he sold out. Breeze would probably have blown it with a man like Kendall, but Poole knew he had the sophistication to pull it off. He was much better than Breeze; so why was he dragging out the shitkicker accent and the good old boy vocabulary?

"Of course," Poole said, "I'm not trying to buy you, Joe. That was just an example."

"Of course," Kendall agreed.

"So what do you want to know?"

"Tell me where you delivered those two canisters."

"That's all? Hell, you know where I took them. Hill Six fifty-one."

"I want to know exactly. You got in the jeep with them and took off for the top part of the hill. They called it Grenoble. It was an old French bunker."

"That's the place, all right. Sounds like you've already got all the answers."

"Not all of them," said Kendall. "I need to know what happened after you got up to Grenoble."

"Why is that so important?"

"Details are always important. Narrative flow, credibility, and all that."

"If you say so. It's your business. Okay, let's see. We stopped the jeep right outside some dilapidated old concrete bunker and some colonel met us."

"Colonel Weiss."

"That's the one. He was expecting me, and as I recall we didn't waste much time on chitchat. He had a couple of men unload the canisters. I had to go along with them because the letter said I was supposed to verify that the canisters were delivered safely and stored in a protected location."

"Were they?"

"If you can call any place in Vietnam protected. We went down into that bunker, and I'll tell you, it was one creepy place. That old bunker must have gone thirty feet down into the mountain. It was like breaking into the burial chamber of a pyramid. The marines were using the top part of the bunker, but I'd swear nobody had been in the bottom of it since the French left. There were even some old, broken wine bottles down there. And it was cold, I remember that. Damned strange down there." Poole felt chilled by the memory and warmed himself with more bourbon.

"And that's where you put the canisters."

"Yeah," said Poole, "one of 'em."

"You mean the second canister was stored someplace else?" Kendall suddenly seemed very intense.

"Uh-huh. The colonel—Weiss?—he didn't want to put both of 'em in the same place. Too many eggs in one basket, he said. That bottom room was right below the place where they stored the ammunition, I think. Anyway, we put the other canister somewhere else."

"Where?" asked Kendall. "Exactly."

"Hell, Joe, it's been a long time. I think we put the second one at the back of some abandoned gun emplacement. There were tunnels all over the place and it was all connected underground, so it's hard to say exactly where we were. What difference does it make?"

147

"More than you'd believe," said Kendall quietly. He reached for his glass and took a long drink.

"Shit, it didn't make any difference at all. They never even used that stuff, as far as I know. That whole trip was for nothing. And I do mean nothing. You write about it, and you'll have yourself one very boring book, I'll tell you that, Joe. Never even used it."

A thought struck Poole. The booze was upon him now, but he could still think. The body got wobbly and the words got blurry, but the brain never quit. Dead drunk, Turner Poole was twice as sharp as Breeze Woodward on the soberest day of his life, if he'd had one.

"Or did they use it?" Poole asked cagily. "You seem to know a hell of a lot more about this than I do, Joe. Did they use that stuff? Is that what this is all about?"

Kendall ignored the question. "Did you know what was in those canisters?"

"Sure I did!" Poole insisted. "I wasn't some hick kid from Texas. I knew what was goin' on. It was biochemical warfare, that's what it was. Biochemical. That means germs, Joe. That's why I wasn't supposed to talk about it, 'cause Lyndon was up to something he shouldn't have been up to. He was gonna give the Vietcong cancer or rickets or some damn thing. Shit, I don't care. You know all about it, don't you? Did they ever use that stuff? Tell me, Joe, 'cause I really want to know if that trip accomplished anything."

"No," said Kendall. "They never used it. They never had the chance."

"That's what I thought. Old Lyndon said it would win the war, but we didn't win that one, did we? So I guess they didn't use it. Made that trip for nothing."

"Tell me about that bunker," said Kendall. "How close were the canisters to the ammunition dump?"

"Who cares? What difference does it make how close they were to the ammo?"

"The ammunition dump blew up that night. The VC hit us, and they blew the hell out of Grenoble. Would the explosion have taken out those canisters?"

"How the hell would I know?"

"You're the only one left alive who would know. How close were they to the ammunition?"

Poole tried to focus on the details of the bunker. He remembered long dark tunnels and dripping concrete walls.

"Well," said Poole, "the one we put in the gun emplacement was clear on the other side of the mountain, damn near. Seems like we walked forever down there, but I guess it couldn't have been more than a hundred yards."

"So that one wasn't near the ammunition."

"Nope. But the other one was right beneath it, down under about ten feet of concrete. Shit, if the ammo went up, that thing's probably still there, buried deeper 'n Big Bad John. All of Lyndon's germs down deep in the ground, just like Lyndon."

Poole gave a short, snorting laugh. Kendall lighted a cigarette and puffed at it deliberately for several seconds. He looked very thoughtful, but Poole had a mind like a bear trap and he knew what Kendall was thinking.

"It *is* still there, isn't it? What are you gonna do, file a complaint with the fucking Environmental Protection Agency? Those old EPA boys'll have a shit fit, you tell 'em we've been dumping germs. They get upset if you just bury some old tin cans in a vacant lot. Bastards tried to sue me, once. Is that what's gonna happen, Joe? You gonna get the EPA on my ass for dumping germs in Vietnam? Well, lemme tell you, the fuckin' EPA will just have to stand in line with all the others. Seems like jus' about ever'one wants a piece of old Turner's hide these days. So I ain't gonna get in a sweat about some can of germs in Vietnam, I'll tell you that."

"The EPA isn't interested," Kendall assured him.

"Well *who*, then, God damn it! Who's after me this time? The DEA? FBI? Some fuckin' congressional committee? Or is the local boys? The cops? The AG? The chickenshit Board of Health again? The Mafia? The KGB? Who the hell is after me now?"

"Nobody's after you," Kendall lied.

149

"Everybody's after me," said Poole sadly. He drank some more bourbon. He looked up at Kendall and pointed his finger at him. *"You're* after me."

"No, I'm not. I'm just writing a book."

"About a coupla cans o' germs buried on some godforsaken mountain in Vietnam? Then how come you know so much about me? Answer me that, old buddy, old comrade-in-arms. Who's been telling you lies about me?"

"No one," said Kendall.

"Bullshit. What's your game, Kendall? You can tell old Turner the truth. What's your price, Joe? Every man's got a price, it says so in the Bible or the Constitution or the Boy Scout oath. Somewhere. How much, Joe? You just tell me who's after me about those goddamn germs and I'll pay you for it. The truth shall make you money. How much?"

Poole fumbled for his wallet and managed to extract a crisp hundred-dollar bill. He dropped it on the table.

"That'll make a nice tip for the waiter," said Kendall as he got to his feet. He stepped around the table and pulled Poole up to standing position.

"Come on, Turner."

"Where we going? You haven't told me the truth yet."

"I'll tell you the truth. We're going to get a cab. You can pick up your car tomorrow. I don't think you should be driving."

Poole protested weakly as Kendall steered him out of the restaurant. Outside, the muggy heat wrapped itself around them and Poole wanted to puke.

"I can drive," Poole insisted, breaking free from Kendall's grip.

"Not with me in the car," said Kendall.

"Fine, suit yourself." Poole spotted his car and set a course toward it. He stumbled once over a curb, but he made it. He looked around, but Kendall was no longer with him. Kendall was standing on the other side of the parking lot, watching.

"Kendall!"

"What?" shouted the writer.

"We're even now, right? I paid for the dinner. You saved my life and I paid for the dinner. Even up, right? No matter what those bastards say, Turner Poole pays his debts!"

Poole got behind the wheel, started the engine, and sped off into the night.

Ginsburg and Hodges were waiting for Kendall when he returned to his hotel room. They were standing in the hallway outside the door, looking like process servers who were paid by the hour. Ginsburg was still wearing a dark suit and tie, straight out of the FBI fashion guide, but Hodges, in a concession to the heat, wore a seersucker jacket and had loosened his tie.

"Can we come in?" Ginsburg asked politely.

"It's been a beautiful evening," said Kendall. "Let's not spoil it."

"Funny," said Hodges.

"We need to talk," said Ginsburg.

"Why? I'm sure you heard every word Poole and I said all evening." Ginsburg stared at him, looking both disappointed and determined. Kendall, drained by the heat and the drinks, decided not to fight it. He unlocked the door and ushered the agents into his room. Ginsburg sat down in the same chair and Hodges resumed his station in front of the television set. Familiar with the scenario, Kendall took his assigned spot on the edge of the bed.

"That was a nice job you did tonight, Joe," said Ginsburg. "First-class."

"Ah," said Kendall, "opening night reviews. What now, drinks at Sardi's?"

Hodges folded his arms across his chest. "Don't be cute," he said. "This is serious business, Kendall."

"You got the information we needed," said Ginsburg.

"Yeah," said Kendall. "Wonderful."

"You don't sound very pleased."

"I just threw my professional ethics in the trash can. I should be pleased by that? What I did tonight would probably have gotten me fired from any decent news organization. Journalists are not supposed to be Judas goats for the FBI."

"Grow up, Kendall," Hodges said scornfully. "It happens all the time."

Kendall stared at Hodges. "Does it?" he asked.

"Count on it."

"Well, if it does, it shouldn't."

"There's nothing wrong with helping your country," Ginsburg pointed out.

"That's not my job."

"Your *job!*" Hodges's voice fairly dripped with contempt. "What job? Come down off your high horse, Kendall. You don't even have a job. Who appointed you the guardian of the First Amendment? You're just some hack writer who stumbled into something that's too big for you to handle. Don't make a crusade out of it. Why don't you just go back home and write some more mysteries?"

Kendall didn't have a comeback for that. There was too much truth in what Hodges had said, and the fact that it was Hodges who said it just made it sting more. He was out of his depth here, the same as he had been in Vietnam. Ever since Ginsburg told him about Nightwind, he had been feeling cold drafts from the empty place at the center of himself.

Ginsburg looked annoyed. He turned to Hodges and asked acidly, "Should I send you out to wait in the car again, Vance?"

"That won't be necessary, Arn. I'll be a good boy." The two agents exchanged a glance that told Kendall volumes about their relationship. Ginsburg was in charge and Hodges plainly hated him for it.

Ginsburg turned back to Kendall. "Joe," he said earnestly, "whatever your feelings may be, journalistic ethics have to take a back seat here, and I think you know that. Finding that second canister of Nightwind is the most important thing you or I will ever do. You should be proud of the contribution you've made. Yesterday we didn't even know *if* Nightwind was ever delivered to Vietnam. Now we know that it was and we know precisely where that second canister is."

"Do we?"

"If what Poole said was accurate, I think it's obvious. The first canister, the one that the Puerto Ricans got, must have been the one stored in the tunnel to the gun emplacement. And the second canister must still be buried under the rubble of the ammunition dump."

"Yeah," said Kendall, "I guess that's reasonable. Sounds like a good place for it."

"If that's where it really is," said Hodges. "All we have is Poole's word for it, and Poole was drunk."

"The second canister hasn't turned up anywhere else," said Ginsburg. "And it seems doubtful that anyone would have bothered to dig out the bottom section of that old bunker. According to Poole, the marines weren't even using it."

"According to Poole."

"That can be checked, Vance. We already have people looking for veterans who served at Hill Six fifty-one, then and later. We'll get confirmation."

"And what happens when you get it?" Kendall asked. "Is that the end of it? Do you just let sleeping bugs lie?"

"No," said Ginsburg. "Someone will have to go there and determine whether or not the canister is still there. We have to *know*."

"That sounds like fun. What are you going to do, send in a bunch of soldiers on helicopters that don't work?"

"I think the operation will be more subtle than that, Joe."

"Then there *will* be an operation?"

"That's not really any concern of yours now, Kendall," Hodges told him.

"Bullshit! Don't think you can cut me out of this thing now, Hodges."

Hodges merely grinned, but Ginsburg seemed sincerely interested in making sure Kendall understood.

"Joe," he said, "your agreement was with us—the FBI.

153

But any clandestine operation in Vietnam itself will be conducted by someone else."

"The CIA, you mean."

"Whoever it is, they are not part of our arrangement. We can't make promises on behalf of other agencies. We intend to live up to our part of the bargain, Joe. You've cooperated with us, you've helped us immensely, and we won't forget that, believe me."

"I don't need brownie points with the feds, damn it. I need the story."

"You'll have to get it somewhere else. I'm sorry, but that's the way it is."

"You should have read the fine print, Kendall." Hodges was grinning again.

Kendall felt as if the rug had been pulled out from under his feet. And he also felt something that was very close to what he had felt when they sent him home from Vietnam: relief. He was out of the game, now. He couldn't strike out if he was sitting on the bench.

"There's one more thing, Joe," said Ginsburg. "You know how dangerous Nightwind is. You must realize the panic that could result from disclosure that a canister of Nightwind is still missing."

"What are you saying?" Kendall was afraid he knew exactly what Ginsburg was saying.

"If we can't find that second canister, Joe, we can't let you publish."

Kendall sprang to his feet and faced Ginsburg. "You lying son of a bitch! That wasn't part of the agreement, you bastard!"

"Nevertheless," Ginsburg said calmly, "unless that second canister is found, we cannot let you publish anything about Nightwind."

"And just how do you think you're going to stop me?"

"Shit," laughed Hodges, "that's the easy part. Kendall, there are already laws on the books that will let us throw you in jail if you so much as talk in your sleep. You wanted in, hotshot. Well, you're *in*, all the way and for as long as it lasts. Come on, Arn, we've wasted enough time with this asshole."

Ginsburg got to his feet and looked at Kendall. As Kendall had suspected, Ginsburg was basically an honorable man; he hadn't enjoyed sticking the knife in half as much as Hodges had enjoyed twisting it.

"We'll be in touch, Joe."

"Right. Gook luck with your book, Arn. I hope it makes the fucking best seller list."

Ginsburg ducked his head and hurried out of the room. Hodges paused at the door and gave Kendall a quizzical look, then he, too, was gone. Kendall was left alone with the wreckage of his story. His exclusive was buried as deep as the second Nightwind canister.

He paced around the room, not sure what to do or even how he felt. He still had the original book, the comprehensive history of a day in January 1968, but now it seemed like a meaningless exercise. When he had seen Poole getting into the helicopter to fly away from Hill 651, he knew he was letting something important get away from him, and was going to settle for something that looked much easier. But even the easy story had turned into a nightmare. Now it was going to happen all over again. The important story had just walked out the door, and the easy history was going to be a constant reminder that he had blown it again.

There had been something cursed and haunted about Hill 651. Everyone who was there that day seemed to have been fated for a grim, eroded future, or no future at all. Colonel Weiss was blown to atoms when the ammo dump exploded. And Captain Bascomb never quite got off the mountain, bumped from his last flight by a frightened kid who shouldn't have been there in the first place.

Frost and Smack had somehow survived that hideous night. Kendall had tracked them down already and knew what there was to know about their pathetic lives. Smack returned from Vietnam untouched, except by the habit that gave him his name. He was now serving twenty-to-life in a California prison, guilty of rape, aggravated assault, armed robbery, and a half-dozen lesser charges. Frost went home to Minnesota with shrapnel in his back and a thirty-percent disability that brought in monthly checks to supplement his welfare payments and food stamps. In 1977, ten years after Kendall first saw him looking for a fight in a penny arcade, Frost found his fight in a home-town barroom. He must have forgotten the lethal lessons they taught him in boot camp by then; what else could explain the fact that a drunken nineteen-year-old kid managed to slash Frost's throat with a switchblade? Frost had staggered out of the bar and bled to death in the same street that had spawned the troubles that took him to Hill 651.

Then there was Turner Poole, visibly disintegrating, and all his money couldn't prevent it. He had spent less than an hour on Hill 651, but it had been enough. The circle was closing now, and Poole was trapped in it. Doing dirty work for presidents was, in the end, no different from doing it for Breeze Woodward or for himself. Dirt was dirt, and Poole had covered himself with it.

And Vitaglia. Kendall had been looking forward to seeing the articulate leatherneck philosopher again. Vitaglia had come home undamaged, but somewhere along the way he must have changed his mind about staying in the Marines. He returned to college in quest of a Ph.D. in philosophy; he never quite got it. Vitaglia died of cancer in 1972.

Which left only Joe Kendall, a second-rate journalist who stumbled into big stories and then ran out on them.

He sat on the edge of the bed and stared into the blank television screen. A dark, warped Joe Kendall stared back at him from the screen, an image as hollow as the man it reflected.

Minutes or hours passed, a time-bending rerun of the acid trip that had first taken him into the frozen, empty gap that was at the core of Joe Kendall. A rerun, indeed: Welcome Back, Kendall. To the place where it all begins and ends—an unmapped wilderness where Vietnam and Boston and Hill 651 and a hotel room in Houston and all the roads between them never existed. Down there, it was all Joe Kendall and nothing but, floating in the darkness and waiting for the next chance to fail.

At last, the image spoke to Kendall.

"Not this time," it said. "Damn it, not *this* time."

Chapter Eleven

With dark sunglasses shielding his eyes from the highway's dazzle, the airconditioner on full blast, and a thermos full of bloody marys on the seat beside him, Turner Poole felt almost human. The big Lincoln cut through the shimmering heat at seventy, gliding in and out of traffic like a skier schussing down a mountain. Poole liked the sensation of speed and motion, to be going somewhere—anywhere—with careless, irresistible momentum. If you went fast enough, nothing could ever catch up with you.

Joe Kendall and Lyndon Johnson had caught up with him last night, and the memory of it was sharp enough to slice through the fog of his vicious hangover. While he slogged through the painful details of getting ready for the day, Poole had reassembled the essential facts of his encounter with Kendall.

Somebody was interested in Nightwind. Somebody was feeding facts to Kendall, and Kendall was using them to pry more information out of Poole. They wanted precise details, and the crap about narrative flow was nothing but smokescreen.

Why should it matter to anyone, after all this time? If someone was trying to smear the reputation—such as it was—of Lyndon Johnson, Poole would be only too happy to cooperate. But no one cared about Lyndon these days, and Kendall hadn't even asked him about his interview with LBJ. It wasn't Johnson they were after.

So, was it Turner Poole they wanted? If they did, they were using one hell of a long fishing pole. They could get him on any of a dozen transgressions, and they didn't need to dig into the history books to do it. They were already dogging his tracks and nipping at his heels, and it hardly seemed necessary to exhume the moldering corpse of Lyndon Johnson. Nobody in his right mind would want to do that.

By the time he reached his office, shaky but functional, Poole had concluded that he was no more than a bit player in this particular drama. That was at once reassuring and disquieting. If Turner Poole was just one flagstone on a long path, where was it leading? Who wanted what?

His tame congressman might have the answer—might, in fact, *be* the answer. Culpepper was beginning to squirm; the Abscam investigation was probably giving half the people in Washington sleepless nights. If Culpepper was running scared, he might be looking for a way to make a deal. If he had somehow acquired knowledge of Nightwind, perhaps he was trading it to the feds for some sort of immunity.

That didn't make a great deal of sense to Poole, but nothing better occurred to him. He decided to call Washington and see what his man had to say.

Culpepper was his usual smarmy self. He had heard it was hotter than blazes back in Texas. He and some of the boys were going to see about getting some federal disaster aid sent down home. Poole told him that he didn't want to talk about the weather; anyway, the heat wasn't so bad when there was a night wind. The reference went right past Culpepper, who was fundamentally not too bright. If he knew anything at all about Nightwind, he would have dithered like an epileptic hen when Poole made that remark. Poole made small talk for another minute, then hung up on the congressman. Culpepper didn't know anything.

Next, Poole had called his man at the Houston office of

the FBI. Ellsworth was a marginally useful bureaucrat
whose one virtue was his acute sense of hearing. He somehow managed to hear whispered gossip in men's rooms
and around the coffeepot without getting close enough to
draw attention to himself. Ellsworth was the sort of man
who was practically invisible, the last man on anyone's list
of bribe takers and stool pigeons. Poole had been paying
him off for five years now, and no one was the wiser.

But this morning Ellsworth had been as jumpy as a
jackrabbit on locoweed; no "How's it goin', Turner," no
casual gossip about the humorous habits of the feds. Poole
never had the chance to ask any questions. Ellsworth was
compulsively formal, curt, and rather obviously scared.
The entire conversation lasted less than a minute.

Poole had replaced the phone receiver and then stared
at the instrument for several minutes. Ellsworth had not
wanted to talk, had, in fact, seemed spooked by the mere
fact that Poole had called him. Ellsworth had never been
afraid to talk before. Perhaps there was a good reason for
his not wanting to take a call from Turner Poole.

The reason was achingly obvious, now that he thought
about it. Poole's line was bugged. An FBI employee who
knew that would not want to be logged as the recipient of
even a casual call from a man under investigation.

The bug didn't surprise Poole. But anyone listening to
his conversations over the last month would have picked
up circumstantial evidence of a flock of crimes, big and
small, in various stages of execution. Why, then, were they
interested in Nightwind all of a sudden?

The question answered itself. Nightwind, and not Turner Poole, was the true object of scrutiny. The feds were
nervous about it for some reason, so nervous that they re-
cruited Kendall to come in and pump him for them.

And all Kendall was interested in, really, was the exact
location of the two canisters. One of them was in a dismal
tunnel and the other, if Kendall had been telling the truth,
was probably still buried under a demolished bunker. That
fact had seemed very important to Kendall.

Now, barreling down the highway to Corpus Christi,

Poole felt immensely pleased with himself. He had seen, finally, the one true Light at the End of the Tunnel. Only it wasn't at the *end* of the tunnel. It was buried in the heart of the tunnel, still there, still waiting.

Colonel Thi was the sort of man Turner Poole liked to do business with. The fact that he was Vietnamese may have had something to do with it. Poole had always found it easier to deal with foreigners than with his fellow Americans. In his days with Breeze Woodward he had been the house expert on Mexicans. They responded equally well to intimidation and small favors and, in general, behaved like stray dogs, grateful for table scraps and accustomed to being kicked. Lately, however, the Mexicans had turned into Chicanos, a very different breed of dog, one that would bite your ankle if you gave it half a chance. As Chicanos, the Mexicans had discovered that they were an oppressed minority and that people like Turner Poole were the enemy. But the Vietnamese were still tame. There weren't enough of them to be an oppressed minority. They still thought of themselves as refugees—stray dogs, in other words.

Poole parked the Lincoln dockside, in front of the pink stucco building that was the home of the Excelsior Shrimp Company. Colonel Thi had chosen the name himself, because he thought it sounded impressive. Poole thought it sounded ridiculous, but he had learned to go along with the strange notions of foreigners. Colonel Thi could call the business anything he wanted, as long as he remembered who was in charge.

Getting out of the car, Poole nearly collapsed. The world went black for a moment, and his knees buckled. He grabbed the car door and held on until vision returned. It was the heat. This had happened a lot lately, a reaction to the shock of moving from arctic air conditioning to a numbingly hot atmosphere that felt like the surface of the planet Venus. When the heat wave finally went away, so would these annoying moments of total incapacity. It was nothing worth seeing a doctor about.

Recovered, Poole reached back into the car for the thermos bottle. The Excelsior Shrimp Company had only one feeble airconditioner, and there would be need for something cool and wet. Poole slammed the door, walked around the car and into the ugly pink building.

Inside, he found Colonel Thi sitting behind a battered wooden desk, reading a copy of *National Geographic*. Two of the office girls, whose real names Poole could never remember, were sitting near the other desk, chattering to each other like birds around a feeder. One of them, Daisy, was a dark, almond-eyed beauty who knew enough English to be interesting—in bed, at least. Poole was sorry that he didn't have more time.

Colonel Thi saw him and sprang up from his chair, beaming. Thi was fat and fiftyish, but he could grin like a little boy when the occasion demanded it. He hurried to Poole and shook hands like a Texan.

"Mr. Poole! You should have let us know you were coming! My wife will be furious that I did not tell her!"

"Well," said Poole, disengaging himself from Thi's grasp, "you just tell her that the next trip, I'll make sure to pay her a special visit. How is she?"

"Oh, she is fine. And my sons are fine, too. They are out on the Gulf today, and they will also be sorry they missed you."

"Boats okay?" asked Poole.

Thi's smile faded. "The boats," he said, "are like boats always are. They float, they go out, they come back in. One of them needs a new propeller and another one needs to have the bottom scraped, and all of them need engine overhauls. Or better still, new engines. You remember, I told you that last month. Now, it is worse. Unless that is why you are here today, to tell us you have bought new engines." Thi looked at him hopefully, but found no comfort in Poole's flat expression.

"No new engines, Colonel. Not now, anyway. Your sons are geniuses with those old engines. They'll manage."

"We always manage," said Thi phlegmatically. "That is what we do best."

"You bet," said Poole. He sat down heavily on a chair by Thi's desk and started unscrewing the thermos top. "You got a glass?"

Daisy quickly found two glasses and set them down on the desk in front of Poole. She smiled at him demurely, then hurried back to her corner of the office.

"Colonel?" Poole started pouring from the thermos, and Thi nodded gratefully. Poole tapped his glass against the colonel's and took a long drink that half emptied the small glass. Thi sipped at his own drink.

"It's about lunchtime, isn't it? Why don't you send the girls out to eat?"

Thi reacted as if the suggestion had come from a commanding general. He spoke a few brief words in Vietnamese and the girls quickly got to their feet and started for the door. Daisy paused at the door and smiled at Poole.

"Khe-tuckee Fry?" she asked. "We bring?"

The thought made Poole's stomach roll over. "No, Daisy, you *don't* bring. You go, you eat, yes?"

Daisy nodded and went out into the blazing day with her girl friend. Poole drank some more of his bloody mary; the stuff was getting warm already. He looked at the colonel.

"Another special delivery, Mr. Poole?" Thi asked unhappily.

"Not exactly," said Poole.

"You know I don't like these special deliveries. We do as you say, Mr. Poole, but I worry for my family. What will happen to them if they catch us?"

"If you don't make any mistakes, Colonel, they won't catch you."

"That is easy for you to say. You are sitting in your big office in Houston while my sons and I are out on the Gulf unloading bales of marijuana."

"Colonel, do I have to remind you that without those special deliveries, the Excelsior Shrimp Company would be floating belly-up in the harbor?"

Thi locked eyes with Poole for a moment, then looked down at his drink. He took another sip.

163

"Mr. Poole," said Thi, "I know it is necessary. But I worry about my family."

"Then why don't you worry about how you'll feed them if this business goes bankrupt? You're a man of the world, Colonel. You know how things work, and just because you're in the United States now, it doesn't mean anything is different. You shipped dope out of Vietnam, and now you're shipping it into the States. What's the difference?"

"The difference is that in Vietnam we had protection."

"You've got it here, too. I told you I'd keep the feds off your back, and I have."

"But that is not enough. We need protection from the other fishermen. They hate us because we are Vietnamese. They pour sugar in our gas tanks and cut our nets and threaten our women. They are like Vietcong."

"Really? Tell me, Colonel, when's the last time somebody threw a hand grenade into your house?"

"They haven't yet," said the colonel. "But tomorrow, perhaps they will."

"And perhaps they won't. I never told you it was going to be easy here. If you don't like it, you could always go back to Vietnam."

Thi frowned and shook his head emphatically. "That," he said, "is something I can never do."

"Why not?" asked Poole. "Did they purge your brother? Isn't he still a big muckety-muck in the party?"

"Even my brother could not help me if I returned. They would shoot me. Family is no longer important in Vietnam."

"Family is always important," said Poole. "If you've got the right relatives, you can't lose. Hell, we've got families right here in Texas that did the same thing as your family. Back during the Civil War one brother would go fight for the North and the other would stay home and fight for the South. That way, no matter who won, there would be somebody in a position to protect the family and its land. Same damn thing you did, right?"

Thi looked at the floor. "It is what my father ordered," he said. "We did not argue with him. We did as he told us. My brother went north with Ho and I stayed and fought for the government."

"And it worked, right? Your family kept its land and nobody bothered you much."

"The land belongs to the people now."

"Bullshit. The land belongs to the people who run the government, and your brother is one of those people."

Thi raised his eyes from the floor and stared at Poole. "Why are you talking so much about Vietnam? I will not go back, Mr. Poole, not ever. I do not want to go back to Vietnam."

"But I do," said Poole.

Thi said nothing. He had been dealing with Americans for twenty-five years, half his life, but he never really understood them. They were not a predictable people. They had strange desires and they acted on sudden impulses, as if there were no history. Americans thought they could do anything they wanted with the future because they had no past. Thi waited for Poole to explain this latest mad impulse.

"Don't look at me like that, Colonel," Poole told him. "You know I don't like it when you go inscrutable on me."

"It is you who are being inscrutable, Mr. Poole. Why do you want to go to Vietnam?"

"I forgot something," said Poole. "Left it behind a dozen years ago. It's still there, and now I want to go and get it. I know it can be done, Colonel. Americans can get into Vietnam now, I checked. It's not easy, but it can be done if you've got a little pull in the right places."

"My brother, you mean."

"You're still in touch with him, right?"

"We received a letter in the spring," said Thi. "He and his family are well."

"Good, good, glad to hear it. Then he can help."

"I don't know," said Thi reluctantly.

"Then find out," Poole said. "And do it quickly. I want to be in Vietnam as soon as I can. Two or three weeks, no more."

"I will try," said Thi.

"Trying isn't good enough. *Do* it. If this thing works out, there will be a lot of money in it for all of us. You can buy some new engines. Or send your sons to Harvard, if that's what you want. Or set up a Swiss bank account like your old bosses did. This is the main chance, Colonel. Don't blow it."

"I will do as you say," Thi said.

"Of course you will," said Poole. "You're a can-do fellow, Colonel. I know I can count on you." Poole clapped Thi on the shoulder and squeezed the soft flesh at the base of his neck.

Thi endured this strange, unseemly American gesture. There were times when Americans made him feel unclean, made his skin crawl. There were times when he devoutly wished that his father had chosen differently and sent him north and let his brother cope with the Americans. It would have been so much easier if that had been his fate.

"I will contact my brother," said Thi. "I will do what I can. But tell me, Mr. Poole, what is this thing you left behind? What is it you want?"

Poole laughed. "Only the wind, Colonel," he said. "The night and the wind."

Joe Kendall had contacts of his own. On the flight back to Boston he compiled a list of people who might be able to help. During his days covering the Movement for *Rocky Road*, he had been in touch with people who were in touch with people who were out of touch. Some of those people were still out of touch, permanently, but others had survived. Once it became clear that the great Revolution was not going to happen, the radicals of the sixties gradually accommodated themselves to the shifting realities of the seventies. Some of them became national jokes, some of them renounced everything they had once stood for, but most of them simply lived their lives the best way they could.

For the first time in years Kendall felt fired up and ready for anything. It was a strange feeling, and one that he didn't wish to examine too closely. An epiphany that occurred in a hotel room in Houston probably wouldn't stand up to a searching analysis.

Still, he felt as if he had passed over some sort of bridge, leaving behind the brown, polluted waters that had been flowing through his life. He didn't know exactly what had caused the change, but there was no denying its existence. Perhaps it had been the sight of Turner Poole. Poole was a benchmark in his life, a reminder of the day when everything fell apart. But Poole, he now knew, was not quite what he seemed to be on that day; if his perception of Poole had been false, then perhaps other images of 1968 were equally distorted. Maybe he had been too unforgiving of himself, maybe he had expected too much of a twenty-three-year-old kid. Or maybe it just didn't matter as much as he thought it did.

Possibly, he should thank Ginsburg and Hodges for his new sense of purpose. For a dozen years the only person who had told Kendall that he couldn't do something was Kendall himself—and Kendall had believed. Now Ginsburg and Hodges were telling him what he could and couldn't do, and Kendall resented it. Self-doubt was a private struggle, and the outcome mattered to no one else. But official censorship was a naked challenge; a couple of FBI bozos were not going to set limits on him. That jerk-off lieutenant at Da Nang had tried, but Kendall found a way to get to Khe Sanh, anyway. If the twenty-three-year-old Kendall could do it, then so could the thirty-five-year-old version.

By the time the plane landed at Boston, Kendall knew exactly what he had to do; in his mind he had already done it. Now it was simply a question of making it happen for real.

Ginsburg flipped once more through the pages of his novel. He was simultaneously attracted and repelled by the damned thing. Nightwind had come alive again, and by comparison, the novel seemed hopelessly trivial. It had been a good defense against the tedium of routine oper-

ations, an escape valve for instincts that had no other out-
let, a lighted stage where great events might take place.

But great events were now unfolding in the real world,
and Ginsburg was a part of them. Ace King, his indestructible hero, had it easy. Arnold Ginsburg, though, was far
from indestructible, and even farther from being infallible.
If Ace King screwed up, a rewrite could solve everything.
If Arnold Ginsburg screwed up, living, breathing human
beings might die.

And Ginsburg was mortally afraid that he had screwed
up.

He opened the bottom drawer of his desk and dumped
the manuscript into it. Ace King was going to be put into
Deep Sleep, his animation indefinitely suspended. Ginsburg
picked up his telephone, punched a button, and asked
Vance Hodges to come in.

"Good morning, Arn," said Hodges. He lowered himself
into a chair and stared at his boss. Hodges had been giving
him that strange, probing look ever since they returned
from Houston. Ginsburg was afraid he knew what was
causing it. Hodges also thought he had screwed up.

"What have you got from Langley, Vance?"

"Just talked to Kieffer. He says the Backtrack operation
will be ready to roll in a week."

"No sooner?"

"Christ, Arn, you know how those guys are. They'd
rather sit around and play with scenarios than actually
take a chance on doing something."

Ginsburg nodded gravely. His colleagues at the CIA
were a difficult bunch to work with. They built up meticulous scenarios and fiddled with hypothetical details until
they were absolutely certain they were ready, by which
time conditions in the real world had changed so radically
that the original scenario was worthless.

"It's a tough one, Vance. They've got to do it right the
first time. Once an attempt has been made, the Viets will
know something's up. If they get to that canister before we
do, God only knows what would happen."

"Kieffer thinks he knows—in his godlike way."

"Oh?"

"One of their scenarios," Hodges explained. "They figure that if the Viets knew about Nightwind, they might be tempted to use it in Cambodia, or possibly even in China. They're kind of intrigued by the ramifications of that. Some of them think it might even be a good thing. Stabilize the region."

"Wonderful. They aren't seriously proposing that, are they?"

Hodges shrugged. "You know the Company, Arn. Exploding cigars for Castro, a pie in the face for Brezhnev. Kieffer says Backtrack will recover the canister, but he won't say what they plan to do with it once they have it."

"Don't they realize the potential of this thing? Hasn't anyone told them how dangerous Nightwind could be by now?"

"Oh, they know. Kieffer assured me that they've been consulting with the White House and everything is going to turn out just fine."

Ginsburg wished he could accept that. It was a measure of how far the world had spun off its normal axis that he could find himself worrying about the CIA almost as much as he worried about the Vietnamese.

"Anything new from Houston?"

"More of the same," said Hodges. "Poole is obviously aware that his line is bugged. He's been doing a lot of running around lately, including another trip down to Corpus Christi. The DEA boys think he's planning a major dope shipment and they're getting ready to pounce."

"What do you think?"

Hodges scratched his left earlobe, tilting his head slightly. "I think DEA is wrong," he said. "I think Poole has Nightwind on his mind."

"And we put it there," said Ginsburg. "Can he do anything?"

"Who knows? His Vietnamese colonel has relatives still in Nam, and he's been in contact with them. The communications have been monitored, but so far there's nothing out of the ordinary. Poole doesn't seem to have told anyone about Nightwind."

"Yet," Ginsburg added. "I don't know, Vance, maybe we should drop the net on him."

"Can't," said Hodges flatly. "I had the same thought, but right now Poole is untouchable. The DEA wants him loose, and so does Trent and his congressional unit. They think they're getting close to nailing Culpepper, and if we take Poole off the streets it would blow a year's work."

Ginsburg shook his head, reflecting on the strange workings of his own government. Every time you had a good reason for doing something, somebody else in the Bureau or the Company or the Agriculture Department had a dozen reasons for not doing it.

"He worries me," said Ginsburg.

"I'll tell you who worries *me*," said Hodges.

"Kendall."

"You got it, Arn. That guy is a flake, and he knows too much."

"We had to tell him, Vance."

"Did we?" Hodges plainly didn't think so, and Ginsburg was beginning to have doubts of his own.

"He gave us some vital information," said Ginsburg. "Without Kendall we still wouldn't know where to look for the second canister."

"Yeah, but we didn't have to deal with him. I think if we'd applied a little pressure, Kendall would have cracked wide open and given us everything we wanted. We didn't have to tell him about Nightwind."

"Maybe. But the way we did it produced the results we needed, so there's no point in second-guessing ourselves."

"First person plural, huh, Arn?"

"When this is over, Vance," Ginsburg told him, a trace of heat in his voice, "you can file any kind of report you please."

"Whatever you say, Arn."

The agents stared at each other for several silent seconds. Ginsburg felt a sudden premonition that Hodges would win in the end. His back was ripe to be climbed over—or stabbed—if not by Hodges, then by some other macho go-getter. The paper clip counters always lost. With a man like Hodges on your tail, the first mistaken judgment could easily become the last. Hodges knew too much—thanks to Kendall, he even knew about the damned book.

"So," Ginsburg said at last, "what is Kendall doing that worries you?"

"It's what he's not doing. He's not making any important calls from his home phone. I think he knows we've got it tapped."

"Under the circumstances," said Ginsburg, "that's not exactly surprising. Kendall's not stupid."

Hodges didn't debate the point. "He is making a lot of calls from his girl friend's phone, but we haven't been able to get a tap in. We've checked her phone records, though, and Kendall has been calling people all over the place—including several calls to Canada and one to Paris. Some of the people he's calling are known subversives."

"He's writing a book," Ginsburg pointed out. "If he's talking to sixties radicals, it's probably just research."

"On Nightwind?"

"What did you expect? As long as he doesn't reveal anything, there's no problem."

"You sure put a lot of trust in that bastard, Arn." Hodges said it as if it were an accusation, which it undoubtedly was. And he was right, Ginsburg did trust Kendall. He couldn't say exactly why, except that he just couldn't picture Kendall going off on his own and doing something foolish. Kendall was a writer, after all, and Ginsburg knew something about what it was like to be a writer. Writers observed, they didn't act. If they felt the urge to do something, they channeled it into their writing. They let the Ace Kings handle the rough stuff. Kendall was safe.

"I think we ought to put him on a leash," said Hodges. "At least until Backtrack is in motion."

"Get a tap on his girl's phone," said Ginsburg, "but don't go beyond that without checking with me first."

"Whatever you say, Arn." Hodges got up and walked to the door, then turned back to Ginsburg. "You writers really stick together, don't you?" Hodges was out the door before Ginsburg could think of a response.

Sara prowled restlessly around his apartment while Kendall packed his suitcase. There was an art to packing for extended trips to faraway places. The longer the trip, the more lightly you had to travel. You couldn't let yourself be distracted by missing luggage or dirty socks. It was necessary to remember that the farther away from home you were, the less people cared about the condition of your laundry. So you packed the essentials and learned to survive without after shave lotion and an extra pair of pants.

"Are you taking your typewriter?" Sara asked.

"Nope," said Kendall, not bothering to look up from the suitcase. "Just a notebook and a couple of ball-points."

"Is that the way you did it before?"

"That's right. Can't carry a typewriter into combat."

"But you're not going into combat this time. Why don't you take the typewriter?"

Kendall sighed and turned to face Sara. She was leaning against the closet door, hands behind her back.

"Why," he asked, "is it so important to you that I take the typewriter along?"

"You might need it," she said. "What if you need it and you don't have it?"

"Then I'll borrow one."

Sara stared at him, pouting, looking more like a little girl than she ever did before.

"Let's have it," he said. "What's all this bullshit about the typewriter?"

"I just want you to have it with you. Maybe it'll remind you that you're not young Joe Kendall, war correspondent. You're a journalism professor at Boston University, and you've got no business chasing off into the boondocks like this."

"Hey, kiddo, who wanted me to write this book?"

"Okay!" Sara threw her arms into the air, as if surrendering. "Okay, I was wrong!"

"Fine," said Kendall, "no typewriter."

"No, I was wrong about the book! Let sleeping dogs lie, Joe. Forget about Vietnam. You can't change it now, so why don't you just let it go?"

That's where she was wrong, Kendall thought, but he couldn't tell her that. She didn't need to know that he *could* change things.

"Ever since you got back from Houston, you've been acting like some kind of speed freak."

"You used to complain that I spent too much time moping. Observe, Sara—I am no longer moping."

"I know," she said, "and it scares the hell out of me. What happened down there, anyway?"

Kendall took a step forward and put his hands on Sara's shoulders. He looked into her eyes and hoped that there was such a thing as ESP. He wanted her to know, somehow, that what he was doing was important. And that he desperately wanted her to be here when he got back. Then, the time for solitude would be gone; then, he would be ready to live.

"It's going to be okay, Sara."

"I wish I could believe that."

"Believe it, it's true. This trip . . . it's just something that I have to do."

"Of course. A man's gotta do what a man's gotta do, right?"

"Go ahead, make fun. Have a good laugh."

"I'm not laughing, Joe. I'm just scared."

That was the difference, thought Kendall. Sara was scared, but this time around, he *wasn't*. It was a fantastic feeling, not being afraid.

"Sara," he said gently, "just trust me. I've been screwed up for a long time, and now I've got a chance to get unscrewed. I can't explain it, but this may be the best thing that's ever happened to me."

He felt her muscles relax, and then she came into his arms and buried her head against his shoulder. He held

173

her tightly and marveled at how good she felt, how good this moment was. He had forgotten that such moments were possible. He had been so busy remembering, he had forgotten the only thing that was really worth remembering. He was alive, and he wasn't alone.

He kissed her, and the moment became even better. Kendall disengaged himself long enough to shove his carefully packed suitcase off of the bed. There would be time for that later. Vietnam would still be there.

Chapter Twelve

Pham Dinh Truong was, by nature, a careful, cautious man. It followed, then, that he was also an observant man. He noticed things, even the little things, because he knew that his well-being depended upon his sensitivity to changes in the world around him—a world in which any change at all was dangerous. Every living Vietnamese felt the same way. The only Vietnamese who did not fear change were the ones who had already been killed by it.

The only way to cope with change was to keep one step ahead of it, to become first what all would become later. The proof of his philosophy was all around him, laboring unproductively in the late morning sun. The people who lived in this barren mountain land were here because the government had designated it a New Economic Zone. The needs of this NEZ were many, but first it needed people, and these the government had supplied. Some came because they believed what they were told, but most came because they did what they were told. Truong, however, had come because seven years earlier he had anticipated the nature of the next great change that was to sweep across his land, and he had prepared himself for it. Those who had not seen the change now worked in this NEZ; Truong was in charge of it.

Truong sometimes reflected that he might have done

better for himself had he been less cautious. But giving up caution meant entrusting one's fortunes to nothing more substantial than luck, and these sad hills hid the remains of thousands who had been neither cautious nor lucky. Nor had they been very wise, when all was considered. They had died so that others might plow up their bones from worthless land that now belonged to all the people.

Truong had been, until 1973, a major in the South Vietnamese Air Force. He had bombed and strafed this same land that now refused to yield a decent crop of soya beans. None of the people who were assigned to the NEZ had ever seen this solemn corner of the country from the air, and if they had, Truong knew, they would never have agreed to resettlement here. From the perspective of the sky the region around Khe Sanh showed its true face— bleak, hostile, eternally changeless. If a million tons of bombs could not transform this land, what chance was there for this makeshift band of reluctant, unschooled peasants?

Even the mighty Americans had failed here. They fought for Khe Sanh because their maps told them that this was a strategic point that had to be held. The Vietnamese knew better—since few of them could read maps, they were not deceived by them—and in the end, after a brief, pointless siege, they simply marched around Khe Sanh and ignored it. Many months later the Americans finally realized the truth about this place, and they rolled up their metal runways and departed.

Leaving Khe Sanh, the Americans were rehearsing for their grudging, bitter departure from the rest of Vietnam. Truong had seen the change coming. It was clear that, before long, Air Force majors who dropped bombs on their own people would not be welcome in Vietnam. So Truong defected to the Communists, and the glorious April of 1975 found him on the winning side.

The nation's reward for winning the war was more war, first in Kampuchea and then against the Chinese—and perhaps again, soon. Truong had not fought (for either side) simply to go on fighting. Shortly after Saigon was taken, Truong permanently removed himself from the fighting by making a bad landing on a shell-cratered field. A disk in his lower spine slipped out of place, the inevitable result of a thousand such landings. A simple operation could have cured him, but the few doctors who remained were too busy amputating mangled limbs and stitching up ripped bellies. Truong didn't particularly mind. He accepted the nagging pain in return for this safe, undemanding post in a forgotten corner of this triumphant nation.

Truong had presided over this bleak domain for nearly five years and was not displeased by his accomplishments. He had kept change to a minimum, assuring himself a comfortable, safe existence. In Vietnam that was all one could reasonably ask.

So Truong, being cautious and observant, immediately noticed the plume of dust on the horizon. It signaled the approach of a vehicle, making its way over the one rock-strewn road that connected this baking plateau with the rest of the world. The workers in the fields and those resting in the shade of their concrete block barracks ignored the vehicle because its arrival was unlikely to have the slightest effect on their lives. But Truong watched it carefully because he was the master of this place, and even a minor change demanded his personal attention.

He stood next to the dusty road and waited. The vehicle was an American jeep, not surprising, but one of the passengers also looked like an American, and that was a great surprise. Truong did not like surprises, and this one worried him. His back began to ache, a sure sign that change was in the air.

The jeep came to a stop in front of Truong. The driver kept the engine running, while the two passengers got off; the American carried a small suitcase and cast his gaze uncertainly over the sights of the NEZ. The other man was well dressed, in creased dark trousers and a crisp white shirt. He approached Truong.

"You are Pham Dinh Truong?" he asked briskly.

"Yes," said Truong, "that is who I am."

177

"I am Nguyen Van Dai. I am from the Ministry of the Interior."

That meant that he was probably from the Public Security Bureau. Truong waited to be told what would be required of him.

"I am escorting an American journalist," said Dai. "He was here during the war, and now he wants to see the old battlefield. I have talked with him and he seems sympathetic. Apparently he has some influence in the government, so he is to be treated with respect. I am told that you speak excellent English."

"I speak it well enough," said Truong. "Does he understand Vietnamese?"

"Very little," said Dai. The man smiled crookedly. "I called his mother a whore, but he did not respond. I think he is safe."

"And what am I supposed to do with him?"

"Show him the battlefield, if that is what he wants. Let him speak to the workers. Make him feel comfortable."

"You will not be staying?"

Dai made a sour face. "My presence is not required. I have better things to do than look at the junk the Americans left behind."

Dai turned to the American and shifted to English. He spoke it reasonably well, like so many people in the south who were younger than forty. Those who were older than forty were more likely to speak French.

"Mr. Joe Kendall," he said, "allow me to present Pham Dinh Truong, who is the director of this district. Mr. Truong will be your escort."

The American extended his hand and Truong shook it, a formal gesture he had seldom used in the last five years.

"Welcome to Khe Sanh, Mr. Kendall. You have been here before, yes?"

"A long time ago," said the American. He looked down at the ground as he spoke, as if he were ashamed. Perhaps he had reason to be.

"This time, I promise no one will shoot at you. Now we are peaceful and productive."

178

"I wasn't a soldier," Kendall said quickly. "I was here as a journalist. I was against the war."

"There is no need to apologize," said Truong.

"I wasn't apologizing. I just wanted you to know."

The three men stood silently for a moment. Encounters such as this were bound to be awkward. Dai used the silence as an excuse to leave. He got back into the jeep.

"I will see you in Quangtri, Mr. Kendall. Enjoy your stay." He looked at Truong and added, in Vietnamese, "Don't let him step on any land mines."

The driver gunned the engine, executed a three-point turn, and headed back the way they had come. Truong and Kendall watched the jeep for a few moments.

"Let me take your bag, Mr. Kendall. This," he said, gesturing to the large concrete building by the edge of the road, "is our administrative office. It is also my home, and you are welcome to stay in it tonight."

"Thank you," said Kendall, surrendering his bag. Truong led him into the building, where a creaking fan did little to cool the air. They went into Truong's office and Truong gestured for Kendall to sit down.

"I'd rather stand," said Kendall. "After that jeep ride, I may not sit down for weeks."

Truong ventured an understanding laugh. "Yes, I am afraid our roads are rather rough. Not like the great highways in America."

"Some of them are pretty rough, too." Kendall looked around the office, but there wasn't much to see, except a few maps and charts that were taped to the walls. He seemed to be at a loss for words. Truong decided that the American was already sorry that he had come here.

"Have you been in Vietnam long, Mr. Kendall?"

"Just two days," he said.

"And will you be staying long?"

"Just a few more days. You see, I'm writing a book about what happened here in 1968, and I just wanted to see if Khe Sanh had changed much."

"Has it?" Truong was genuinely interested.

179

"It's hard to tell," said Kendall. "Nobody is shooting; that's certainly a change."

"Yes," said Truong, "now we are planting crops and building a strong, new nation."

Kendall smiled slightly. "Mr. Truong, that sounds like what we would call the party line."

Truong returned the smile. "It *is* the party line. What else is there to say about this boring place?"

Kendall seemed to relax a little, which is what Truong wanted. He knew Kendall would not be comfortable with an official recitation of facts and statistics and the clumsy slogans people like Dai always used on foreigners. Kendall was here for something entirely different.

"Your English is excellent," said Kendall.

"I had much practice," said Truong. "While you were here in 1968, Mr. Kendall, do you know where I was? I was in San Antonio, Texas, learning to speak English and fly American airplanes."

"You learned well."

"The English better than the flying, I think. These days, however, I have little need of either skill. It is good that you are here. Don't say this to Mr. Dai, but sometimes I miss the Americans. Does that surprise you?"

"Yes, it does."

"From the time I was ten years old," said Truong, "there were always Americans here. My father sometimes said that he was sorry the French left. And I am sometimes sorry the Americans left. Perhaps the next generation will be satisfied just to be Vietnamese."

"You have children?"

"I did," said Truong. He paused, then decided that he might as well tell him, so that Kendall would be spared the embarrassment of asking. "My wife and my son were killed eight years ago. A rocket attack."

"American?"

"Vietcong. It doesn't matter. The war killed them. Tell me, Mr. Kendall, what is it you wish to see? The big American base?"

"Well, yes, I'd like to see that. But I really came to see

a little camp on a hill a few kilometers from here. That's where I was in 1968."

"There are many hills and many camps. Do you know the name of this one?"

"I don't know what the Vietnamese called it. The marines called it Hill Six fifty-one."

Truong nodded. It was as he had suspected when he first saw the dust on the horizon.

"I know the place," said Truong. "There is a road that goes near there, if you don't mind another bumpy ride."

"That's okay," said Kendall. "I would really appreciate your taking me there. I don't suppose you get many visitors who want to go to a place like that."

"Not many," said Truong. "In fact, none at all, until today."

"So I'll be the first."

"No, Mr. Kendall," said Truong as he opened the door, "the second. Shall we go?"

Houston and Boston were far away now, and somewhere between there and here, the strange, surging confidence Kendall had felt began to erode. Now it was gone entirely. As the jeep bounced along the narrow mountain road, Kendall wondered how he had got into this, and now that he was in it, how he could get out of it.

The idea had seemed so clear and simple when he first thought of it. Just hop in a plane, get off in Vietnam, truck on up to old Hill 651, and find the second Nightwind canister. He didn't want to do anything with it, he just wanted to see it and confirm with his own eyes that the wild stories Ginsburg and Poole told him were true. And, incidentally, he would tread the bloody earth of Hill 651 and, in so doing, somehow disperse the lingering demons that had haunted him for a dozen years.

Turning the idea into reality had been surprisingly easy, and unexpectedly enjoyable. He had uncorked his bottled-up skills and found that he could get things done if he tried. He had tracked down his old friends from the peace movement and found that many of them were still politically active. The old subterranean network was creaky from disuse, but it still existed.

A friend in Toronto led him to a French diplomat in Paris who had good contacts with the North Vietnamese and NLF delegations at the peace talks. The diplomat was still in touch with his Vietnamese friends, who were now members of the government. One of them, in fact, was on the politburo, and that man had graciously arranged a visa for Kendall. The Vietnamese were glad to welcome American journalists back into their country, because they still had hopes of getting the American economic aid that had been promised in 1973. The Vietnamese knew the importance of American public opinion, and they were well aware of the power of the American media. Any American journalist who could be counted on to write sympathetically about Vietnam was a positive asset.

Kendall flew to Bangkok, and then on to Hanoi. Nguyen Van Dai attached himself to Kendall like a limpet and took him around to meet all the right people, all of whom were friendly and eager to prove that there were no hard feelings. Dai showed him a war memorial in the center of the city. It consisted of the tail of a B-52 that had been shot down during the Christmas bombing, on display like an enormous stuffed bird. The point was clear: the Vietnamese were a strong, united people who dealt harshly with foreign invaders, but were willing to let bygones be bygones and have peaceful relations with everyone—even with the cowardly beasts who bombed babies and hospitals from forty thousand feet.

The tour was interesting, but when Kendall let it be known that what he really wanted to see was Khe Sanh, Dai turned surly and uncooperative. Dai was stuck with Kendall, but Dai had no desire to go tramping around on some forsaken battlefield in the treacherous mountains of the south. Dai interpreted his instructions as liberally as possible, delivering Kendall to Truong at Khe Sanh, then retiring to whatever comforts were available in Quangtri.

Truong was a curiosity. Speaking with him was almost like conversing with an American. As he drove, Truong bombarded Kendall with questions about the States and what it was like there now. Truong liked Big Mac hamburgers, Coca-Cola, Hollywood movies, and *Star Trek*. He had been impressed by the vast, open expanse of Texas and the towering peaks of the Rockies. He hoped to see America again someday.

Kendall suspected that Truong was intentionally dominating the conversation in order to keep him from asking questions. But Kendall really only had one question, and that would be answered soon enough. If Kendall was the second visitor to Hill 651 today, then who the hell was the first?

The obvious answer was that Kendall had blundered into the CIA operation to retrieve Nightwind. If his arrival blew the mission, Ginsburg and Hodges would chop him into little pieces and feed him to dogs when he returned—if he did return. What would Truong be thinking by now? He might well be thinking that it was Kendall who was the spy.

The whole trip was beginning to seem like a fool's errand. It had cost him money he couldn't afford to spend, and even if everything went smoothly, the most he could expect to accomplish would be a quick glance at a pile of rubble. And if things didn't go smoothly, he might accidentally tip off the Vietnamese to the existence of the second Nightwind canister. Sara had been right: the expedition was nothing but macho nonsense.

But he was here now, and it was far too late for second thoughts. The jeep, with much grinding of gears, was winding through the thick green valleys, slowly climbing toward Hill 651. The sky was a brilliant, endless blue, a dazzling contrast to the wet, gray cloak he remembered. Scattered over the hillsides, though, were pungent reminders of the way it had been here in the old days. The bent, truncated rotor blade of a helicopter protruded from the foliage at the base of a hill. The stripped carcass of a truck rested silently among the rocks and boulders that had been scraped away from the roadbed. They were like the bones of dinosaurs, patiently waiting to become fossils in this open-air museum of unnatural history.

Truong pointed over the windshield at a dark, bulky mass of earth and rock. "There it is," he said. "You can see the road that leads to the top. It is a terrible road, but I think we can make it if this jeep holds out. We have many jeeps, but your country won't sell us spare parts."

Kendall stared at the hill. He was seeing it now as the Viet Cong had seen it, a forbidding prominence rising out of the green shelter of the jungle. He tried to imagine what it would be like, knowing there were five hundred well-armed soldiers up there. What could possibly propel a man up those slopes, into the fiery maw of the American defenders? Who could be crazy enough to attack such a place?

Twelve years ago he had been on top and had seen the crazy men who defended this isolated citadel. Were the attackers on that blazing night just as insane as the defenders? Did the man who died with scraps of Kendall's T-shirt clutched in his fist know what he was doing? He must have; fury like that burned away the fence between the insane and the merely desperate. It had to have been born in some volcanic cauldron that fed on the elemental fires of the earth itself.

Seeing the view from the bottom of the hill, Kendall finally understood what had happened that night. He knew that history had declared Tet a military failure. The MACV flacks had recited casualty figures that proved beyond any rational doubt that the offensive had been a catastrophe for the Communists. It had taken them three years to recover to the point where they could launch another offensive. Tet was unquestionably a defeat for the Vietnamese.

But from the bottom of the hill, a different, more basic truth was revealed. The men who charged up that deadly slope knew, before they took their first step out of the safety of the jungle, that they would never make it to the top. This place could never be taken by storm in a thousand years. But taking it wasn't the point. *Trying* to take it was what it had been all about. If Hill 651 could not be taken in a thousand years, the attackers would nevertheless try for a thousand years, and a thousand more. And each screaming assault had really been no more than a question. Are you willing, they had asked, to defend this place for a thousand years?

And the answer, finally, had been No.

It came down to a question of will—not the strutting, comic will proffered by Pattons and Liddys, and not the strident political will espoused by fevered ideologues. This was something altogether different, something fundamental. It was a will that accepted and insisted upon harmony and balance, and anything that intruded upon that balance was not to be tolerated. The force that drove men up this hill was the same as the force that drove oceans against continents, eternal and irresistible.

In these haunted Eastern hills, Kendall felt the tug of yin and yang. He was no oriental scholar, but he knew what he had encountered. An American army in this place was simply a rock on the shoreline, and if the rock didn't understand its fate, the ocean certainly did. And Kendall, no more than a pebble in this roaring tide, began to feel a strange sense of peace seeping into him.

Should the pebble feel bad because the tide sweeps it away? Kendall smiled suddenly. He had become his own Zen master, asking questions that ultimately answered themselves, if he would only realize it. If the pebble was swept away, then it was in the wrong place, and the ocean was merely helping it get to the place where it belonged. There was no need to rage against the ocean.

Nor was there reason for the pebble to hate itself for being a pebble. Curious things were happening, down here at the bottom of the hill. Looking down from the top, he had seen only half of the world, yin or yang, he didn't know which and it didn't matter. The missing half had suddenly slipped into place, and in the unity of things, distinctions disappeared. Those empty, drug-inspired boxes he had seen in himself at last made sense. From the top, looking down, that awful void had seemed to be a destination. But from the bottom of the hill, the void was a totality, the place of undisturbed balance and harmony. If it was a destination, it was also a starting point.

The jeep rocked to a halt. Truong killed the engine and looked at Kendall. "This is as far as we can go, I think. Better to walk from here, if you don't mind."

"I don't mind at all," Kendall told him. "In fact, I would consider it a privilege to walk up this hill."

Truong raised an eyebrow. "That is a strange thing to say."

"It's been a strange day."

"Indeed," said Truong. "Strange, indeed."

The four Vietnamese workers they had picked up at Khe Sanh were handy with pick and shovel, but they sure as hell weren't in any hurry. There was no reason they should have been, but Poole felt that Colonel Vinh might at least have provided them with some motivation. What good was it to be a colonel if you couldn't make a bunch of peasants work harder?

Vinh sat on an upended slab of concrete, eyes hidden by a pair of aviator sunglasses. He looked as if he were in attendance at a particularly engrossing chess tournament, and each move was worthy of hours of studied concentration. If his fat brother Thi acted like that, Poole would have thrown the son of a bitch into the Gulf.

"Can't you get them to work faster?" Poole asked impatiently.

"Your canister, if it is there, will not move by itself, Mr. Poole. It has been there twelve years, and a few more hours will not matter."

"The sun will be down in a few hours."

"Then we will come back tomorrow," Vinh answered placidly.

"Fuck tomorrow. I'm going down there."

Vinh shrugged, as if it were all the same to him if they reached the canister tomorrow or next year. Poole threaded his way past the broken blocks of concrete that littered the entrance to the bunker. He switched on his flashlight and played it over the floor of the shattered tunnel. He promptly banged his head on the sagging roof.

Poole swore with each step. Hunched over, sweating like a stuck pig, jet-lagged, and thirsty, he couldn't recall the last time he had been in such a foul temper. If the canister wasn't there, the explosion of the ammo dump was going to look like a firecracker compared to the pyrotechnics he felt blossoming inside himself. Guided by the sound of lazy digging, Poole slowly made his way down into the remains of the Grenoble bunker.

At least it was cooler down here, cool and dark like the inside of a marble mausoleum. He might be safe here from the dizzy spells that had been bothering him. It was just the goddamn heat that was doing it to him. After he got through here, he was going to move to Alaska, where everything was sharp and cold and white.

If not Alaska, then maybe Sweden. He wasn't convinced that this thing, however it broke, was going to get him off the hook with the feds, or with anyone else. But if he had the canister, he would at least have some monstrous big leverage. He could trade, he could deal, he could even threaten if the situation called for it. One way or another, he was going to settle all accounts.

Poole reached the place where the fallen concrete blocked the way. The four workers, frozen in the flickering shadow of an oil lantern, were grinning at him like idiots. As far as he could see, they hadn't accomplished one damned thing since the last time he was down here, an hour ago.

"Well?" Poole demanded.

One of the workers pointed to a huge block of concrete that was wedged into the tunnel opening. Smaller chunks blocked access to the big slab. The worker started to explain things to Poole in his rapid, singsong language, but Poole wasn't interested in excuses in any tongue.

"Work!" he said.

The lantern seemed to be going out, and blackness crept in from the edge of things. Poole sagged to the cold rock floor of the tunnel. The Vietnamese stared at him.

"Dig!" he commanded. Obediently, they returned to their work, leaving Poole alone in the gathering darkness.

Shit, he thought, this has got to stop. He was only forty years old and he had a hell of a lot of things to do. He wasn't going to put up with fainting spells and vapors.

There were good doctors in Houston, great ones, in fact. He supposed there were also good doctors in Sweden. When he got out of here, he could go to one and get a shot, B-12 or something. Vitamins, blood sugar, whatever the hell it was, money could certainly cure it.

His vision began to clear, and the tingling in his limbs faded away. He could move again, and it was always best to be in motion.

"I'll be back," he told the workers. "You just keep digging."

Poole trudged slowly back up toward the light. It was hotter than hell up there, but at least it wasn't dark. He stumbled over some loose rocks and banged his knee once, but managed to avoid hitting his head again. Emerging from the bunker, he found Vinh still sitting on his concrete slab like Buddha himself. It took Poole a moment to realize, as his eyes adjusted to the light, that Vinh was no longer alone.

Joe Kendall stood there, looking as surprised as Poole felt. The Vietnamese official he'd met earlier today stood next to Kendall, an evil smile on his face.

"Mr. Poole," said Truong, "you look very tired. Are you okay?"

"Uh . . . yes, I'm fine, I'm just, uh, hot."

"Yes," said Truong agreeably, "it is hot. Mr. Kendall and I had to walk all the way up the hill. Oh, I apologize for my bad manners. Mr. Turner Poole, this is Mr. Joe Kendall. He is also an American. This is quite a coincidence, is it not?"

"Quite," said Poole. He looked at Kendall and thought rapidly. Poole stuck out his hand and smiled oafishly.

"Nice to meet you, Mr. Kendall. My name's Turner Poole and I'm in salvage. You know, we left a lot of valuable stuff behind here, and I'm trying to help the government decide what to salvage. Like germanium. Radios and electronic equipment with germanium components. You know, the price of germanium has just gone through the roof lately, and some of this junk might be worth a lot of money now. So me and Colonel Vinh here, we worked out a deal to salvage the stuff. Say, you're not the competition, are you?"

Kendall shook Poole's hand and nodded. "No," he said, "I'm not the competition, Mr. Poole. I'm just a writer, here to see what the place looks like now. Don't worry about me. You just go ahead with what you were doing."

Poole felt relieved that Kendall was willing to play the game. But Vinh was still hiding behind his sunglasses and it was impossible to tell whether he was buying any of this. And Truong . . .

Truong just stood there, smiling.

Chapter Thirteen

This, thought Kendall, is going to be one hell of an awkward evening.

Vinh and Poole had returned to Khe Sanh in the jeep with Kendall and Truong, leaving the workers with the light truck that had brought them to the top of the hill. In theory, the workers were to continue the excavation until sundown, but nobody really believed that.

Vinh was taciturn and enigmatic, saying little in English or in Vietnamese. Poole played at his role as the talkative Texas salvage expert, but it was clear that he lacked conviction. Truong was still the affable host, and seemed to be hiding some vast inner amusement. For his part, Kendall was determined to keep his mouth shut and contribute as little as possible to whatever was going to happen.

Truong served them dinner in his home, which was surprisingly comfortable, considering that it consisted of two rooms on the second floor of the administrative building. The dinner, a tasty chicken concoction, was cooked by a shy young Vietnamese girl who obviously worshiped Truong. She understood a little English and giggled when Kendall complimented her.

"She was a prostitute in Saigon," Truong explained after she had left. "So were her mother and her sisters. Her life here is much healthier."

"She seems very shy," Kendall observed.

"She is embarrassed by what she used to be. And since all Americans look alike to her, she is probably afraid that she may have met you before. She was very young then."

After dinner they sat down on Truong's padded rattan furniture and stared uncomfortably at one another. With the windows open the room was airy and well-ventilated, and the evening breeze rattled the bamboo shades.

Truong went to a cabinet and produced a bottle of Scotch. "Colonel Vinh," he said, "I hope you will not ask where I got this."

"You got it on the black market," said Vinh. "Where else would you get it? Do you have ice?"

"Sadly, no."

"Doesn't matter to me," said Poole. "I want to thank you for your hospitality, Mr. Truong."

Truong served the drinks. Kendall sipped at his own and kept a watch on Poole.

For a time Truong entertained his guests with a recitation of facts and statistics demonstrating the great progress that had been made by this New Economic Zone. As a journalist, Kendall was obliged to pay attention; he even took a few notes. Some of Truong's boosterism might eventually find its way into the book. Meanwhile, Poole concentrated on his drink and Vinh maintained his tight-lipped impassivity.

When Truong finally wound down, Vinh said a few sharp words in Vietnamese and got to his feet; Truong did likewise. "Please pour yourself more drinks, gentlemen," he said. "Colonel Vinh and I will be in the office. There are some routine administrative matters we must discuss. I hope you don't mind."

"Not at all," said Poole. Truong and Vinh left the room, and Poole immediately refilled his glass.

"Go easy on that stuff," Kendall advised.

"Shove it," said Poole. "What the hell are you doing here, anyway?"

"I'm not salvaging germanium."

Poole brightened. "You liked that one, did you? I thought it was pretty good, myself."

"You don't really think you're fooling anyone, do you?"

"I'm here, aren't I? I got this far."

"With Vinh's help, I presume. He knows, doesn't he?"

"Knows what?" Poole asked innocently.

"You really are a piece of work, Poole. Who the hell is Vinh, anyway? What's your connection?"

"You're so smart, you figure it out."

Kendall took a stab at it. "I'd say he has some connection with your little Vietnamese colony in Corpus Christi. He's some sort of bigwig down in Ho Chi Minh City, and you've got some sort of deal with him. What is it, Poole? You trade him Nightwind for money? Or does he just get a percentage of your action?"

"Neither," said Poole. "I don't like to give away points in my operations. Colonel Vinh got twenty-five thousand in cash up front, and he'll get another fifty when I'm safely out of the country."

"With the Nightwind canister."

Poole nodded and took another swallow of Scotch.

"What then?" Kendall asked.

"That doesn't concern you."

"The hell it doesn't. Don't you realize how dangerous that stuff is? Why do you think they stored it in such a remote location in the first place? They didn't want to take a chance on exposing their own men, Poole. And as dangerous as it was in 'sixty-eight, it's even more dangerous today."

"Are you trying to scare me, or what?" Poole sounded determined to be unimpressed.

"You don't know what's involved, Poole. Nightwind is incredibly dangerous."

"Bullshit. How do you know so much about it, anyway? Did the feds fill you in so you could pump me? Look, Kendall, I wouldn't be here if you hadn't shown up on my doorstep and started asking strange questions. You as much as told me that at least one of those canisters is still here, right? Well, if the marines left it behind, then it doesn't really belong to anyone, now does it? I seem to be the only living person with any clear claim to it. If I dig it up, it's mine by right of salvage, if nothing else."

"And what are you going to do with it?"

"Wheel and deal, boy, wheel and deal. It's what I do best."

Poole seemed impervious. For all his Texas manner, it seemed to Kendall that Poole resembled nothing so much as a nineteenth-century British magnate, out east of Suez for a little fun and games with the wogs.

"Have some more Scotch," Kendall said, passing the bottle to Poole.

"You wouldn't be trying to get ol' Turner drunk, would you, Joe? Better men than you have tried." Nevertheless, Poole accepted the bottle and refilled his glass.

"Do you really think they're going to let you walk out of here with Nightwind?"

"Why not? They don't even know what the hell it is. And Vinh wants his money."

"What about Truong?"

Poole dismissed Truong with a contemptuous flick of his wrist. "Bush leaguer," he said. "Vinh could have him for breakfast."

"Maybe," said Kendall, "but chew on this for a while. One of the Nightwind canisters was removed four years ago. Truong was in charge here four years ago."

Poole straightened up in his chair and became more alert. "What are you saying, Joe? That this Truong guy found the first canister?"

"Who else?"

"Then what's he doing here now?" Poole demanded. "Why in hell would he still be in this rathole?"

"I don't know," Kendall admitted. "I haven't figured that out yet."

"You be sure to let me know when you do."

While Poole tended to his drink, Kendall set his mind on the problem. Ever since they found Poole at the top of Hill 651, Kendall had the uneasy feeling that Truong knew exactly what was going on. He seemed secretly amused by it all. That might make sense if Truong had found the first canister but didn't know about the second one; he would think that Poole and Vinh were trying to dig up something that was already gone. And if that were the case, then Kendall would give a lot to know what Truong and Vinh were talking about downstairs.

If Vinh told Truong about the second canister, things could get very interesting. The four of them would see all the cards—all but one. Kendall was still the only one who knew just how dangerous Nightwind could be. Somehow, perhaps he could use that knowledge to steer the course of events.

Which left the question of precisely what that course should be. If his knowledge equaled power, the responsibility that came with the power felt weighty and unfamiliar. Kendall was used to reporting events, not influencing them. A ghastly variation of Heisenberg's principle was in play here; you couldn't observe something without affecting the object under observation.

Nightwind was too important to be left to the clumsy machinations of any of them. The ideal solution would be to delay everyone until the CIA did whatever it was they were planning to do. But that didn't look like a very practical option. Outside of murdering Truong, Vinh, and Poole in their sleep, there simply wasn't anything Kendall could do to slow down the game.

With great reluctance Kendall concluded that if anyone got the second canister, it should be Poole. That, at least, would get the canister out of Vietnam. Poole might be dealt with later; one way or another, Nightwind would be recovered.

And that would make Kendall the ultimate winner. He couldn't publish unless the second canister was safely in the hands of the U.S. government. Self-interest and prudence, then, dictated that he should help Poole. And since Poole already seemed to be on top of the situation, the best help Kendall could give would be to keep his mouth shut and say nothing.

The irony didn't escape him. His supposed power to influence events was an illusion, after all. The most and least he could do was nothing. He was dead on the balance point, one foot on yin, the other on yang. He dare not disturb the fragile order of things.

Echoes of Vitaglia's voice came back to him. Be sure you're right, and then go ahead—but you can't be sure you're right, so you go ahead anyway. The alternative was Zeno's discredited paradox about the impossibility of any motion at all. But Zeno seemed to be in charge here, not Davy Crockett. For Kendall, motion *was* impossible. The pebble would have to let the ocean decide what was to happen.

But the pebble could still worry. Kendall did.

Poole presently fell asleep on the couch. Kendall removed Poole's boots and maneuvered him to what looked like a more comfortable position.

Truong and Vinh returned from their private conference. Vinh looked at Poole, stretched out in slumber, snorted, and immediately retired to Truong's bedroom without so much as a glance at Kendall.

"There is a cot in the office," said Truong. "You must be very tired, Mr. Kendall."

Kendall realized that he was. He was still jet-lagged, and the events of the scorching day had left him exhausted. He followed Truong downstairs to the administrative office. He sat down heavily on the edge of the cot—former property of the United States Marines—and began unlacing his boots. Truong watched him.

"Would you tell me something, Mr. Kendall?"

"What?"

"This afternoon, you said it would be a privilege to walk up that hill. I have been wondering why you said that."

Kendall dropped a boot on the wooden floor. "Twelve years ago," he said, "I was on top of that hill while some of your countrymen were trying to get to the top. They didn't make it, and this afternoon I saw that they never really had a chance. But they still tried. They were very brave men. I don't think I ever realized that before."

"And that is why you came here?" Truong asked. "To walk up that hill?"

"In a way," Kendall answered cautiously.

"You had no other reason?"

"I'm collecting material for a book."

"So you said."

"It's true."

"I'm sure that it is. You're not like Mr. Poole. You didn't come here to salvage germanium—although I suspect that you know the value of germanium."

"Do you?" Kendall asked him.

"This is my district. It is my responsibility to be aware of all our resources."

Kendall removed the other boot. "What would you do with the germanium, if you had it?"

Truong sat down in a chair and leaned forward, toward Kendall. "As a representative of my government," he said, "it would be my responsibility to turn it over to the proper officials."

"Like Vinh?"

"Colonel Vinh is a very powerful man."

"Colonel Vinh is a weasel. He's corrupt and greedy."

Truong smiled, a brief flash of white teeth, quickly concealed again by his straight, thin lips. "Colonel Vinh was a hero of the revolution."

"Do you think that matters now?"

"Of course not," Truong replied. His tone changed subtly, as if he had suddenly removed some unneeded garment. "What matters is that Colonel Vinh is still powerful."

Kendall studied Truong. He was not sure he could read the subtle ideographs of an Oriental face. Talking with Truong was like talking with an American, but Truong was not an American. He was Vietnamese.

"You always go with the winners, don't you?"

"What sense would it make to go with the losers?"

196

"The Vietcong killed your family, yet a year later you joined them."

"I told you before, the war killed them. I had cousins who were killed by an American air raid. To whom should I be loyal, Mr. Kendall?"

"You seem to have answered that question already. In America we call it looking out for number one."

"Yes," said Truong, "I know. That is one of many things I learned in America, besides the English and the flying. I learned how to look out for number one. Is that such a terrible thing? Isn't it what Americans do? Your leaders change as often as ours do, and somehow your people adjust, the same as I have done."

"We do things a little differently."

"Not so different. I was there in an election year, Mr. Kendall. I saw how you did things in 1968."

"Not one of our vintage years."

"Your leaders were shot, there were great riots in the streets. And when it was all over, you had a new President and the people were loyal to him. And when Nixon lost the mandate of heaven, as we would call it, again there was a great change and your people adjusted and were loyal to the next new leader. And this year you will do it again and it will be the same. Why should you expect it to be different here? I accept change and adjust to it. If the Chinese should conquer us next year, I will adjust once more. I don't understand why you question this."

"Neither do I," Kendall confessed. "Maybe I'm just too tired to think straight. But this business of loyalty—I think it must go deeper than you want to admit. Take a good look at Turner Poole tomorrow. He's real good at looking out for number one, Mr. Truong. A goddamn expert."

"Is that why he is here . . . to salvage the germanium?"

"Poole is here because he is a very desperate man. I think you should let him salvage whatever the hell he wants and help him get out of this country just as fast as possible."

"That is undoubtedly what Colonel Vinh wants."

197

"Then go along with it. Don't play any games, Truong. Just let it happen."

"You think I might interfere?"

"I think you will always look out for number one."

"You may rely on it." Truong got to his feet. "Have a pleasant sleep, Mr. Kendall. I hope that cot will be comfortable."

Truong turned off the overhead light and left the office. Alone in the dark, Kendall wondered if he had said too much. He supposed he would find out tomorrow.

In the morning Truong was gone. So was the jeep.

Poole was hung over and didn't seem to appreciate what had happened. Kendall kept his own counsel. Vinh, however, was coldly furious. He swore vehemently in Vietnamese and every few seconds he cast suspicious, challenging glances at the Americans.

"He has gone to the hill," Vinh declared.

"Maybe he just wanted to get an early start on the digging," Poole suggested hopefully. Vinh didn't think the comment rated a response.

The colonel turned his back on Poole and walked briskly toward the workers' barracks, across the dusty roadway. His short, choppy gait looked vaguely comical to Kendall. Vinh collared the first worker he encountered and began demanding answers.

"Christ," said Poole, "I wish I'd thought to bring sunglasses. That sun is killing me. Do you suppose Vinh has an extra pair?"

"Why don't you buy the ones he's wearing?" Kendall suggested.

"Don't start with me, Joe," Poole warned. "I can't handle that this morning. What the hell is going on around here?"

"Truong is looking out for number one, I'd say."

"You think he's going to split with the canister?"

"Wouldn't you?"

"Truong doesn't know shit," Poole insisted.

"Truong," Kendall corrected, "knows everything."

Poole, his hand shielding his eyes, turned to look at Kendall. "Damn it, Kendall," he said, "you knew he was going to do this, didn't you?"

"I thought he might."

"Then why the hell didn't you do something about it?"

"What would you suggest?"

"You could have told me."

"You'd already passed out, Poole."

"Well, Vinh, then. You could have told Vinh."

Kendall looked across the highway at Vinh. The colonel was making angry, threatening gestures to a small knot of farmers.

"Vinh wouldn't have listened to me," said Kendall. "Last night Vinh probably thought he'd bought Truong. That was what their little conference was about, I'd guess. Vinh thought he had a deal, but Truong probably figured he could make a much better deal on his own. You know how these things work, Poole."

"Yeah," Poole protested, "*I* know, but *Truong*? He's just some gook bureaucrat. What the hell does he know?"

"He knows how to survive," said Kendall.

At length Vinh commandeered a truck from the farmers. It developed that Vinh did not know how to drive, and Poole was obviously having trouble just keeping his eyes focused. Having no alternative, Vinh ordered Kendall to drive. The three of them crowded into the cab of the truck, a little blue Toyota pickup, and started up the road to Hill 651.

The morning was hot and bright, the road rugged and dusty. Inside the cab the heat quickly became intense. After five miles Kendall stopped the truck and Poole pushed Vinh out of the way and threw up into a ditch. Vinh looked from Poole to Kendall and said nothing. Poole shakily got back into the truck, and Vinh let him sit next to the window. The journey resumed.

They reached the base of Hill 651 and still there was no sign of Truong. Kendall set the emergency brake and got out. Poole didn't budge.

"You don't mean we have to *walk* up the fucking hill?"

"Either we walk up, or we walk home. The engine is already overheating."

Poole stared at Kendall in anguished disbelief. Vinh waited for Poole to move, and when he didn't, calmly reached across to open the door and shoved Poole out. In silence Vinh started climbing. Kendall followed, and a few moments later Poole brought up the rear.

On this morning it was no privilege to climb the hill. Driving on the rough road had absorbed most of Kendall's attention, but now there was nothing to keep him from thinking about what was happening. If Truong had got away with the Nightwind canister, he could be on his way to almost anywhere. Laos was barely five miles away. And Truong was a flier; if he could get his hands on an airplane, there was no telling where he might go. China, perhaps, or to the Pol Pot cadres in Cambodia. He knew Truong wouldn't hesitate to sell the canister to the enemies of his own people.

They reached the summit, near the wreckage of the old command bunker, and still there was another half mile to Grenoble. If Truong was up there, he was on foot. Vinh never paused, but Kendall stopped to wait for Poole, who was lagging far behind. Even from a distance, the Texan looked awful. He was drenched with sweat and his face was mottled with pink and white patches.

Poole looked as if he wanted to say something to Kendall, but he couldn't seem to muster enough energy to make the words come out. Kendall had nothing at all to say to Poole. He resumed the hike, and Poole had no choice but to follow.

Vinh reached the old French bunker well ahead of the Americans. He descended into the wrecked tunnels and was lost from sight. By the time Kendall and Poole arrived, he was still in the tunnel. Poole collapsed onto a slab of concrete.

"Come on," said Kendall, "we've got to go down there."

"Vinh," Poole gasped, "Vinh will tell us."

"You trust Vinh?"

Poole didn't answer, but even in his depleted condition, he couldn't escape the logic of the question. He groaned feebly, got to his feet, and followed Kendall into the tunnel. They had no light, so Kendall improvised with his cigarette lighter, turning up the flame and keeping it going until the heat singed his thumb. Their progress was slow and fitful, but the random noises from deeper in the tunnel told them that Vinh was not far away. Soon they saw a flickering, reflected light shining off the dull concrete, and they followed it to its source. They found Vinh holding a kerosene lantern left behind by Truong or the workers. At his feet, on the floor of the tunnel, was the long metal canister Kendall had first seen a dozen years ago.

"Jesus Christ almighty!" Poole breathed. "It's still here!"

"Idiot!" snapped Vinh. "It is empty."

Vinh lowered the lantern and allowed them to see. The blunt cone of the canister rested against the tunnel wall, two feet away from the long tube of the cylinder. The cone had been unscrewed, and the reflection from the lantern danced over the curved, gleaming interior of the empty canister.

"Oh my God," Poole mumbled.

"It was Truong," said Vinh angrily. "This was done recently. Truong has taken what was inside."

Vinh raised the lantern and stared hatefully at Poole and Kendall, his jaw muscles twitching. Kendall saw why Vinh always wore sunglasses; without them, his eyes looked small and piggy.

"Which one of you told him?" Vinh demanded. "I did not tell him what was inside. He would not have known to open the cylinder if someone did not tell him. It was you, Kendall! You told him!"

"No," Kendall answered quietly, "I didn't."

"Then how did he know? How could he know?"

Kendall knelt and examined the canister. He gestured for Vinh to lower the lantern.

"He knew," said Kendall, "because four years ago he opened the first canister."

"The *first* canister?" Vinh looked up at Poole, who was

still standing. "You didn't tell me there was another canister!" Vinh shouted. He turned back to Kendall, seeing that Poole was too stricken to provide any answers.

"How do you know this? Did Truong tell you? Answer me, Kendall!"

Kendall ignored Vinh's rage. It was beginning to make some sense now, and he didn't want to be sidetracked by Vinh's display of spleen.

"Truong must have found the first canister, or heard about it from one of his workers," Kendall explained calmly. "That was four years ago, and he didn't *know* what was inside. But he could make an educated guess. See these letters and numbers?"

Kendall pointed to a row of figures that had been stenciled in white paint along the rim of the canister. "Truong was a South Vietnamese pilot," said Kendall. "He was familiar with standard American military abbreviations and designations. If he had worked with Agent Orange, he would have known the designation for a biochemical weapon. With his experience, I think it must have been pretty obvious to him what was inside. He opened up that first canister and probably sold the contents to some terrorist organization. He didn't know exactly what he had, but he knew it was valuable. Or maybe he didn't. Maybe he didn't get much money for it, and that's why he was still here. I'm just guessing, now."

"Go on," said Vinh. His voice carried the tone of a military command. "If there was a first canister, how did he know about this one?"

"He didn't. When you guys showed up and started digging, he probably thought it was a great joke. He knew what you were after, and he thought he already had it. But then—"

"Then *you* arrived," said Vinh, pointing an accusing finger at Kendall, "and you told him!"

Kendall pushed Vinh's hand aside. "I didn't have to tell him. When I showed up and wanted to see the same hill, he could see that something was going on. And you two were digging in a completely different spot from the place where the first canister was found. He didn't have to be clairvoyant to figure that there was probably a second canister. So he came up here last night, probably with a couple of workers, and dug it up for himself. Since he already knew what was inside, he opened it up and carted away the hockey pucks—that's what they called the disks inside—because they'd be easier to move than the whole cylinder."

"You have figured this out too easily," Vinh declared. "You know too much. You are a CIA agent!"

"Oh, bullshit," Kendall answered wearily. Vinh, for all his dark theatricality, was such an obvious small-minded asshole that he didn't even want to deal with him.

"We will shoot you! That is how we treat CIA—"

"Vinh," Kendall said tersely, "if I were a CIA agent, you and Poole and Truong would all be dead by now, and I'd be over the border with the goodies. And don't threaten me, Colonel. You can't afford to let anyone hear the truth about what's happening here—they'd probably shoot *you*. So kindly can the CIA bullshit. Hell, I almost wish I were an agent. Maybe I'd know what to do next."

"We must find Truong!" Vinh announced, as if he had solved some great mystery. "He cannot be more than a few hours ahead of us. The workers at the NEZ will know where he went. We will—"

Vinh was stopped short by the dull, hollow thud of Turner Poole collapsing. Kendall got to him quickly and rolled him over onto his back. In the dim light of the lantern Kendall could see that Poole was still conscious, but his breathing was labored and ragged. Kendall lifted him up and propped him against the tunnel wall. Poole's head lolled to one side. Not knowing what else to do, Kendall slapped him smartly on the cheek.

Poole moaned, and the moan became a deep, anguished sob. Tears glinted in the uncertain light as they rolled down his face.

"Oh, Jesus!" he cried. "Oh, Jesus, I'm dying! I've got cancer, I know I do! It's all ruined, and I'm dying!"

"Cancer?" Kendall couldn't accept it, yet there was

something hauntingly plausible about a man like Poole contracting a disease like cancer. It was the disease of the times, and Poole was quintessentially a man of his times.

"Oh, Christ!" Poole wailed.

"Poole, listen to me! Do you have any medicine? Didn't the doctors give you any pills?"

"There aren't any doctors. But I've got cancer, I know I do! I can feel it. I'm dying. Everything's falling apart and I'm dying."

Poole was using more energy proclaiming his imminent death than Kendall would have thought a cancer victim would have available. He relaxed a little. Poole wasn't dying.

Kendall slapped him again, harder this time. "Poole! Listen to me! You're not dying and you don't have cancer!"

"Yes, I do," Poole insisted, "I know I do."

"No, you don't. You're out of shape, you're an alcoholic, you're hung over, and you're probably on the verge of a heatstroke. But you're not dying, Poole. You just want to, that's all."

Poole halted his moaning, not sure how to respond to Kendall's accusation. He closed his eyes, put his hands to his face, and sobbed some more.

Kendall turned to Vinh. "He just needs a little rest," he said. "We'll have to stay here for a while. It's cool here."

"But Truong is getting away!"

"That's the breaks."

"Leave him!" Vinh demanded. "We will leave this worthless son of a bitch here!"

"No, we won't," said Kendall. "And you're not going anywhere without us, Vinh. You can't drive, and I've got the key, anyway. So just relax and rest your bones for a few minutes. I'll take care of Poole."

"If I had a gun, I would shoot him!"

"Joe!" Poole called, his voice quivering. "You won't let him leave me here, will you?"

"Relax, Poole. Nobody's leaving. Nobody's going to get shot. We're going to rest for a little while, and then we're all going to leave together and try to find Truong. Isn't that right, Colonel Vinh?"

Vinh snorted contemptuously, and after a few seconds of defiant staring he grabbed the lantern and stomped resolutely away, toward the top of the tunnel. The light grew dim, and then was gone altogether. Kendall flicked his lighter and held it in front of Poole.

"I can't keep this on all the time. But don't worry, Vinh's not going anywhere. We'll get out of here when you've got some strength back. At least it's cool down here."

Kendall let the flame go out. The darkness was complete.

"It's falling apart," Poole said softly. "And I can't stop it. I can't do *anything*. What went wrong, Joe? I used to be able to do everything, and now I can't do *anything*."

Kendall wondered whether he could do anything, either. Then it came to him, in the black silence, that he was already doing something. He was doing what the tough, desperate men who had once occupied this broken citadel had done. Plans and policies didn't enter into it. Courage and convictions were not a part of it. When those glittering gold and ivory acid-boxes were shattered and the debris was swept away on the tide, you couldn't crumble like Poole, because at the center of it all, the night was irreducible. And you couldn't run, as a young correspondent had once run toward the crest of this haunted ridge, because there was nowhere that was not a part of this place. In the end, you just hung on. You kept your balance and you did whatever had to be done. Down here in the darkness, at the center of things, there were no choices.

Chapter Fourteen

Dawn was spectacular on the South China Sea. The climbing sun exploded on the horizon, sending pink and orange shafts of light through the gaps in the cloud banks piled up in the east. The sea itself seemed to glow from the radiance of a submerged fire, and the last bright stars of night were reflected in the chuckling waters lapping against the metal hull of the boat.

On the foredeck an infant began to cry. Somewhere else another child took up the song, and soon there was a disorganized chorus at work, counterpointed by the heavy stirrings of waking families and the aimless, clanking labors of the ancient engines and the bored crewmen who attended it. The noise would crescendo over the next hour, and by then it would be too hot for movement, too hot even for the wails of sick and hungry children. Everything would stop by then, except for the syncopated chugging of the engine. Perhaps that would stop, too.

Truong leaned against the railing outside the bridge and let the torpid morning breezes cool his face. The relief wouldn't last long, but it was enough to rouse him from the languid stupor of the night. His thousand-dollar cabin received little air, and at night the pitiful families clustered on deck had the better of it. But during the day he would have shelter from the endless sunshine; by noon many of the two hundred refugees aboard would gladly kill him for that room, before the sun killed them.

But the night could kill, too. Up by the bow the first of the night's victims was being rolled overboard, into the waiting sea. Several more would follow. The activity was ignored by all but those directly affected by the loss, and even they watched the burials with a passivity that bordered on indifference. On this, the fifth morning of the voyage, death had lost its novelty—if it had any to begin with. These people had seen death in every imaginable form, and they seemed to realize that they would see much more of it before they reached their destination.

Smoke from the morning cookfires drifted back toward the bridge. There were fewer of them today because there was less to cook. In two days there would be no need for fires at all; nothing would remain but a little rice and some dried fish. The boat was supposed to reach Mersing by then, but Truong already had his doubts. Last night he had seen the distant beacon of the gas-jet fires on the horizon. He knew the fires were part of the drilling operation at Trengganu on the Malaysian coast; but if that was the source of the fires, then the boat was not where it should be. Mersing might still be three or four days away, and much longer than that if the engine should fail.

The captain emerged from the deckhouse and stood next to Truong, sniffing the air. "If wind don't change," he said, "we get smoke right in our face. Got to change course, then."

"Are you sure you're on the right course now?" Truong asked him.

The captain frowned at Truong. "Hey! Who is navigator here? Who has sailed this sea for twenty year? You or me?"

He waited for an answer, but Truong didn't feel like giving him one. The captain's name was Schmidt, and he was the fruit of a union between a German—or perhaps, Dutch—sailor and an Indonesian prostitute. He had his father's name and profession and his mother's opportunism and a fat, swarthy face that captured the worst of both of them. He spoke a dozen languages, none of them well, and captained a ship that flew the Greek flag and bore the name of a Roman emperor, *Augustus*. The man was a foul, polluted international sinkhole, and Truong despised him.

But Schmidt and his Mediterranean rustbucket were all that was immediately available in Da Nang. Truong knew where to look—he kept track of such things—and had found Schmidt barely an hour after arriving in the port city. Schmidt, of course, had been amenable to a deal, and before nightfall Truong was safely aboard the *Augustus*. For a thousand dollars of American cash, and the promise of another thousand upon arrival in Mersing, Truong secured a small but private cabin in the aft corner of the deckhouse. For another five hundred Schmidt agreed to sail on the morning tide instead of waiting another day to pick up a few more families. The latecomers weren't likely to have enough money to make the delay profitable, and profit was the only thing capable of motivating Schmidt.

The other voyagers carried with them as many of their possessions as they could—light enough cargo—but Truong brought aboard nothing but a small valise and one large, leather suitcase. The suitcase must have weighed fifty kilos, but Truong managed to lug it aboard without help. If someone knew just how heavy it was, they would suspect he was smuggling out a large quantity of gold.

Ounce for ounce, his cargo probably wasn't as valuable as gold, but it would serve. The twenty-four thick platelike disks—Truong thought of them as skeet, which he had shot at in Texas—ought to be worth ten thousand dollars apiece, as Truong calculated the market.

The market consisted of a man named Raphael Alonzo, or at least, that was what he called himself. He was a man of mixed blood and unmixed loyalties: Alonzo sold implements of death to anyone who had the money to buy them. He was utterly loyal to money.

Truong had met Alonzo once before, in 1976. When the workers combing the ruins of the bunkers atop Hill 651 found the canister, they immediately reported it to

Truong. Although he had never seen an object quite like it before, he suspected its true nature. He contacted a man he knew in Ho Chi Minh City, a Chinese merchant named Le Kuan. If anyone knew what to do with such a find, it would be Le Kuan.

Le Kuan, in turn, got in touch with Alonzo, who operated out of an import-export company in Singapore. Alonzo and Le Kuan arrived in Khe Sanh a week later, and Truong showed them the canister. He told them that he suspected it contained some sort of nerve gas. To his surprise Alonzo told him it was not nerve gas, but rather a new form of bacterial weapon. Inside the canister, said Alonzo, there would be a dozen or more devices that the Americans referred to as hockey pucks, a reference none of the three men really understood. Each hockey puck contained a bacterial agent and an explosive charge to disperse the germs once the puck was ejected from a helicopter. The pucks, however, were basically harmless because the charges were not armed for detonation until they were inserted in the ejection mechanism.

Alonzo didn't say how he knew all of this, but he spoke with such authority that Truong couldn't doubt his word. Alonzo had been dealing in weapons for so long, and had such excellent sources of information, that he frequently knew more about exotic new weapons than the armies to which they belonged. It was said that he had sources in both the Pentagon and the Kremlin.

Truong supposed that the existence of men such as Alonzo was inevitable in a world where weapons were the number one item of trade, but he was slightly awed to meet such a man. It gave him a glimpse of a world beyond the one he knew, a world where all the numbers ended in long strings of zeros, where anything at all was possible.

Under Alonzo's direction Truong opened the canister. Alonzo was pleased to find a full two dozen of the devices; he said that his informant had been too conservative. Alonzo reached into his pocket and pulled out twenty five-hundred-dollar bills. He gave them to Truong, thanked him, and said that another forty thousand would be paid as soon as the shipment reached Singapore. Le Kuan would deliver the money.

Alonzo and Le Kuan departed with the hockey pucks, and Truong settled down to wait for his money. He waited more than a month, until impatience got the better of him. He went down to Ho Chi Minh City in search of Le Kuan, but the merchant had vanished. Some said he was dead and some said he had left the country, but all agreed that Le Kuan was gone for good. Truong returned to Khe Sanh and resumed his life.

He used the money sparingly, saving most of it for an emergency that might never come. He knew that ten thousand dollars wasn't really enough to buy very much of a new life outside of Vietnam, and the life he had wasn't so bad. He had plentiful food, women whenever he wanted them, and no visible enemies. Until the arrival of Poole, Kendall, and Vinh, he gave little thought to leaving.

But the second canister changed everything. Colonel Vinh was a man who could destroy him, and if Vinh knew about the second canister, then he could easily enough find out about the first. Truong considered letting Vinh and Poole take the canister and do as they liked with it, but in the end, he realized that such a course would not be safe. Vinh wasn't likely to leave anyone in a position to inform on him.

Truong attempted to strike a deal with Vinh, but Vinh was not receptive to the idea, which sounded a lot like blackmail to him. Vinh grudgingly offered Truong five thousand dollars to keep his mouth closed. But Truong knew how such deals worked now, and he realized that he was much more likely to see the point of a knife than the five thousand dollars. And five thousand dollars was nothing. Vinh was clearly not sophisticated in these matters, and the American, Poole, had probably taken great advantage of him. Truong saw that he had only one course.

He hesitated just once, after his conversation with Kendall. The American journalist, unlike Vinh and Poole (and Alonzo and Le Kuan) treated Truong as an equal, as a man of experience and insight. He was interested in Truong himself, and not merely what Truong might possess. Kendall's disapproval had a strange sting to it. He seemed to speak from knowledge and, uniquely in this company, from some sense of morality.

Truong knew about American morality, the God-and-country hypocrisy of people who wiped out entire villages at the touch of a button. He had no use for those who proclaimed unalterable answers. But Kendall had only questions. His experience on Hill 651, whatever it was, seemed to have given him access to some deeper level of meaning that he was still trying to understand. Kendall was an intriguing man, and for a few moments Truong seriously considered playing the game his way.

But Kendall was also naïve if he thought that philosophy mattered now. In a land where three million had died horribly, philosophy offered no protection. That was something that Truong understood and Kendall didn't. Kendall spoke of loyalty, but in Vietnam one might as well be loyal to a sinking ship.

Now, standing on the bridge of this wallowing scow, the thought came back to him and brought a hard, rueful smile to his lips. For the next few days he truly and unavoidably would have to be loyal to a ship that might begin to sink at any moment. In this he was no different from the huddled refugees on the foredeck. For the first time, possibly in his entire life, he felt at one with his people. It was an odd, disquieting sensation, and one he did not particularly care for.

Schmidt suddenly elbowed Truong in the ribs. It was something stronger than a mere nudge, but not enough to be considered cause for offense. The captain was merely clumsy, handling his body the same way he handled his boat.

"You got some big deal cooking in Singapore, right?"

"If I do," Truong said coldly, "it's none of your business."

"Everything on this ship my business," Schmidt insisted. "You want message, you tell me what you got going."

"Did my message come in last night?"

"First you tell me."

"Do you want that thousand dollars when we reach Mersing, Captain?"

Schmidt shrugged. "Maybe we don't get to Mersing," he said. "Or maybe ship gets there but you don't. So you tell me now."

Truong wanted to hit the fat half-breed, but he knew that would be foolish in the end. There were five crewmen aboard, and Truong had seen two AK-47 automatic rifles in the captain's cabin.

"If I tell you now," said Truong, "you might throw me overboard. I'll tell you before we dock in Mersing."

Schmidt thought about it for a few seconds, then gave in—rather too easily, in Truong's estimation.

"Okay," said Schmidt. "I show you message now, you tell me deal later. I trust you now, right?" Schmidt removed a crumpled piece of yellow paper from his breast pocket and handed it to Truong.

It was the reply he had been hoping for. Alonzo had received Truong's message, radioed two days earlier. Truong was worried that Alonzo might have disappeared by now, but apparently he was still in the same business at the same address.

"Will inspect shipment on arrival," the message read. "Providing papers as requested."

"Very big deal, yes?"

"It's none of your business, Schmidt."

"If you say so," said Schmidt. "Just like those round things you got in suitcase, eh? Not my business. But before long, you tell me, right?"

Truong said nothing, and after a moment Schmidt laughed uproariously and returned to his post on the bridge. Truong stared at him and realized that the captain was more dangerous than he looked. That nudge in the ribs had been more than a loutish greeting. He was checking for a concealed weapon, the same as he had checked the cabin. It was fortunate that Schmidt had nudged him in the right side rather than the left; if he had, he would

212

have found the pistol that was tucked into Truong's belt beneath the loose khaki shirt. He didn't know what the hockey pucks were, but he would certainly have recognized the gun.

The day was hot already. On the foredeck they were erecting their little cloth or canvas sunshades, for all the good it would do them. Truong decided to return to his cabin. Everything would be safer there, and he wouldn't have to look at the ugly captain, or at the people on deck who were about to die.

He found a young woman waiting at his cabin door. She was small and very pretty, even though her face was blistered from the unrelenting sun. In her arms she held a baby, no more than a year old.

"Please," she said. "Please help me." Her eyes were large and desperate.

Truong wished she would go away, but he found himself saying, "What do you want from me?"

"Please let us stay in your cabin. It will be cool there, and I must keep my baby out of the sun. He will die out on the deck when the sun gets high. I will do anything for you if you will just please help me."

She was bargaining with the only thing she possessed, her own body. Truong had struck such bargains before, with the displaced whores who had been removed from the city and taken to the NEZ at Khe Sanh. He could tell that this woman was no whore, but she was willing to become one, and her price was not money. If it had been, Truong probably would have accepted the offer. But something about the way she held the baby reminded him of the way his wife and son had looked, so long ago. He seldom thought about them, but now that their memory had been evoked, he felt a strange, stabbing anger. If she had lived, he wondered, would she have offered herself in such a way, for such a reason? He knew the answer, and he hated it.

Truong opened the door for her. Inside, there was room for only the narrow bed. The woman looked at Truong uncertainly, then sat down on the bed, at the far corner of the room. Truong entered and closed the door behind him, but did not sit down. He stood and watched as the woman unbuttoned her blouse.

He felt oddly relieved to realize that the unbuttoning was not for him, but for the baby. She held the child up to her breast and lightly stroked his hair. Her voice barely a whisper, she hummed some song that Truong didn't recognize.

Truong watched her in silence for many minutes. Finally, he opened the door and quietly slipped out into the companionway. As hot as it was on deck, it would be better there. If he stayed in the cabin, he would have to say something that he didn't know how to say. He had tried to say it several times, but the words wouldn't come. He could think of no way to tell the woman that her baby was already dead.

"Safe once again," said Kendall, "in the arms of American bureaucracy."

"Speak for yourself," said Poole. "If I had a brain left in my head, I'd get the hell out of here."

Kendall looked around to see if anyone was listening, but no one was. That figured. He had nearly been forced to manhandle the clerk at the reception desk just to be noticed at all. Bureaucrats were true to their colors at all times and places, even if the place was the American Embassy in Kuala Lumpur.

"Poole," Kendall said in a harsh whisper, "if you so much as take one step toward the door, I swear I'll break both your legs."

Poole knew he meant it. Kendall had been cajoling, threatening, and generally controlling Poole's every action since the morning he collapsed in the bunker on Hill 651. Poole wouldn't admit, even to himself, that he was afraid of Kendall, but circumstances forced him to defer to the journalist's demands. Poole wasn't sure he cared anymore.

But barging into an American embassy and demanding to see the CIA resident was a little more than Poole's nerves could accept just now. Kendall certainly had balls,

ilence she followed him back to his cabin. They sat
er on the bed for a long time without moving or
ng. At last, she embraced him. Truong could feel
ed, and found that he shared it. They made love
assion and gentleness, as if it were to be for the first
st time.

r, she spoke a little. She was from a small village
Da Nang. Her husband had been a schoolteacher un-
e old regime, but the Communists, after reeducating
lecided that he would be more useful as a soldier.
d been killed last year in Kampuchea. With the gold
iven to her by her husband's parents, she purchased
e for herself and her child on this boat. Now that
ld was gone, she was alone in the world.

ough she never said so, Truong felt that she wanted
take care of her. She assumed he was just another
e, one who had enough money to buy a cabin, but
refugee. Truong wondered if it was true. He didn't
f himself as being like the people on the foredeck,
haps he was, in ways he didn't fully understand. In
s as a pilot he flew over the people of Vietnam
feeling as if he belonged to them. But in a ship
re all bound for the same destination, and it didn't
whether they slept in a cabin or under a tattered
canvas on the deck.

since his first sight of Ly, holding her child, she
inded him of his wife, dead these eight years. Now
was gone, but the memory remained, overlapping
atever was the reality of this moment. He was
her as he had been drawn to no other woman,
s wife, whose face he could no longer hold in his

couldn't sleep that night, and after sunrise he
on the deck and watched the dwindling, ragged
vaken. He looked into their faces and wondered
were, these people, and how they had come to
And he wondered about the strange bond he was
to feel with them. Surely, it went beyond shar-

but no one was going to arrest Kendall. Poole, on the
other hand, faced a future he didn't even want to contem-
plate. Yet all he wanted, really, was to be home again.
To achieve that goal, he was willing to do as Kendall
instructed.

Again, on that goddamned hill, Kendall had probably
saved his life. As with the mortar shell, there was no way
to be certain what would have happened if it hadn't been
for Kendall, but there was a very good chance that Vinh
would have either killed him on the spot or left him there
to die of his own anxiety. But Kendall had taken charge
and somehow managed to get him off of that bastard hill
and back to Khe Sanh.

There, in Truong's office, Poole lay on the cot, conscious but uncaring, while Kendall hammered out an
agreement with Vinh. The colonel was a very angry man
by that point, but Kendall finally managed to get him to
listen to reason. According to the story of the NEZ workers, who were probably too afraid of Vinh to lie to him,
Truong was headed for the coast. His obvious next move
was to get himself and the Nightwind pucks aboard a ship.
With Vinh's power and resources, it ought to be possible
to find out which ship he was on, and where it was bound.

Unless he was willing to abandon everything, Vinh
couldn't pursue Truong himself. But Poole and Kendall
could, and Poole's money would make it worthwhile for
Vinh to help them. And Vinh's own self-interest made it
highly desirable for him to get Kendall and Poole out of
the country as soon as possible, before anyone could start
asking questions.

In the end, Vinh accepted an offer of twenty-five thousand dollars to help them pick up Truong's trail, with
twenty-five thousand more to be sent to him when they
caught him. Poole was too weak to protest Kendall's ex-
travagance with his money, but it didn't seem to matter,
really. All the money in the world wasn't going to save
him now, but if another fifty grand could just get him
home, he would settle for that.

Poole had suffered no more debilitating attacks after

that morning, not even in the humid heat of the coastal plain. They drove first to Hue, the nearest port, and began the search. After two days Vinh was convinced that Truong had not been in Hue, so they moved on to the next port to the south, Da Nang. While Vinh went around town asking questions, Poole stayed with Kendall at the seedy hotel where the few foreigners remaining in Da Nang congregated. Kendall allowed Poole two drinks a night, and after he enforced the limit with a painful half nelson, Poole was willing to acquiesce to Kendall's rules.

The wait in Da Nang had been torture, and Poole was in no condition to stand up to torture. His willpower seemed to have been sucked right out of him. The conviction remained that he could no longer do anything, that the world in general and Poole's life in particular had disintegrated. He wanted no more adventures; the juice had turned sour and poisonous. A man could take only so much, and after that he had a right to collapse if that was what he wanted.

Ahead of him lay God knew what miseries—probably a long trial and a longer prison sentence. The vultures had been flapping around him for months, and now that he was down and helpless, they were sure to land. The hell of it was, he didn't even know where it had all gone wrong. Hill 651, maybe.

Kendall tried to cheer him up, after a fashion. He pointed out that they might still be able to recover the Nightwind. There would be no money in it this way, but the government might be persuaded to view Poole's odyssey as the loyal act of a patriotic American who earnestly desired to undo any damage he might have caused by his naïve actions on behalf of President Johnson, so long ago. That was Kendall's scenario, at least, and Kendall was a writer, a specialist in scenarios. Maybe it could be made to work. Maybe a grateful government would forgive him his past transgressions if he promised to stop importing marijuana and swindling land speculators and bribing officials and all the dreadful rest of it. Maybe.

Vinh found what they were looking for. He reported

that Truong was almost certainly abo_tus_, which was bound for Mersing on There was no way to be certain that on that ship, and it was equally uncertion was actually Mersing. It was alstain that Vinh was telling the truth, buPoole to fork over the twenty-five thou

After that things moved swiftly. VinHo Chi Minh City the next day, andthey were on a flight to Bangkok, withto Kuala Lumpur. And now they weremanding to meet with the CIA residentamazed by it all. But nagging at himthat Kuala Lumpur was even farther frSanh. Somehow, he was still moving inabsolute wrong direction.

The clerk returned to the receptiomechanically at Kendall.

"Mr. Wilson will see you now," heme."

"Let's go," Kendall told Poole.

Sure, thought Poole, why not? Wlose?

Her name was Ly Tran Chi, andwhat he was going to do with hercabin for over a day now, leavingdropped her baby over the side intchad happened during the night. Trthe day on deck, and when he .retisunset, Ly said quietly that it woultake the child outside. Truong weher way to the railing at the porbreath, looked up at the moon, th

"Help me," she said.

She leaned over the railingTruong. She watched him for a fant, then bent forward and kigo, and Ly Tran Chi's son fell in

ing passage on a rusting boat, but he could make no more sense of it than that.

Sometime before noon the engine stopped. The boat rocked back and forth in the hot sea as the waves slapped against the hull. Truong went to the bridge and asked Schmidt what was happening. Schmidt assured him that the problem was minor, repairs were being made, and they would be under way again very soon. Truong didn't believe him.

He scanned the horizon and spotted two small ships in the distance. He watched for a few minutes until he was certain they were approaching. Other people noticed them, and someone ran up to the bridge and asked if the ships were coming to tow them. Schmidt laughed.

Truong went back to the cabin. Ly woke as he entered. He took the pistol from his belt and handed it to her. She didn't want to take it, but he insisted.

"Use this if anyone but me tries to come in."

"But why?"

"Thai pirates," he said. "I think the captain was expecting them."

"Are you sure?" she asked. "Why would he expect them?"

"Because they will rob us and he will get a share. I have heard stories about this. They may even kill everyone on board. I don't know. But use that gun if you have to. Don't let anyone come in and don't let them take anything."

Truong kissed her, then went back to the bridge. The two ships, fishing boats by the look of them, were little more than a kilometer away now. Schmidt was watching their approach.

"Captain," said Truong, "I think the time has come for me to tell you about that deal."

"Now?" asked Schmidt. "Very busy now."

"Yes, now. In your cabin."

"Talk here." He nodded to the first mate, a slim, boyish-looking Filipino. "Use English. He don't understand."

"No," said Truong, "in your cabin. I have something to show you. Something that will interest you very much."

There was only one thing that would interest Schmidt very much. If Truong wanted to let him in on his big deal, now was obviously the time. Schmidt said a few words to the mate, then led Truong down the steps to his cabin belowdecks. He closed the door and grinned at Truong.

"Now," he said gleefully, "you tell me about this big deal, right?"

"Right," Truong agreed. He slammed his fist into Schmidt's ample gut. The captain doubled over and Truong brought his knee up, connecting with bone, snapping the head back. Schmidt toppled to the deck.

The gun cabinet was locked, and Truong didn't want to make a lot of noise, so he spent several minutes rifling the captain's desk and locker before he found the key. He took out the two AK-47's and three ammunition clips. He inserted one clip in a rifle and stuck the other two into his belt. As an afterthought, he removed the firing pin from the second rifle. Before going back on deck, he looked through a porthole at the approaching ships. They were only a hundred meters or so off the starboard bow. There seemed to be a lot of men on deck, but no one was fishing.

All five crewmen were on deck when Truong came up the companionway with the rifle. They seemed to know the routine. The people on the foredeck were excited but apprehensive, lining the railings and chattering in worried tones. The men on the fishing boats were smiling. For a moment Truong wondered if he could be mistaken. Then he saw the glint of a shiny rifle barrel and he knew that he was not.

Truong emerged from the shadows, slipped into the deckhouse, and grabbed the first mate from behind, holding his forearm tightly against the boy's throat.

"You speak English?" Truong demanded. "Viet?"

"English," the boy gasped.

"Good. When I say to, you tell those crewmen to put

their hands in the air and keep them there, or I'll kill them. Understand?"

The boy nodded. Truong let him go and stepped back out on deck. He leveled the rifle at the nearer of the two boats and fired a long burst. The noise, so familiar, was deafening for a moment. He saw the bullets chipping away wood just above the waterline of the fishing boat.

"Now!" he yelled to the mate. The boy shouted something in Tagalog, and the crewmen, clustered on the foredeck, hesitantly raised their arms. One of them was too slow, and Truong fired a quick burst over his head.

"Search them!" Truong called in Vietnamese. The refugees were no strangers to the procedures of warfare. Many hands grabbed at the crewmen. Confident that the crew would present no problems now, Truong turned his attention back to the two boats.

The first boat had sheared off, but the second was still coming on. It was too slow to make a successful attack on anything but a ship that was dead in the water, as this one was. At the bow of the fishing boat, two men were setting up a machine gun.

Truong took careful aim, timing the burst with the rising swell. The boat pitched upward, and Truong squeezed the trigger. He emptied the clip into the oncoming pirates. The two gunners fell forward, into the water, and were lost from sight. The other men on deck ran toward the stern.

Truong pulled out the empty clip and inserted a new one. His target was already turning away. He waited to see what they would do next, but they had already done everything they were going to. The Thai marauders were used to defenseless, sometimes cooperative prey. There would be other, easier days, and there was no profit to be made on this one. They ran.

A cheer went up from the foredeck. Truong stared at the people there and realized they were cheering for him. Embarrassed by this display, he awkwardly raised the barrel of the rifle in acknowledgment.

After instructing the first mate to stay where he was and

do nothing, Truong returned to the captain's cabin. Schmidt was still unconscious on the floor. Truong brought him to life with a sharp kick to the rib cage.

It took a few minutes for Schmidt to understand everything that had happened. He picked at the dried blood on his chin stubble while Truong explained what he wanted. Finally, Schmidt went to his desk and took out the appropriate map. He pointed to their location.

The closest destination that made any sense was Bidong Island, just off the Malaysian coast. Trengganu was closer, but too many questions would be asked there. At Bidong there was a swarming refugee camp, and Truong figured he could find safety in numbers. Alonzo would be waiting at Mersing, far down the coast, but a radio-message could establish the new rendezvous point.

Truong stabbed at Bidong Island with his index finger. "How long?" he demanded.

"Four hours, five, maybe six. After dark, maybe. But patrol boats there. Maybe they don't let us land."

"Then we'll beach the ship there if we have to. They can't stop that."

"Beach *Augustus*?" Schmidt was horror-stricken at the very idea.

"From now on," Truong told him firmly, "you do everything I say. Or I'll kill you."

"Goddamn bastard pirate! Goddamn mutineer!"

Truong calmly smacked Schmidt in the mouth with the barrel of the rifle.

"Everything I say," Truong repeated.

Schmidt rubbed his chin and nodded sullenly. "Everything you say."

Truong waited on deck until the engine was started again and the three nonessential crewmen were tied up. Then he handed the rifle to one of the refugees, a man who said with a mixture of pride and shame that he had once fought under General Giap. When he was sure the *Augustus* was on the correct course, he returned to his cabin.

"It's me," he said.

Ly flung the door open and wrapped her arms around him. "I was so worried!" she said.

"Everything will be fine now," he soothed.

"Yes, yes!" She stepped back and looked into his eyes, and Truong again felt the awkward sensation he'd had on deck when the people cheered him.

"But what will happen to us now?" Ly asked.

Truong took her back in his arms and held her tightly, but he didn't answer. He didn't know the answer.

Chapter Fifteen

The camp on Bidong Island was hauntingly familiar. It was as if some unimaginable force had scooped up part of old Saigon—the shops, the squalid back alleys, Tu Do Street whores, the black market, the nameless wartime ghettoes—and transplanted it all to this festering tropical island. More than forty thousand people were packed into a couple of square kilometers, clinging to the steep slope of a bulky, forbidding mountain on the edge of the sea. No one at all had lived here two years ago, and now the makeshift refugee camp had the air of permanence, as if it intended to become an impoverished scale model of Hong Kong or Singapore.

Truong felt as if he were in a waking dream, where places never seen are remembered from a past that never happened. He found himself looking for familiar landmarks, knowing full well that what he sought no longer existed and what he recognized was no more than an illusion. Yet it was all real, from the stink of human waste intermingling with incense and cooking fish, to the cardboard shanties and the ringing litany of the crippled beggars in the streets.

Only the Americans were missing.

Truong found everything he needed in a surprisingly short time—or, perhaps, not so surprising, since everything anyone needed was readily available here, for a price that few could pay. Truong could pay, and within two hours after the *Augustus* had moored at the end of the jetty, Truong and Ly were established in a four-meter-by-four-meter room on the first floor of an ungainly three-story shack that was constructed of rough-cut lumber, corrugated cardboard, and plastic sheeting. This was a prime location, not far from the water distribution point on the beach, and Truong paid the owner fifty dollars to rent it for a week. The landlord thought he had made a killing, because no one got out of Bidong in a week. Truong could have bought the entire building for five hundred.

The ship had come into Bidong at night, unchallenged by the Malaysian patrol boats. There were a few Malaysian soldiers on duty as police, but they were quickly and cheaply bought. Technically, the camp was run by the United Nations High Commissioner for Refugees, and the UN did manage to provide some minimal rations and medical facilities, but in fact the refugees ran the place themselves. Two committeemen who greeted the boat were told the story of the voyage of *Augustus*. It was a familiar tale to them, but Truong's successful seizure of the ship and battle with the pirates caused a minor sensation. Truong could not afford notoriety, so he paid off one of the committeemen and slipped ashore unnoticed.

Ly came with him. She carried part of his load of the heavy, deadly skeet without asking what they were, leaving Truong a free arm to carry one of the AK-47's in a bedroll. They settled into their room and made love on a hard bamboo mat. Afterward, Truong lay on his back and thought about the way his life had suddenly expanded, and about the things he must do to make a future for himself, and for Ly.

In the morning Truong gave Ly some money and sent her out to buy food and Western clothing for herself. When she returned, he left her with the rifle and went out to acquire the things he needed. A Chinese tailor took his measurements and promised that his three-piece suit would be ready that same afternoon. In the next hour he bought some toilet items, a pair of glasses, and a gold wedding band.

Truong was accumulating props. When he left Bidong, it would be in the guise of a prosperous, westernized diplomat, complete with papers, apparel, and a wife. Ly, he thought, was an ideal prop; even if people were looking for him, no one would be looking for a man and wife. It was a convenient reason for taking Ly along; he wasn't quite ready to admit to himself that there might be other reasons.

He returned to the shack and ate the meal Ly had cooked on the kerosene stove. Then they made love again, and by now it felt as if they had been together all their lives.

That afternoon he took a chance. They left their belongings unattended and went out together to sit for the photographer Truong had found that morning. When they returned home, they had everything they would need.

The next day was to be their last on Bidong Island. Alonzo was due to arrive at noon. There was a rude airfield hacked out of the jungle on a flat spot on the flank of the mountain, a kilometer inland from the edge of the camp. In a final exchange of messages from the *Augustus*, they had arranged to meet there. If all went well, they would soon be bound for Singapore.

When it was time for him to leave, Truong explained as much as he could to Ly. She was to guard their baggage and threaten to use the rifle if she had to. He didn't expect trouble, but if trouble came and threats would not avail, she should get out and leave their bags behind. He expected to be back in an hour, and then they would leave together.

Truong walked slowly through the muddy paths of the camp. He felt conspicuous in his new suit, even though he had left the vest and tie in his suitcase. They would be needed later, but for now all he needed was the jacket with its hidden inside pocket that the tailor had sewn according to his specifications. One of the skeet fit into it, and although the weight of it was annoying, it was impossible for anyone else to tell that it was there.

His pace became slower still. He should be in a hurry to get out of this dungheap, but some invisible force was tugging at him. If he wanted to, he realized, he could stay, he and Ly together, and make their lives here. Bidong was not going to disappear; it was becoming, almost in spite of itself, a living, growing nation. It was in some ways like the first colonies in the Americas, an implausible refugee community, a magnet for human flotsam, built out of nothing on the fringe of nothing. Bidong, somehow, would endure. These people—his people—would survive. Truong could stay and share their strange adventure. With the money he already had, and the money that Alonzo was bringing—or even without it—he could build something here. What, he didn't know, but the uncertainty was actually a part of the allure. In this new land the future remained to be written.

Truong came to a complete stop. Had he made a decision without realizing it? He looked at the people around him in the buzzing street and tried to imagine what it would truly be like to live here. Did any of them share this bizarre vision, or were they simply marking time and waiting for the day when they could leave? Did it even matter?

Then he saw something that made the whole question foolish, no more than an idle, naïve fantasy. Fifty meters away two Caucasians were walking toward him. There were other Caucasians in the camp, UN workers and doctors mainly, but these men were different. They walked slowly, plainly looking for something, or someone. Truong didn't recognize one of them, but the other, there was no mistaking. It was Joe Kendall.

Truong quickly ducked behind the corner of a cardboard shack and tried to think. The Bidong dream had been stupid from the beginning because he had allowed himself to forget the obvious. Kendall was bound to follow him, probably Poole too, and by now they could have alerted the UN authorities or the Malaysians or, most likely of all, the CIA. He was surprised that they found him so quickly, but now that they had, there must be no more surprises.

Truong ran down a parallel alley, toward the Americans. He found a hut which seemed substantial enough for his purposes and stepped into it. Inside, there were several small children and two women. He took a ten-dollar bill from his pocket and handed it to a wide-eyed eight-year-old boy. He assured the women that no harm would come to them, then told the boy what he wanted. The boy looked at his mother for a moment, then ran out into the street. Truong positioned himself next to the doorway and told the women to keep silent. He pulled the pistol from his pocket, raised it above his head, and waited.

The boy came running back in a minute later. Then the first American stepped into the dark room, and Truong brought the butt of the pistol down onto his skull. The man pitched forward; before he hit the ground, Truong was standing in the doorway, the pistol pointed at the head of Joe Kendall.

Very slowly, Truong stepped back into the hut and beckoned Kendall to follow. He did, looking more surprised than afraid. Keeping the gun on Kendall, Truong took another ten-dollar bill from his pocket and threw it toward the women. He told them to tie up the other man and gag him. After a few seconds' hesitation one of them grabbed the money and started to do as she had been instructed.

"Now," said Truong, "what shall I do with you, Mr. Kendall?"

"Do you really want an answer?" Kendall asked.

"No, I've already decided. I was just making conversation. You are a more resourceful man than I would have expected."

"So are you," said Kendall. "Nice threads, Truong."

Truong took a second to understand the American

idiom, and when he did, he smiled. "Traveling clothes, Mr. Kendall. There are some things I must ask you, but I have an appointment I don't want to miss. You will have to come with me. I have seen many American movies, so I know all the foolish, heroic things you are probably thinking about doing now, but please don't. You are not a man I would want to kill, but I will if I have to."

"I believe you."

"Good. Now we will go." Truong told the women to keep the man tied up and, preferably, unconscious. He would return soon and give them more money if they did as he told them. If they didn't, he would set fire to this shack.

Holding the pistol in his coat pocket, Truong walked along behind Kendall, directing his course with terse orders in whispered English. It wouldn't do to attract too much attention.

They soon came to a narrow mud road that had been cleared from the jungle. They were alone here, and Truong came up alongside Kendall so they could talk. He asked Kendall how he had found him.

"It wasn't really that difficult. Your friend Colonel Vinh traced you to the ship. Poole and I flew to Kuala Lumpur and learned that your ship landed at Bidong instead of Mersing. And here I am."

"And where is Poole?"

"Poole's sick. We left him in Kuala Lumpur. Hell, Truong, you saw him. The man was a wreck."

"What about the other man, the one who was with you? Who is he?"

"His name is Winslow."

"That doesn't tell me very much, Mr. Kendall. He is a CIA agent, isn't he? You couldn't have gotten to Bidong without help. He is CIA, isn't he?"

"No," said Kendall, "I wouldn't work with pigs like the CIA. Winslow's just some UN worker."

"You are lying," Truong responded, his tone sharp and threatening. "You may not like the CIA, Mr. Kendall, but you would go to them because you had to. How many others are there?"

"Just the two of us."

"Really? And how did you get here?"

"We flew in this morning."

"Which one of you is the pilot? In case you didn't notice, we are going to the airfield now, so you might as well tell me the truth."

"Okay, there's a pilot, too. He's with the plane, but he's just some Malaysian charter pilot. He doesn't know what's going on."

"But he is at the field. That is good to know. Now you're beginning to be helpful, Mr. Kendall."

They walked along without speaking for a few minutes. They listened, instead, to the wild noises of the jungle. After a time a new sound was added, the whine of an airplane coming in for a landing.

"Your appointment?" Kendall asked.

"Yes," said Truong.

"And you're going to sell the pucks. The Nightwind."

"I have no use for them myself. I will make a great deal of money. It is the great American way."

"Truong, listen to me. There are some things you need to know about what's inside those pucks. The stuff you sold four years ago killed a lot of people, but what you have now could be even more dangerous. Fantastically dangerous. It could kill everybody on this planet. I swear to you, that's no lie."

There was a hint of desperation in Kendall's voice. Kendall sounded sincere, but a desperate man would say anything and make up the wildest of stories.

"You make no sense," Truong replied. "Why would your government build a weapon that could kill every person on earth? It is insane."

"Of course it is. Just like the thousands of H-bombs we've got. Insane, but nevertheless, we have them."

"I still don't believe you. Why would they send such a potent weapon to Vietnam?"

"Because they screwed up," said Kendall. "You've worked with the American military, Truong. You know how incompetent they are. The stuff in those pucks is an accident. It's a virus or a bacteria of some kind, and in the time it sat in that bunker, the bugs mutated into something more dangerous than the original bug. They don't even know what the hell it is now, but they know it kills."

"And that was why they sent it to my country. To kill Vietnamese."

"Yes, but—"

"Enough!" Truong commanded. He pointed to the clearing ahead of them. "We are at the airfield. I apologize for what I am about to do, Mr. Kendall. In some strange way, I almost think of you as a friend. And because you are almost a friend, I am now going to hit you on the head hard enough to make you unconscious. If I don't do this, you will see the men I am meeting, and if you do see them, they would surely kill you. So if you should wake up, I strongly advise you to pretend that you are still asleep. And Mr. Kendall, I want you to know that I will look forward to reading this book of yours."

"Truong, you can't—"

Truong hit Kendall in the side of the head with the butt of the gun. Kendall managed one faltering step, then dropped into the mud of the road. Truong pulled him into the foliage.

He went to the edge of the airfield and waited to be seen. A few hundred meters away, two airplanes were parked. One of them was attended by a single man, as Kendall had said, and three men were standing under the wing of the other plane, a twin Otter. One of the three saw him, and they began walking toward him.

Truong looked back at Kendall, lying in the underbrush. Conceivably, he could hide Kendall completely before Alonzo got here. But that wouldn't do; he couldn't take the chance that Kendall might wake up before he and Ly could get away. He would have to let Alonzo and his men stand guard. He owed Kendall nothing, after all.

Alonzo was a man of about fifty, slim and sallow-faced, with shining black hair that was combed straight back over his sweating scalp. He looked vaguely Latin, but a man from Singapore might have literally any sort of racial background imaginable. The two men with him, though, were Chinese, large and heavy. One of them carried a black briefcase.

They stepped onto the road, and Alonzo immediately noticed Kendall. "Who is that?" he demanded.

"An American journalist," said Truong. "He is not a threat, so long as he remains unconscious. He saw nothing, and he knows very little."

One of the Chinese went over to check Kendall. After some rough prodding, he seemed satisfied.

"We will deal with him later," said Alonzo. "Did you bring the merchandise, Major Truong?"

Truong removed the puck from his inside pocket. Alonzo took it from him and examined it thoroughly. Finally, he nodded and handed it back.

"It is the same as the others. You have the rest?"

"In the camp."

"Then get them."

"First, the money. The last time, I never got my share."

"That was the fault of Le Kuan. I was not responsible. In a business like mine, one must be scrupulously honest because the people one deals with seldom are. I am sorry you were cheated before, but it was not my doing."

The Chinese with the briefcase opened it and held it up for Truong to see. Inside, there were neat stacks of hundred-dollar bills.

"You can count it later, in the plane," said Alonzo. "But I assure you that it is all there."

Truong nodded, and the Chinese closed the briefcase. "Now," said Truong, "the papers."

Alonzo removed two black folders from his pocket. "As requested," he said. "Two Malaysian diplomatic passports. I should charge you extra for the woman's, but since you suffered unfairly in our last transaction, I give it to you as a gift, with my compliments."

Truong took the passports and studied them. As far as he could tell, they seemed to be genuine, lacking only the photographs to make them complete. He put them into his pocket.

"Not yet," Alonzo said quickly. "When you return with the merchandise. If you keep the passports, I can't be sure that you will return." Alonzo held out his hand.

"No," said Truong. "You brought two strong men with you as insurance, Mr. Alonzo. I have no bodyguards, so I will keep the passports as my insurance." He stared grimly at Alonzo.

Alonzo returned the stare, but relented after a few seconds. "Very well," he said. "Now you go and get the merchandise and your woman. My man will go with you. Don't be long."

Truong turned and started back down the road. One of the big Chinese came with him. It was going well, he thought. They were going to make it.

Poole hated this. He felt as if he had landed on the surface of some hostile, alien planet. Dozens of slanted eyes followed his every movement, peering out of dark doorways, trailing along behind him. A zone of silence seemed to surround him; the humming, indistinct Oriental voices all stopped when he drew near and resumed when he had passed. Swarthy faces regarded him with suspicion, and even the naked children sitting in the filthy puddles stopped whatever they were doing and looked up at him with an awful, instinctive loathing.

He shouldn't be here at all. He should be in the first-class lounge of a 747, somewhere over the Pacific, sipping bourbon and trying to make a date with a stewardess. He should be home, in his own bed.

Somehow, he had let Kendall force him to come to this cesspool. Telling the CIA everything hadn't been enough for Kendall—he had to come and see for himself. Kendall argued that the two of them were the only ones who knew what Truong looked like, so they both had to come. Poole

233

didn't see why the hot shit CIA couldn't just whip up one of those composite sketches, like the police did when they were looking for some two-bit rapist. They didn't need him. He wasn't even sure he could identify Truong if he tripped over him. He might be able to deal with these slopes one or two at a time, but to pick out one from thousands was an impossible task.

Walking through these infested streets made Poole think of his trips into the Mexican barrios for old Breeze Woodward. The Mexes looked a lot alike, too, and their faces held the same suspicion and resentment he saw here. But the greasers, in the old days at least, were also afraid, and that made all the difference. Poole could walk tall among them, and the switchblades didn't frighten him because both he and the people who held them knew that the entire police force, and the Texas Rangers if need be, would like nothing better than an excuse to come in and stomp these chili beans. One riot, one Ranger, the saying went, and damned if it wasn't true.

But these awful gooks and chinks weren't afraid. Like big-city niggers, they'd lost the Fear. It was as if they'd seen absolutely everything a white man could do to them, and it no longer impressed them.

Briggs, the CIA agent, didn't seem to feel it. Maybe he'd been out here too long. He spoke fluent Vietnamese, and he walked around this place like John Wayne himself, as if he could still call in an air strike if anyone gave him shit. Briggs's display of balls didn't make Poole feel one bit safer; hairy-chested assholes like Briggs never got themselves hurt, just the people around them.

Poole waited outside the tumbledown shacks while Briggs went inside and looked for likely candidates. If he spotted one, Poole had to go inside too and try to make an identification. Standing alone on the street was bad for his nerves, but going into those shanties was indescribably worse. The stench enveloped him and made him want to puke, and his jitters got so bad that it was all he could do not to shit in his pants.

Briggs had been inside this latest hut for a long time now, and Poole could hear the incomprehensible interrogation. The people in the street were still staring at him, and if he forced himself to stare back, they didn't look away. Poole wished Kendall would show up. Maybe he could talk some sense into him now. Maybe he would realize by now that whatever the hell it was he wanted, he was not going to find it here.

The agent emerged from the shack and grinned at Poole. "Paydirt," he said. "Folks in there came in on the *Augustus*. They say there's a guy who could be Truong who lives in that building down there, the one with the blue plastic sheet on the side." Briggs pointed to the shack he meant.

Briggs started down the road, but Poole hooked his elbow. "Wait a minute," he protested. "Aren't you going to wait for Kendall and Winslow?"

"What for? We can handle this."

Briggs strode away, leaving Poole no choice but to follow. He was damned if he was going to stand here by himself.

By the time they reached the building where Truong was supposed to be, Poole could feel another attack coming on. His heart was thumping like an oil rig, and bright sparks danced around the edges of his field of vision. He could picture himself collapsing into the shit-covered street, lying helpless under the angry sun. Maybe it would be cooler inside. Maybe there would be a floor to fall on.

"You coming?" Briggs asked him.

Poole could only nod. Briggs pushed aside the burlap mat hanging in the doorway and went into the dark hovel. Poole followed.

It took a second for his eyes to adjust to the gloom. A woman was sitting on the floor, next to a flickering kerosene lamp. She looked up at them, and Poole could instantly see that this one did feel the Fear. This one had a reason to be afraid. This was the one, and it was going to happen right here. He knew it, and she knew it, too.

235

She darted toward the opposite corner of the tiny room, moving like a she-cat in the night, her claws bared. She had something in her hands now, a rifle, and as she straightened to fire, Briggs was reaching for his own gun. Poole stood paralyzed in the light of the doorway. The rifle flashed and Briggs fired and the noise was like a thunderclap on the west Texas prairie, and it went rumbling on and on as they fell, chain lightning on the dark summer horizon.

Poole felt a bee sting on his leg, and as he fell forward, he watched in astonishment as a big leather suitcase exploded a split second after Briggs's final shot hit it. The sound was like more thunder, far away, echoing from the next county on the soft evening breeze. He found himself lying facedown on the rough wooden slats of the floor, and sprawled next to him was Briggs. Half of his head was blown away, and his one blue eye stared silently at the woman who had killed him. Poole could see her, too, on her back, absolutely still, her outstretched arm resting on the overturned kerosene lamp. Flames were spilling out of it, licking across the floor and up the cardboard walls.

And it was snowing. White specks filled the air and drifted down to him, like the last lazy flakes of a blue norther sweeping in across the rolling plains. It was pleasant to watch, sparkling and dancing in the firelight.

The flames were getting close, and he was going to have to move, somehow. There was no pain, but the drifting snow flecks tickled his nose and made his eyes water, and his head felt like a big balloon, blowing up to a fantastic size, till it seemed it would float away on the high prairie winds, huge as the endless Texas sky.

As soon as he saw the smoke, Truong knew it was over, forever. From a hundred meters away he could see the flames, too, boiling up out of the rooftops. He had seen it so many times before, from the air, from the ground, sometimes even in his dreams, the smoke and the flame marking the end for someone in a nameless village or scorched rice paddy.

He ran toward it, Alonzo's big Chinese lumbering after him. He got close enough to see that at the center of the fire was his own flimsy shack, disappearing in the napalm-orange glow. He stopped, unable to move a step closer to the fire, the eternal, irresistible fire that had scoured his land and his people. It was the same fire, he recognized it instantly, and he knew that it could never be stopped until its work was completed once and forever.

The Chinese kept going. Maybe he thought there was something to salvage, but Truong knew better. Nothing was safe from this fire, and nothing survived it.

People were staggering back from the blaze, stumbling away to some imagined safety. Some of them had already fallen, and they lay in the mud, their limbs twitching. More of them fell as Truong watched, and he realized that Kendall had been telling the truth, after all. The Americans had improved on the fire; even this all-consuming fire wasn't enough to satisfy the Americans. They wouldn't have enough until everything that breathed lay cold as stone, never again to rise up and threaten their awful destiny.

The Chinese had turned around and was coming back to Truong. At first he ran, but his feet became tangled and he dropped to his knees, his hands clutching at his throat, a look of terrible surprise in his eyes. He collapsed into the mud, his limbs jerking wildly.

Truong ran. He felt not a particle of fear, because he knew it was already a thousand years too late for that. He ran because he knew what he had to do, what was necessary, and if he was to accomplish this mission he had to move quickly.

He pounded up the narrow road, feeling the spreading death at his heels. It had certainly touched him, and in the end it would catch him, but not before he did this one last thing for his people. For Ly. For his wife and for his son who had been consumed by the blaze before he had a chance to know it for what it was. But Truong knew. It was the breath of a dragon, and the dragon still lived.

At the top of the road Alonzo and the other Chinese

were waiting. Sprawled in the middle of the road was the Malaysian pilot of the second plane, a dark red splotch on the back of his white shirt. Truong slowed to a trot, then halted completely a few steps from Alonzo.

"What is happening?" Alonzo demanded. "Where is Ching? Where is the merchandise?"

Truong looked at him. The man wanted his merchandise, so he could spread it to the corners of the world.

"It is all gone," Truong panted. "Gone, like Ching and my people, gone, gone."

"What happened? We saw the smoke . . . so did this pilot. We would have killed him anyway, but . . . *Tell me*, damn you! What happened?"

Truong pulled the gun from his pocket and pointed it at Alonzo. The Chinese started to go for his own weapon, but stopped when he saw that it was too late.

"You are the worst of all of them," Truong said.

"What are you saying? Put that gun down!"

"A dragon can't help being a dragon. But you are just a dog, Alonzo. You do the dragon's work so you can grow fat on the flesh of the dead."

"You are babbling! Tell me what happened in the camp! Did it escape? Are you infected? Is that why you babble about dragons? Tell me!"

Truong tried to think of a way to explain it. But explanation would change nothing, and it was growing late. He had no time for dogs. He shot Alonzo and then he shot the Chinese. They fell into the road and lay next to the dead pilot.

Truong looked to the underbrush at the edge of the road. Kendall was still there, facedown.

"Kendall!" Truong shouted. "I know you are conscious! Look at me!"

A few seconds passed, and Kendall began to move. He rolled onto his right side and looked up at Truong. Bits of dirt clung to his face. His eyes were wide, but showed no sign of fear. He was simply waiting.

"It is the end," said Truong.

"What happened down there?"

238

"The breath of the dragon has killed my people," he said. "It goes on killing them like before."

"Nightwind?" Kendall's mouth sagged open. "Oh my God," he whispered.

"Not God," said Truong. "The dragon."

They looked at each other. Truong was breathing hard, the gun wavering in his hand.

"It got loose, didn't it? The Nightwind."

"Yes," said Truong, "it is loose. I brought it here, and now it is loose. What have I done, Kendall? What have *we* done?"

Kendall had no answer.

"I don't know if what you said is true, Kendall. I don't know if this thing will kill the world. But it has killed *my* world. And it will go on killing until I stop it."

Truong reached into the hidden pocket of his coat. He pulled out the puck and held it up for Kendall to see.

"I saved one," he said. "I saved one for the dragon."

"What dragon?"

"You should know, Kendall. You should know what you are."

"I don't understand."

"You will. Everyone will."

"Are you going to kill me?"

Truong hesitated. It still wasn't completely clear to him. The details remained to be decided.

"No," he said finally. "I thought I was going to, but it would be pointless. I can't kill every American I see. But I can kill the dragon."

"What dragon? Where?"

"In his lair," said Truong. "That is where I will kill it. I know you don't believe in dragons, do you, Kendall? But we Vietnamese do. We have seen them all our lives, and we have felt their breath."

"I still don't understand."

"But you will. When you do, maybe you will put it in your book, if anyone is left alive to read it. Say this, Kendall. Say that the war is not over yet. There is one more battle to be fought. In the dragon's den. Good-bye, Kendall. Don't go down there, or the dragon will kill you, too. It eats its young, you know."

Truong put the Nightwind back into his pocket. He paused for a second, then picked up the black briefcase. He ran toward the plane. He could fly an Otter, he thought. It would be good to fly again, one last time.

One last time for everything.

Chapter Sixteen

Manhattan appeared beyond the left wing tip. The glass castles of the Trade Center were ablaze in the sunset, and the dark stone monoliths of Wall Street looked like the sheer rock ledges of a mountain stronghold—like the lair of some ghastly mythical beast. A dragon, perhaps.

Kendall didn't know. It was all a guess now, hunches and hopes piled on top of intuition and fear. He was playing blindfolded chess, and all he knew for certain was that there was a black knight loose in his back row, and the final checkmate could come with a single deadly move.

Next to him, Ginsburg adjusted his seat belt. Ginsburg was a nervous flyer, and he had put away four martinis since leaving San Francisco. He acted like a man who was used to having the bottom drop out from under him, an event that could happen on the ground just as suddenly as it could in the air.

They hadn't talked much during the flight. Kendall had talked himself out in San Francisco and, before that, in Kuala Lumpur and on the overgrown jungle airstrip on Bidong Island, and it seemed that the more words he spoke, the less they meant.

The first words had been the important ones, shouted into the microphone of the airplane on the Bidong field. It took him ten precious minutes to figure out how to operate it correctly, and it was another half an hour before he got a static-ridden response in a language he could understand. He didn't know what to say, so he kept calling "Mayday!" over and over until something happened. He finally established contact with the radio operator of a supertanker somewhere in the South China Sea. More minutes passed before he could get a link to the American Embassy in Kuala Lumpur. He didn't know who else to call.

At the embassy Mr. Wilson, the CIA resident, was unavailable. Kendall tried to explain the situation to some nameless underling, but the man refused to understand what was happening. Kendall swore at him and demanded that he get Wilson, but the urgency never seemed to penetrate.

And as the minutes passed, Kendall watched the wind in the trees, wondering what would happen when it changed. Nightwind was loose, and down in the camp they might all be dead by now. His own turn could come at any moment. His head throbbed in pain from Truong's blow, and it hurt to think. He wanted to run, to plunge into the jungle and hide himself from the invisible killer that might be only seconds away from him.

But he stayed. Somewhere in the middle of it all, a calmness descended on him. He had been here before—not Vietnam, but Vietnam under another name. An island, not a hill, but the terrain was familiar. He kept his balance, he did what had to be done because that was all that could be done.

At last, he reached Wilson. He told him what had happened, as coolly as if he were phoning in a high school football score. Who, what, where, when—the why of it would have to wait for later editions. Wilson understood what it meant; help was on the way.

Help didn't arrive for hours. In the meantime, panicked refugees from a camp of refugees found their way to the airfield and clustered around Kendall, as if he could provide answers. From a woman who spoke a little English, he learned that there had been shooting and a fire, and people had suddenly begun to fall over and die. All was chaos down there, and anyone who ventured too close to the fire quickly became ill. What sort of fire was it, she wanted to know, that killed without burning?

As the sun went down, planes began landing at the airfield—UN teams, Malaysian army officers, and Wilson and his little crisis squad from the embassy. Kendall explained as much as he could to Wilson, then let the CIA carry the ball. He was just a journalist again. He even took some notes.

He spent the night trying to sleep under a wing of the airplane. If he slept at all, he had nightmares that were indistinguishable from reality. By dawn a decontamination team from the U.S. Seventh Fleet had arrived. The situation was officially under control. Kendall flew back to Kuala Lumpur with Wilson.

They debriefed him at the embassy. He had little to add to what he had already told them. Poole was dead. The two agents, Winslow and Briggs, were dead. Alonzo the death merchant was dead. Many people in the camp were dead or dying. And Truong was alive, on the loose with the last remaining container of Nightwind, in quest of dragons.

Kendall thought he knew where Truong was going. In his ravings about dragons Truong's mission had taken on overtones of legend and myth. Kendall knew nothing about Vietnamese mythology, but he remembered from an anthropology course that there was really only one basic myth, and it was shared by every culture in every time. From Aeneas to Ahab, to Dorothy and Frodo, the evil power had to be confronted and slain in its own lair. The passage into the underworld was inevitable. Truong was going to America.

Kendall followed him. When he landed in San Francisco, he was met by Arnold Ginsburg. The FBI agent alternately cursed him and thanked him. He had received a full report on the events of the last two weeks, and he didn't know exactly what to make of it all.

"If we didn't need you," he said angrily, "I'd throw you in jail right now."

"On what charge?"

"We'll think of one. But first, we have to find this Truong character. You're the only one who's seen him. We've got some photos of him from his cadet class, but they're a dozen years old. I don't think they'll be very much help. You're the only one who can make an eyeball ID, Kendall. We need you."

Kendall didn't feel like being needed, by the FBI or by anyone else. More than anything, he needed to get away, to sleep for a week and have a chance to figure out what had happened to him. He felt as if all his anchor chains had been cut, and his internal compass was spinning like a roulette wheel. He needed to call time out and get his bearings. But Ginsburg and Truong weren't going to give him the opportunity.

So now he was descending toward the runway at Kennedy airport, bound for a convocation of dragons. The world he knew had gone creaking ahead in his absence, and he read the newspapers with a Rip Van Winkle double sight, out of synch with the times but surprised that so little had changed. The hostages were still being held in Iran. The Red Sox were, indeed, out of the race, two weeks before Labor Day. Ronald Reagan was the new Republican nominee when he left, and no one seemed to have had any second thoughts about it in the meantime. John Anderson was still talking about making a quixotic third-party run. And this week the Democrats were meeting in New York to nominate Jimmy Carter for a second term.

It was Tuesday already (or again—time zones and the international date line had left him adrift). The newspapers were full of Monday night's rules fight on the convention floor, the outcome of which had assured Carter's victory in the balloting on Wednesday. And tonight, Ted Kennedy was going to mount the podium at Madison Square Garden and deliver a speech that everyone agreed would be the dramatic high-point of the convention.

On page 7 of the newspaper there was a small, three-paragraph story, datelined Kuala Lumpur. It told of a cholera epidemic in a refugee camp on Bidong Island. More than six hundred people had died, and there were two thousand more confirmed cases. United Nations and World Health Organization officials were on the scene, and it was stated that the epidemic had already run its course, that the worst was over. It was not front page news.

Ginsburg had told him what the newspapers didn't. As far as anyone could tell, they had been very lucky. The fire had apparently destroyed most of the Nightwind agent before it could escape. What did get loose was a short-lived variant of the old Nightwind B, together with small amounts of some new strains that seemed to be especially dangerous. Everyone who had been within fifty meters of the fire had died quickly, their central nervous systems overwhelmed by a massive dose of the deadly bug. Those within a radius of two hundred meters of the fire had fallen ill with symptoms that were very similar to those of Legionnaire's disease. Outside of that zone there were only a few scattered cases, and most of those seemed to be mild.

"The problem," Ginsburg had said, "is that none of this really tells us anything about the bug that's in the puck Truong has. We know that there was mutation in the second canister, but we can't predict what happened in any single puck. What he has might be completely harmless. Or it might be one of the new strains seen at the camp. Or it could be something utterly different. Truong could have the doomsday bug. We just don't know."

If there was one ray of hope, it was that Truong himself might be sick. They didn't know how close he had been to the fire, but there was at least a chance that he was infected. Without treatment he might be dead in a few days.

Kendall doubted it. Truong was not going to be stopped before he had a chance to slay the dragon. Myths didn't work that way. Lying in the mud while Truong pointed a gun at him and decided whether he was to live or die, Kendall had somehow known that this wasn't the end. Truong must have known it, too. They were going to meet again. Kendall knew it as surely as he knew anything.

* * *

Arnold Ginsburg was thinking about retirement. He'd have his twenty years in soon, and with his government pension and maybe a part-time job, he ought to be able to manage. He'd get his son through college, one way or another. And maybe he could make some money from his science fiction novel. If he were able to write full-time, he might be able to complete it and sell it. Lately, the novel had been occupying his thoughts more and more. He was in control in that make-believe world, and he could make Ace King do whatever he wanted him to. He didn't have to contend with rebellious mavericks like Joe Kendall or scheming, contemptuous co-workers like Vance Hodges. And nothing of any importance depended on how well he did his job. That was the main attraction. The responsibility for crazed, runaway Vietnamese killers would no longer be his.

He found that he couldn't even handle Kendall any longer. On landing at Kennedy they were met by Vance Hodges, who traded sneers with Kendall. They were supposed to go to the FBI suite at the Waldorf, but Kendall refused to cooperate. He had made other arrangements, he said. His girl friend had a brother who was a graduate student at Columbia and had an apartment on the Upper West Side. Kendall was going to stay there, and no amount of arm twisting and naked threats could make him change his mind. Ginsburg finally caved in, moved as much by Hodges's growing belligerence as by Kendall's obstinacy. If he let the impasse continue, somebody was probably going to get hit, and Ginsburg would be left to pick up the pieces. So he let Kendall go, after getting him to promise that he would meet them at the Garden at nine.

Hodges drove him into town. Hodges was pissed off and he didn't care if Ginsburg knew it.

"You're really losing it, Arn," he said. "How the hell can you let Kendall go off on his own like that? The last time we did that, look what happened."

"What happened," Ginsburg said wearily, "is that we

246

got a line on Nightwind. If Kendall hadn't gone to Vietnam, Poole or Truong would have gotten the stuff and we'd have twenty-four pucks to worry about instead of one."

"And those people in the camp would still be alive."

"That wasn't Kendall's fault. You can lay that one at the feet of our friends in the Company."

Hodges changed lanes suddenly, leaning on the horn as he did so. "I'm really getting tired of the way you stick up for that bastard," Hodges growled.

"And I'm getting tired of your goddamned second-guessing. Put a lid on it, Vance. Just keep your personal feelings out of it and give me a report on where we stand. Do we have anything new on Truong?"

"He's here," said Hodges.

"What? Is that confirmed?"

Hodges nodded. "Yessir," he said formally. "Monday morning on a Tokyo flight. He's traveling with a Malaysian diplomatic passport. Breezed right through customs."

"Are they sure it was Truong?"

"Positive. Tracked him from both ends. He flew from Kuala Lumpur to Tokyo, no doubt about that. The plane he swiped was found at the airport there. The bastard moved too fast. He'd landed and gotten aboard the plane to Tokyo before the Malaysians even started looking for him. From Tokyo he got a Pan Am flight to New York. The plane refueled in Anchorage, but no one got off. So he's here."

Kendall had been right. Ginsburg wasn't sure he believed all that nonsense about dragons Kendall had fed him, but apparently Truong did believe it, and that was all that mattered now. In a way, it was a relief to know he was here.

"How about the Garden tonight? Have they distributed the pictures?"

"For all the good it will do. The convention is the worst goddamn mob scene I've ever seen. Eight thousand press passes, delegates, VIPs, visitors, plus all the usual crazies. The Secret Service is running scared. They don't want

Kennedy to speak tonight, and they want Carter to stay the hell out of town. Naturally, nobody's paying any attention. Business as usual."

"Naturally." Ginsburg had seen enough of politicians to know that the Secret Service and the FBI together couldn't even protect them from themselves, let alone the random Oswald or Bremer. If the politicos insisted on going out and shaking hands and making speeches, as if it were still the nineteenth century and radio and television hadn't been invented, then every now and then some of them were going to get shot.

But this was frighteningly different. However much damage a lone gunman—or a covey of sharpshooting conspirators—might do, it would be nothing compared with what Truong might unleash. An assassin could do his worst and kill a President, but the nation would survive. But Truong could conceivably kill the entire leadership of the Democratic party, and Ginsburg wasn't sure the nation would get over that without convulsions that would shake the Constitution itself. He could even kill an entire city—and what would the United States be like without New York?

He could do worse than that. He could kill the whole country. He could kill the whole world.

Hodges leaned on the horn again. "Goddamn New York drivers," he mumbled.

For what seemed like the hundredth time that day, Truong noticed someone wearing one of the curious T-shirts with the printing, I (followed by a heart-shaped emblem) New York. What were they trying to say, he wondered. I bleed for New York? Maybe they were trying to say that they loved New York, but how could anyone love such a place? Certainly, no one he saw on the crowded streets looked as if they were in love with the city or with anything else.

He knew that even other Americans regarded New Yorkers as a crazed and dangerous breed. Truong had seen Saigon at the height of the war, when it was overflowing with soldiers, refugees, whores, beggars, and American businessmen, but in less than two days in New York he had seen things that made Saigon look safe and placid. Sick, dying old men in overcoats slept on the sidewalk in front of gleaming, opulent skyscrapers. He had seen whores earning their money in parked cars on busy streets and haunted young men masturbating in the shadows of subway platforms. And the blacks, who had seemed so alien in Saigon, did the most bizarre things here without attracting the least attention. He saw one young black, wearing nothing but iridescent purple shorts and roller skates, gliding along a congested sidewalk while carrying a huge stereo cabinet on his shoulder. He sang along with the blaring music and weaved through the crowds without ever missing a beat or colliding with anyone or anything. It was nothing less than a circus performance, and no one noticed.

That was probably just as well. In the midst of all this no one was going to pay any attention to one quiet, unobtrusive Vietnamese in a business suit.

Truong stood on the corner of Forty-second Street and Broadway, the place known as Times Square. It was a loud, bright, confusing place, and Truong was grateful that he had been to America once before. If he had had no idea what to expect here, he would easily have been overwhelmed by it all. This was nothing like San Antonio, of course, but at least he had some idea of how Americans did things in their homeland.

Across the street, there was an enormous can of deodorant mounted atop a building; every few seconds the can sent a spray of steam gushing into the air. Was this display designed to sell deodorant, he wondered, or was it simply some manifestation of the Americans' need to make public the most intimate functions of their bodies? Other intimate functions were certainly on display all around him, from the lascivious movie posters to the immodest dresses of the whores. Everything was for sale here.

He could put an end to it. He tried to imagine what it

would look like when the moment came. The whores, the policemen, the rowdy blacks, all of them, would put their hands to their throats and look at each other in surprise, as the people in the camp had done in their final moment. Then they would stagger and fall and lie on the sidewalks twitching horribly; if there were survivors, would they even notice? Or would they step or skate carefully around the bodies and go on with their incomprehensible business? And if there were no survivors, would the giant can of deodorant continue spraying its ridiculous steam into the poisoned air?

It would be something to see. But Truong knew he wasn't going to see it, because there was no way the act could be accomplished without killing himself first. It didn't matter, though, because he knew he was already dying.

He first noticed it in Tokyo while waiting to board the New York flight. It felt like a tickle in the back of his throat; it made him want to cough, but coughing didn't make it go away. He decided it was simply the infamous Tokyo air pollution, which was even worse than New York's. The sensation returned somewhere over Canada, and then he ascribed it to the effects of breathing pressurized air for the better part of two days.

By the time he reached New York, he could no longer deny that something was happening to his body. He had a fever, alternating with strange, sudden chills, and sometimes his sense of hearing faded in and out. When he ate, the food felt heavy and rocklike in his stomach. He found a Vietnamese restaurant in Manhattan—there were many of them, he discovered—but the familiar fare rested no easier than the steak and potatoes the airline had served.

When he reached Manhattan, he quickly learned that there were no hotel rooms available in the entire city. With the convention in town, the nearest empty room was probably over in Jersey. After all he had gone through to get to Manhattan, he didn't want to take a chance on going to someplace as confusing as New Jersey. He might not be able to get back.

Inspiration struck him. He was traveling as a Malaysian diplomat, so why not play the role to its logical conclusion? He went to the United Nations building, found that it was quite easy to get in, and began searching for a comfortable place to pass the night. He found it in a pleasing nondenominational chapel for the delegates. He took a seat in the corner and soon fell asleep. No one disturbed him.

He knew he couldn't risk trying the same ploy tonight, if it came to that, but there were all-night theaters where he could sleep and bus station rest rooms where he could wash and shave. But if all went well tonight, there would be no need for any of it. He and everyone else in New York would be dead by midnight.

His original plan had been to go to Washington, to the very heart of the dragon. He would pose as a tourist and get into the White House or the Capitol and explode the puck there. Or perhaps, the Pentagon. If the germs were as deadly as those that had been released on Bidong, it might not matter where he chose to detonate the device.

On the plane to New York, however, he learned of the Democratic convention. He remembered the 1968 Democratic convention, which he had watched on television in the barracks in Texas. There had been violent riots in the streets, with dense clouds of tear gas wafting over the people in Chicago. If the present convention was anything like that one had been, his task could not be easier.

They would all be in one place. The President, the senators and congressmen, the rich bankers, and the local party cadres. It was an opportunity too good to miss.

He would like to have got the President, even though this Jimmy Carter had nothing to do with the war or Nightwind. The names and faces changed, but the dragon was always the same, always hungry, ever ready to feast on the burned flesh of a billion nameless victims. The dragon, it seemed to Truong, cared little whether the President's name was Johnson or Nixon or Carter. The dragon endured, the dragon was in control.

But Carter, he learned, would not be in New York until

Thursday night. Truong wasn't sure he would still be alive by Thursday. He was getting weaker with each hour, and it would be foolish to wait.

Tonight, he could get Senator Kennedy, brother of the man who had sent the first troops to Vietnam. There would be justice in this, although he knew that if he simply waited, sooner or later this Kennedy would undoubtedly be killed by one of his own people. The dragon was immense and powerful, but sometimes it drove its own children to acts of madness. Given enough time, it might someday destroy itself. But how many others would die before that day came?

Truong had seen enough of Times Square. It was getting late and he knew that Kennedy would be speaking soon. He wanted to be there in time, but he didn't want to have to wait. He walked down Broadway, knowing the course to his destination from the maps he had seen in the subway. Broadway and Thirty-first, eleven blocks.

There were many people on the sidewalk. Some of them seemed to have something to do with the convention, judging from the name tags and badges they wore. Truong knew he was going to need identification to get into the convention, but he had a plan to deal with that. The Nightwind puck in his inside right pocket was balanced by the weight of the pistol in his left pocket.

As he walked, he asked himself if perhaps he had carried this business of the dragon too far. He was not, after all, some superstitious peasant; he was a modern, educated man, a pilot, and an administrator. Dragons were for people who thought the earth was flat. He was not here to slay a dragon. He was here to commit an act of terrorism, to assassinate the leaders of the most powerful nation in the world.

Yet to view it all in terms of politics was somehow misleading. It denied the reality of what had happened to his people. The truth could not be reduced to tons of bombs and body counts and the number of orphans and missing limbs. More was involved than mere statistics and machinery. The war itself was a living entity, and it went on killing his people long after the statisticians stopped counting. There were no numbers that could calculate the misery of the people aboard the *Augustus* or the unending agony of life in the squalor of Bidong. The computers in the Pentagon and the politicians in the White House had never planned for murdering Thai pirates and sun-killed babies, yet these were as real as the B-52's and the defoliants. There was something more here, something organic, evil, and elemental.

It existed, and it required a name. Dragon would serve as well as any other. He could not set out to destroy an attitude or slay this nameless, cancerous thing in the American soul that compelled them to rise up and lay waste to distant strangers who could do them no harm. But if he thought of it as a dragon, then it became possible to kill it.

So, a dragon, then. Ly would have understood. The people on the boat and the workers in the NEZ would have understood. His wife would have understood. His son would have understood. And perhaps, when the act was accomplished, perhaps then, at last, the Americans would understand.

Broadway was too crowded. Crime happened all the time in the streets of America, but this particular crime would require shadows and darkness. Truong turned to the right and made his way along a side street. He would come to the convention along a less conspicuous path, and hope that he would find someone else who had the same thought. If he couldn't find what he needed in the street, then he would have to go into the building itself.

He was looking for an Oriental photographer. There were many of them here, he knew, mostly Japanese. But Americans who couldn't tell a Vietnamese from a Malaysian probably couldn't make the distinction between a Japanese and a Vietnamese. We all look alike, he thought. Once he had chosen his victim, it would simply be a matter of separating him from the pack and, in some dark place, taking his cameras and his credentials.

He could see Madison Square Garden in the distance, now, several blocks ahead of him. Somewhere to his left, he heard the sounds of a demonstration—chanting, shouting, angry voices on bullhorns. Perhaps it would be like Chicago, after all.

Truong found his spot. He stepped into the dark alcove of a building and checked his line of sight. In one direction he could see all the way to the Garden; in the other, up to Broadway. If he concentrated, he would be able to see his Oriental photographer. Then he would have to run to get ahead of him and cut him off. The running might be a problem. It was hard to catch his breath now, as if his lungs were unable to accept the oxygen he needed.

Suddenly, a sharp metal point pressed against his throat. Two men had appeared from nowhere, out of the shadows and the night. They were black, and Truong could barely see their faces. All that was distinct was the glittering knife blade.

"Okay, chink," said the man with the knife. "Gimme yo' wallet!"

Truong hesitated, and the man pressed the blade into his flesh until it seemed that it would take no more than the additional weight of the wind to make it slice through his skin and into the veins of his throat. He would be dead before he could get his hand on the gun in his pocket.

The second man grabbed the hand of the knife wielder and pulled it away. "Hey, wait a minute!" he said. "This ain't no chink! It's a fuckin' gook, man!"

It made no difference to the first man. "Who the fuck cares?" he asked. "Get his bread."

"Shit!" said the second man. He grinned at Truong. "You from Nam, man? You ever been in Ben Tre? Nha Trang?"

"No," Truong whispered. "I lived in Khe Sanh."

"Fuckin' marine country. You VC, man? You don't talk like no VC. Betcha was ARVN, right?"

"Yes," said Truong.

"What is this shit?" the other man demanded. "Get his fuckin' bread and let's get the fuck outta here."

"Hey, this here's a fuckin' *veteran*, man. Gotta have some *respect* for us Vietnam vets. Ain't that right, gook?"

"The *bread!*"

"Sorry 'bout this." The man reached into Truong's jacket and pulled out the leather wallet. "Don't like to hassle no Vietnam vets, even if they're fuckin' gooks. But you know how it is, man. *Shee-it!*" He looked into the wallet and saw Truong's money. "Un-fucking-believable, man! Dude must have five thousand bucks in here! Lookit this!"

The man with the knife turned to stare at the sheaf of bills. The knife wavered a few inches from Truong's throat.

It was a move they had taught him in San Antonio. Truong's left hand flashed out and closed around the wrist of the man with the knife. Truong twisted quickly to the left, then brought his right elbow up into the face of the startled black man. The impact jarred them both, but Truong was ready for it. In an instant the knife changed hands. A moment later it was hilt deep in the gut of the mugger.

The second man dropped the money and stepped back, watching wide-eyed as his partner slowly crumpled to the sidewalk. Truong wrenched the knife free, feeling the give of the soft tissues as the blade sliced through them. He held the dripping blade toward the second man, the Vietnam vet.

Their eyes locked. Truong's searched for an opening, while the black man's eyes seemed to be looking for an explanation. This was his turf, his own deadly jungle where he owned the night the way Charlie owned it in Nam . . . yet here was this fucking *gook* . . .

He backed up a step and started to turn, to run, but he hesitated and looked back at Truong one last time, still not convinced that any of this could really be happening. Truong slashed at him, the knife raking across the man's rib cage. He reversed the arc, brought the knife back to the man, point first, and drove it in just below the breastbone.

Truong released the knife and watched the vet stagger back, hands clutched around the protruding hilt. He tripped as he stepped over the curb and wound up on his back in the gutter, where hundred-dollar bills were still fluttering listlessly. Truong watched the man begin to die. Until this moment it had all happened very quickly, but the dying would take time.

Truong knew he couldn't wait for it. The man would have to do it alone.

He ran. The clop of his shoes on the pavement sounded like machine guns echoing in the concrete canyons. There were lights up ahead, Broadway lights, and Truong ran toward them. People were there, too, more Americans, more killers, more targets. It was a free-fire zone now.

Truong came to a halt a few yards from a crowded street corner. The heavy Nightwind puck bounced off his hipbone as it swung with his jacket. Truong grasped at it and started to remove it from the hidden pocket. It had to be now. He felt weak and nauseous and he knew that the dying had begun for him, too. He might never make it to the Garden, to the dragon's nest. But they were all the same, the people here on the street were caught in the free-fire zone the same as their leaders, and they were all going to die. Now or later, it no longer mattered to Truong. They killed from bombers, they killed with missiles, with longrifles and sixguns, with liquid fire, with invisible poison. They killed on battlefields, they killed in hospitals, they killed on streetcorners. They killed Indians and buffalo, they killed krauts and nips and dinks and slopes and gooks, they killed everything they ever touched. They deserved what was about to happen to them, they all did.

Someone bumped into him from behind, and he almost dropped the Nightwind. Truong tried to recover his balance and ended up leaning unsteadily against a building.

"I'm sorry!" exclaimed a young woman. She was blond and tiny, no larger than Ly had been. She was with a young man. Both of them wore blue jeans and T-shirts. Truong tried to focus on them.

"Are you okay?" asked the woman. She looked honestly concerned.

Truong nodded, but the woman actually came closer and put her hand lightly on his shoulder. "Are you sure?" she asked. "I'm really sorry. I wasn't watching where I was going. Did I hurt you? You look . . ."

"I am fine," Truong said quickly. "It is just that . . ."

"I'm going to find a cop," said the young man. "Maybe you need an ambulance or something. Stay with him, honey."

"I didn't think we hit that hard," said the girl. "Did I hurt you? You look awful! I'm sorry, but—"

"Leave me alone," Truong whispered. He lurched away from her, found his balance, and walked quickly into the flowing crowd. He could hear the woman protesting behind him until her voice was lost in the roaring traffic.

He was moving up Broadway, he realized, away from the Garden. It didn't matter. It was already too late, the night had got away from him. The young woman had ruined it more completely than the two dead muggers. The stupid girl didn't seem to realize she was standing in a free-fire zone. She was as stupid as his wife had been.

Thursday, then, when the President was in town. He could wait, he could stay alive if he had to. He had more money waiting for him in the locker at Grand Central Station. There were theaters to sleep in, restaurants where he could eat. After all he had come through, he could find a way to survive for two more days. Even in New York.

Chapter Seventeen

Kendall checked to make sure he had all his passes—his press pass, his police pass, his FBI pass, his floor pass. Walter Cronkite himself didn't have such a collection. Security at the Garden was incredibly tight, and without the proper bits of laminated plastic not even Miss Lillian could get onto the convention floor.

Ben, Sara's brother, looked at Kendall's credentials. "Man," he said, "you must have some connections. A friend of mine in the journalism school couldn't even get a one-day press pass."

Kendall didn't comment. Ben had been asking entirely too many questions, and Kendall hadn't answered any of them. He hadn't been a particularly gracious guest.

Sara already knew better than to ask too many questions. She had come down from Boston on Wednesday, bringing him some fresh clothing. Ben surrendered his bedroom to them and slept on the couch, but Kendall had hardly been in the apartment. He was at the Garden all night Tuesday, and staggered back to Ben's place around noon on Wednesday for a three-hour nap that was interrupted by Sara's arrival. Wednesday night was the same, and now, late Thursday afternoon, Kendall was operating on less than ten hours sleep in the last four days. Ben offered him some speed, but he declined. He was already strung out from coffee and adrenaline, and Dexedrine would probably make him jump right out of his skin.

Standing in front of the bathroom mirror this afternoon, shaving, he wondered if some part of himself had already gone over the wall for good. He wasn't sure he recognized the person he saw reflected; the image bore no obvious relationship to Joseph Kendall, assistant professor of journalism. But he had seen this haggard character before, and he remembered where. It was at the Da Nang press center, after a four-day trip to Hue, just before the fever hit him. Hue following Tet was a Hieronymus Bosch hallucination, a junkyard of human spare parts and exploded lives, a place where to see anything at all was to see far too much. He had been there again, searching for Truong, and now he was still searching for Truong and still in Hue, still on Hill 651. He was spread too thin, too much of him was holding down too many untenable positions, and his bones were beginning to show through.

His glimpse of yin and yang, that karmic tour of the inside of the icebox—close the door, and the light stays on!—didn't mean much in the stone realities of New York. If the inner Kendall was finally in tune with the universal vibes, the gristle-and-bone Kendall was picking up nothing but static and garbled transmissions from traffic helicopters. Truong was walking around New York with a chunk of doom in his pocket, and some maverick fragment of Kendall was with him. He had seen too much again, and staring into the gun barrel on Bidong, with death on a rampage all around him, he had heard a few notes of the mad song that was playing inside Truong's brain. He felt the rhythm of it, and one toe, at least, was tapping along with it. He understood Truong.

But understanding wasn't the end of it. There was logic and unity and harmony wrapped up in this awful music, and it was seductive beyond reason. Truong was dancing to the beat, and Kendall felt it in his bones. It was the dragon's song, nothing less.

When he found Truong, would he stop him—or would he surrender to the music of the dragon, and help him?

Just to think such a thought, to admit the possibility that Truong was right, made Kendall want to throw up. He had spent too much time out on the edge, like the death-loving lurps in Nam. Sooner or later, he would have to come back or—rock 'n' roll heaven, here—kick out the jams and go all the way over.

And tonight was the night.

"Are you all right, Joe?"

He looked up from the stack of passes and saw Sara standing next to him. She looked better than his best memories of her, soft and blond and smooth, like a painting hanging on the wall of one of the classiest museums. Perfect and distant.

"Yeah," he said, "I'm fine."

"You look awful."

"I love you too, kid."

She gave him a peculiar look, as if he had suddenly begun speaking in Swahili or Navajo.

"Sara?" he asked. "Do you want to get married tomorrow?"

She blinked twice, her mouth ajar. Then she laughed. "Why not tonight?"

"No," he said, "tomorrow."

The laughter faded. "Why tomorrow?"

"Because tomorrow, I'll be ready. What about it? Do you want to get married tomorrow?"

She started to ask if he was serious, but stopped short. His face had already answered that question.

"Okay," she said after a moment. "We'll get married tomorrow."

They stared at each other. Kendall wondered if he was coming back from the edge, or pulling Sara out there to join him.

"Don't I get a kiss or something?"

He kissed her and held her so close that neither one of them could breathe. Somewhere in the background, brother Ben cleared his throat and mumbled that he just remembered that he had to go pick up his laundry. The door clicked shut behind him.

Sara pulled back from him a little and touched noses. "Ben must think we're crazy," she said. "Are we?"

"I guess we'll find out tomorrow." Kendall released his grip on her. "I've got to go."

"Joe? Can you tell me what's going on?"

"Tomorrow," he said.

"Why can't you tell me now?"

"Because it isn't finished yet."

"And it's going to be finished tonight?"

"One way or another." He kissed her again, and then was out the door before she could ask any more questions. He wasn't sure, but he thought he felt better than he had in years.

Ginsburg dabbed at his nose with a tattered scrap of tissue. The room that had been commandeered for Nightwind security was tiny, some sort of equipment locker where they stored the extra basketballs when the Knicks weren't playing, and too many people were in it smoking cigarettes. The standard security apparatus had a big room with dozens of telephones, but Nightwind was a late addition to the team and had no great status. Few people had so much as an inkling of what was happening, and Ginsburg and his men were looked at with suspicion by the rest of the FBI and Secret Service personnel. They all had the old photo of Truong and instructions about what to do if they found him, but there were too many other things to worry about. The Communist Workers Party was out in the street demonstrating noisily right now, and if they weren't exactly Abbie Hoffman and the Yippies, they were still a powerful distraction. And inside on the floor they were busy renominating Mondale and waving to the TV cameras, waiting for the President to arrive and make his acceptance speech.

Ginsburg had scarcely been out of this makeshift office for three days. A television set with the sound turned down was his only visual link with the rest of the world. His telephones, meanwhile, were ringing constantly, bringing reports from various checkpoints where nobody really

261

had anything to report. There were also some walkie-talkies that kept picking up network floor reporters chatting with their producers and New York cops shooting the breeze. There weren't enough frequencies to go around, and everything was spilling over into a jumbled electronic stew.

There was still nothing definite on Truong. They knew he had spent Monday night at the UN, but his trail disappeared after that. Ginsburg had a private fear about what had happened, and it was too awful to talk about yet. If Truong had been infected, he might be dead by now. He pictured him lying cold in some back alley, amid the trash cans, his body being picked over by faceless scavengers. They might find the puck and take it, thinking it was some sort of goddamn Frisbee. Ginsburg saw them in his mind's eye, brainless teen-age thugs flipping the puck back and forth, setting it spinning. And sooner or later, the spinning would trip the centrifugal switch, and the puck would explode . . . and New York would begin to die.

On the possibility that Truong had collapsed, Ginsburg had ordered a check of all the hospitals in Manhattan. He had received sketchy reports of virtually every male Oriental admitted in the last forty-eight hours, but none of them seemed to fit. There were heart attacks and traffic accidents and muggings, but nothing that vaguely resembled the symptoms of Nightwind. The only report that was even mildly interesting was of an Oriental who had been found unconscious in an alley without a trace of identification on him. But a follow-up revealed that while the man remained unidentified, he was suffering from a fractured skull, and was Japanese, to boot.

On top of everything else, his chair was about as comfortable as a concrete block. And the card table he used for a desk was wobbly. He blamed the Democrats, of whom he was heartily sick. Maybe if Reagan won, the Bureau's budget would be increased enough to allow them to get some decent portable office equipment.

Vance Hodges returned from a check of the outposts. Ginsburg tried to keep Hodges out of the office as much as possible, and Hodges was happy to comply. After a couple of months of close contact he was near the breaking point with Hodges. Something was going to have to give, and Ginsburg knew that in the end, it would probably be him. Hodges was just too good at Bureau politics, and Ginsburg, the paper clip counter, wasn't likely to prevail. He wasn't even sure that he wanted to.

"Anything from the hospitals?" Hodges asked.

"Nothing. The unidentified guy turned out to be a Japanese mugging victim."

"Remember Pearl Harbor."

"What the hell is that supposed to mean?" Ginsburg snapped.

"Nothing," said Hodges. "Don't get so uptight, Arn. Have some coffee."

"I've *had* some coffee. Right up to my eyeballs. What have you got from the checkpoints?"

"More nothing. Christ, Arn, if I had something, don't you think I'd have told you?"

"I wonder." Ginsburg instantly regretted saying it, but he couldn't call it back. Hodges, whatever his faults, was a pro. He wouldn't let personal antagonisms interfere with the job. Hodges looked at him with disgust, then walked away to another corner of the room and lighted a cigarette.

A few minutes later Kendall came in. The agent at the door knew him by now, but still made him show his pass. The resentment against Kendall was universal, possibly Hodges's doing, but more likely the natural result of the agents' suspicion of the press in general, and particularly of this oddball journalist with the spooky, otherworldly look in his eyes. Ginsburg knew what Kendall had been through in Asia, but he, too, found that look unnerving. He had seen it before, in a collection of *Life* World War II photographs. It was the classic thousand-yard stare.

"How are you doing?" Ginsburg asked him.

Kendall didn't answer. He went to the coffee urn and filled a paper cup. He took a sip, then collapsed onto an empty chair next to the card table.

"This isn't going to work," he said.

"Why not?"

"It just isn't. It's wrong, somehow. It feels—I don't know—off key, I guess. I could stand out there at the door all night and I wouldn't see him."

"How do you know that?"

"It's just a feeling. Anyway, I feel like a jerk standing there. I keep seeing people I know and they keep asking me who I'm working for."

Worried, Ginsburg quickly asked, "What do you tell them?"

"I tell them I'm free-lancing. But that doesn't explain why I'm standing by the door instead of out on the convention floor interviewing people. Journalists don't usually cover a big story by doing imitations of cigar store Indians."

"Nevertheless, Joe, we need you there. You're the only one who can make a positive ID, and that's the place where Truong is the most likely to show up. Stay with it another hour, Joe. At least until we get Carter and Kennedy in and out in one piece."

"Yeah, yeah." Kendall's head rocked forward. He was on the brink of total exhaustion, and Ginsburg just hoped that he could hold out a little longer.

Hodges came over. "Well, Jimmy Olson, catching forty winks, are you?"

"Leave him alone," Ginsburg told him.

"He should be at the door."

"He will be. He needs a break."

"And meanwhile Truong could be walking right in."

"He's not," said Kendall.

"Really? You know something you're not telling us?"

Kendall slowly raised his eyes and gave Hodges a devastating stare, launched from some hardened silo of his soul. Even Hodges felt its radiation. He stepped back. Kendall got to his feet and walked from the room.

Hodges looked at Ginsburg and grinned nervously. "That guy," he said, "is getting spookier by the minute. I told you in the beginning, he's a flake."

"Lay off of him," said Ginsburg. "We need him."

"Sure, sure. Can't say anything bad about another member of the great fraternity of writers, eh, Arn?"

"And lay off of me too, damn it!" Ginsburg exploded. "I am sick to death of this crap about writers!"

"I'll just bet you are. You're afraid I'll blow the whistle on your great exposé novel. The Director would be plenty pissed if he found out what you're up to, Ginsburg."

"What the hell are you talking about? What exposé?"

"C'mon, don't try to deny it. You've as much as admitted you're working on a novel."

"Okay, I'm working on a novel. So what? It's got nothing to do with the Bureau."

"Bullshit. You just want to cash in, like that Snepp character at the Company, and all those Watergate guys. I know what you're up to."

"I'm not," Ginsburg protested. "I swear. It's not that at all."

"Then what is it?" Hodges demanded.

"It's none of your business," said Ginsburg. "But I'll tell you anyway, just to get you to shut up. It's a science fiction novel, Vance. Space opera. It takes place in the thirty-fourth century. There's not one word about the Bureau."

Hodges's expression changed. His eyes softened, and a look of genuine curiosity appeared.

"No kidding?" he asked.

"No kidding. Now you know. Have a good laugh."

"What's it about?"

"I just told you. Space opera."

"No, really. I mean . . . hell, Arn, I thought . . . I mean . . . aw, shit, Arn, I'm sorry. I'd really like to read it sometime. I'm a sci-fi freak myself."

"What?"

"Really, Arn. I saw *Star Wars* twelve times. I love that stuff. Ever since I was a kid."

"Me, too," Ginsburg admitted.

"You didn't seem like the type. This really surprises me,

Arn. I think it's great. I mean, really. Hell, if I'd known
. . . why didn't you just say so?"

"Why didn't you? You never said a word about science
fiction, Vance. Or anything else, for that matter. I've
known you, what, six years, and I don't know one thing
about you."

"It goes both ways, Arn."

"I suppose so." Ginsburg leaned back against the chair
and smiled ruefully. He was so locked into his job, so
careful about the paper clips, that he never stopped to
really look at the people around him. And Hodges, apparently, had been the same way.

"Did the Bureau do that to us?" Ginsburg asked.

"I don't know," said Hodges thoughtfully, knowing, at
last, what Ginsburg meant. "Maybe it does that to everybody. Or maybe everybody's just that way to begin with.
Weird, isn't it?"

Ginsburg nodded.

"Space opera, huh?"

Ginsburg felt a laugh coming up from somewhere deep
inside. He pushed it back down. He'd hold it for later.
Some other time he'd tell Hodges how Ace King had
saved a thousand planets from destruction. Right now
Flash Ginsburg still had to save this one.

He was nearby. Kendall didn't know how he knew it,
but he knew it.

Kendall had powers, now. There was nothing supernatu-
ral in it, nothing for the *National Enquirer*. He had simply
gone beyond himself, exceeded the normal limits. It was
like one of those sleep deprivation experiments, where the
subjects begin to have waking dreams and freaky insights
into the nature of things. Out on the edge things come to
you, whether you ask for them or not. Ever since that ka-
leidoscopic night on Bidong, when the jungle was populated with the ghosts of people not yet dead, he had been
getting ready for this. He was stropped and honed, thin as
the edge itself. His body was one huge antenna, dendrites
flashing like Tet fireworks, his nerve endings registering

minute changes in the environment, right down to the random motions of atoms. He was tuned in.

His brain was in overdrive, filtering out the torrent of incoming data, narrowing it down to the irreducible essentials. He walked through the milling throngs of conventioneers and cops, taking it all in and hearing nothing. None of this mattered, it was just chaff. Truong was still alive, and he was here. The whole overflowing arena was empty, except for the two of them.

He passed by his assigned post at the main entrance to the floor of the Garden and didn't even pause. This wasn't the place, at least not yet. Truong had to get here, first, and if Kendall was there waiting for him, he wouldn't appear. Truong knew they were there ahead of him, he expected that. But he wouldn't expect someone behind him, and that was where Kendall intended to be.

He took an escalator down to ground level and pushed on out into the street. It was a warm, sullen night, thick with the breath of ten thousand people. Out here was where it began.

He waited on the sidewalk, he didn't know how long. He was watching, but he knew he wasn't going to see Truong out here. This power, if it was real and not just the final rumbling echo of Vietnam and all that happened there, this power made for strange, giddy sensations. Some madmen, Kendall realized, stay mad by choice, because it was an incredible high to be this strung out. The lurps knew. Frost and Smack had known, and the acid was nothing but an audiovisual aid, a bus token to explore Edge City in more detail.

A cop finally approached him and demanded to see his identification. Kendall had that, did he ever, and he waved plastic at the cop. Satisfied, the cop walked a few feet away, but kept his eyes on Kendall.

The cop had broken the moment, but that was all right. It was time to come back down now, enough sightseeing on the edge. You couldn't stare into the face of sudden mass destruction for too long without hurting your eyes or turning to stone. Anticipating the apocalypse was hard work.

No more sneak previews of madness, then. He knew where Truong's mind was at now, dancing to the dragon's song, and it was simply a question of finding the rest of him.

Truong, sick and dying, weaker even than Kendall, would come this way, into the huge hatbox of the Garden. He'd have checked it out by now, he'd know the terrain. Kendall showed another cop his ID and went back into the building. Truong had done the same by now. Plastic was easy enough to come by.

Back up the escalator, grateful for the free motion. Strength was getting scarce now, and the puck would weigh on him like an anvil. The escalator deposited him at the top like a piece of driftwood. A moment to think, now.

Signs and arrows, cops everywhere. But he wouldn't come this far without knowing he could go farther. He would have protective cover of some kind, cameras maybe, or press passes. Whatever it took, Truong would have it. He had come ten thousand miles for this, and no ticket taker was going to keep him from going the final mile.

Kendall moved slowly toward the main entrance to the floor. Truong would have moved slowly, too, saving the energy that remained for whatever final exertion might be required. Not too slowly, though, or people would notice, the way they noticed Kendall now. He picked up his pace.

He stopped at another checkpoint, blocking the broad corridor. Again, it was easy, a wave of the plastic. But Truong would be getting nervous now. This would be farther than he could have come before. He wouldn't have risked the final roadblocks on a dry run. He was in unknown territory now, and he wouldn't know exactly what to expect.

He might be thinking that this was it. He would wonder if exploding the puck out here would be enough to do the job, to get Carter and the delegates. If he read the papers, he would know that most of the people at Bidong had survived. Distance was crucial. He had to get close, or it wouldn't work. Kendall walked on.

The puck Truong had was still a mystery, it could hold anything. Did Truong know that? Kendall didn't think he had been specific enough for Truong to know anything about the independent mutation in the separate pucks. He might suspect that the fire had moderated the results at Bidong, but he couldn't be sure. He would want to get as close as he could.

Kendall came back to the main entrance to the floor. Everything there was familiar to him, but he saw it now with Truong's eyes. He stopped and looked. Dozens of big, beefy New York cops. Secret Service and FBI by the score, obvious to anyone. Metal detectors, X-ray machines. Even the cameras were being X-rayed. Some of the people trying to get in were being frisked. A few were being turned away because they didn't have the proper ticket for tonight.

Inside, the President was speaking. Kendall listened to the high, thin tones and the singsong rhythm. He was so close, now. The words tumbled out.

". . . Hubert Horatio Hornblower—uh—*Humphrey!*"

Kendall heard it and laughed. God, it was perfect, the Hube gone and in the process of being forgotten. It was amateur night in there, the ultimate Gong Show act. Was this the voice of the dragon?

No, damn it, it wasn't. Would Truong realize that? Would he understand the Looney Tunes rhetoric of American politics and see it for the pathetic charade it really was? The man was an ex-Vietcong after all, and must have a passing acquaintance with the tenets of Marxism. There were no dragons inside the Garden tonight, just chameleons.

He couldn't get in, and there was nothing to get in for. Truong would see that. So where, then? Wall Street? Were the financial lions really the dragons?

Undoubtedly they were—but where were they? On the floor of the stock exchange Truong might hope to kill a

269

thousand brokers and clerks, but the dragon itself would be untouched. Maybe he could pick off the Chase Manhattan, but one bank wouldn't be enough. There were too many of them, too many grasping capitalists to be done away with in a single blow. He'd already killed one of them, and Turner Poole's death hadn't made the slightest difference. Whose would? Kendall could find no answer, and if he couldn't, neither would Truong.

Where?

It was slipping away. He had to get back inside the man's head. Truong the provincial official, Truong the black market dealer, Truong the pilot—the American-trained pilot. Pilots always had alternate destinations, in case they couldn't land where they wanted. If the Garden was a wave-off, then Truong . . .

Kendall had it. He turned and sprinted back down the corridor, through the checkpoints, to the escalator. He shoved people aside and took the steps three at a time. A cop at the bottom of the escalator made ready to stop him, but Kendall whipped out his badges and shouted: "Gangway! I'm on deadline!"

That was good enough. It had been good enough to get him on a helicopter once. But this time it was true.

Kendall ran, down another escalator and into the immense plaza of Penn Station. It would have to be the train. It was too late for the Eastern shuttle; Truong wouldn't know that, but he wouldn't have the strength or the know-how to get to La Guardia. But he would know by now that the station was just below the Garden.

He looked up at the signs and schedules. Gate 9A.

He walked to his left and searched for the gate. The station was crowded, even at this hour. He spotted Gate 8A. And there, next to it, was 9A.

And sitting on a bench, thirty feet away, was Pham Dinh Truong.

Kendall stopped and spun around. If Truong saw him, he might set off the puck right here.

There was a row of telephones against the wall nearest to him. Kendall trotted toward them and dug into his pocket for a dime. Now, if he just hadn't forgotten the number of Ginsburg's line.

Someone else answered after three rings.

"This is Kendall. Get me Ginsburg!"

"Just a sec." There was a long, yawning silence at the other end. A loudspeaker was announcing the departure of a train, but Kendall had one ear against the receiver and a finger in the other so he could hear, and he missed the number of the train. But he could see Truong, still sitting on the bench a hundred feet away. He looked as if he were asleep.

"Kendall?" It was Ginsburg.

"I've got—"

"Where the hell have you been?" Ginsburg demanded. "We've got a line on Truong. That Japanese mugging victim was a photographer with convention credentials. He—"

"Shut up!" Kendall shouted. "I've got him!"

"What? Where?"

"I'm in Penn Station, downstairs. I can see . . . Oh, Christ, he's moving. He's getting on the train. The Washington train."

"Which one?"

"The one that's leaving right now. I gotta go."

"Are you sure it's him?"

"Yes, damn it, I'm sure! I gotta get on that train."

Kendall dropped the receiver and ran toward Gate 9A. Truong was already out of sight. Kendall ran after him, down the concrete ramp and into the dark cavern.

Chapter Eighteen

Kendall stepped aboard the last car as the train began rolling forward. He had waited on the platform as long as he could, making sure that Truong didn't get off at the last second; Truong might have seen *The French Connection*. Everything Kendall knew about the mechanics of a chase—probably everything most people knew—he had learned at the movies. Spending so much time with the FBI had taught him caution, but not technique.

The train had seven cars, plus the engine. They must have a radio aboard, he figured, so as soon as Ginsburg could get his act together, the train would be stopped. Kendall's job, as he saw it, was to find Truong and make certain that he didn't jump. And he had to do it without being seen.

Kendall stood in the aisle at the rear of the car. A lot of people were aboard—probably party soldiers from the Washington bureaucracy headed home. The President had been renominated and their job here was finished. No need to run up the hotel bill for another night in the Big Expensive Apple. With so many people on the train Truong was going to be difficult to pick out from behind. He was still wearing the same business suit he'd worn on Bidong, a nondescript gray that would blend right into this crowd.

He was systematic about it. When he was certain that

Truong was not seated in the rear half of the car, he walked slowly forward and slipped into a seat on the right side of the aisle. A Catholic priest was sitting next to him. Kendall craned his neck and tried to take inventory of the people ahead of him.

"I see you were at the convention," said the priest.

"What?" Kendall was thoroughly spooked by the sudden remark. In the movies, he thought, the fucking extras keep their mouths shut.

"Your badges," said the priest. "I can tell by all those badges you're wearing. A newspaperman, huh? I used to be a sportswriter for my college paper back at Georgetown, but that was years ago. They still played the single wing in those days. Are you a football fan?"

Kendall bolted into the aisle. Truong wasn't in this car. He had to keep his mind on what he was doing, to get back inside Truong's head.

He moved into the next car and followed the same wait-look-and-advance procedure. This time the only empty aisle seat in the middle of the car was next to a kid with a punk rock hairdo and a black T-shirt that read, Boogie Till You Puke. Kendall gave him a quick, threatening glance, the kid returned it, and Kendall got back to business. No sign of Truong ahead, but a conductor was slowly moving to the rear, taking tickets.

For a moment Kendall wondered if he should try to enlist the conductor's help. He dismissed the notion quickly; they'd be in Trenton before he could explain what was happening.

Kendall intercepted the conductor and handed him a ten-dollar bill. "Philly," he said.

"You'll have to wait till I get to you, sir."

"Fine," said Kendall. "I'll be up ahead." He walked on, leaving the conductor waving the ten at him.

He paused between the cars. He'd checked two, that left five. The train was moving slowly, rocking heavily from side to side. It was pitch black outside and Kendall figured that they were still in the tunnel under the river. He tried to calculate what Ginsburg would be doing by now. How quickly could he move, and where would they stop the train? Logically, they should do it somewhere in the middle of the vast Jersey garbage flats. That could be anywhere on the other side of the river, in five minutes or fifteen, depending on how quickly they could get organized. His job, then, was to spot Truong in the next five minutes and stay with him, out of sight. It seemed easy enough.

Kendall made short work of the third car and moved ahead to the fourth. Another conductor met him inside the door.

"Ticket, sir?"

Kendall pointed to the rear. "The guy back there got it."

"I'll have to see your seat stub."

"Oh, shit. Here." Kendall fished another bill out of his pocket, a five, and gave it to the conductor.

"Where to?"

"As far as it takes me. Look, could you speed it up? I'm in kind of a hurry."

"Why?" the conductor asked as he methodically punched his ticket book. "Wherever you're going, you're not gonna get there before the train does."

Kendall didn't try to argue, but a thought occurred to him. "I'm looking for someone," he said. "A Vietnamese man. He's somewhere up ahead. Wearing a gray business suit. Have you seen him?"

"Don't think so," the conductor replied. He handed Kendall the ticket. "Why don't you just sit down until all the tickets are taken? Make my job a lot easier."

Kendall decided not to fight it. He took an aisle seat at the rear of the car and resumed his search. He didn't see anyone in this car who could be Truong. The conductor opened the door and moved on to the car to the rear. Kendall got up again and went forward to the fifth car.

With two to go, now, it was fifty-fifty. He peered through the dirty glass of the rear door and tried to concentrate. The window was so scratched and smudged that it was difficult to see anything. When he was as sure as he could be that Truong wasn't in the rear of the car, he opened the door and stepped inside.

Moving slowly, Kendall made his way up the aisle. Outside, lights were passing by; the train was out of the tunnel. The reflections from the inside lights made it impossible to tell exactly what was out there. Kendall checked the reflections ahead of him, hoping for a glimpse of Truong. No luck. Truong had to be in the last car.

His nerves were stretched to the breaking point now. Ahead, past one more set of doors, lay Truong and the last Nightwind puck. It was almost over. Kendall paused between cars, opened the top half of the exit door, and stuck his head out into the night, feeling the cool caress of the wind.

He realized that he was humming something, audibly. Had he been doing that all the while? With a start, he recognized the tune: "I'm Getting Married in the Morning." Indeed, he was. His sudden proposal to Sara had jumped out of nowhere, but it felt right. By tomorrow he'd be free from the past and ready to start living a life that meant something. If there was a tomorrow.

That would be up to Truong. Kendall had been walking around inside Truong's brain for days. He knew exactly what Truong was thinking and what led him to this train. There was only one place, in the end, to release the Nightwind—the place where the dragon had hatched this poisonous egg; the place where free-fire zones had been invented, where meticulous men in spotless rooms unleashed their corrupt lusts and lived out their fantasies of boundless power. The place where they kept the Hot Line to the Pit itself. Truong was going to the Pentagon.

Kendall had been in the Pentagon, perhaps Truong, as well. Access was simple. Thousands of civilians worked there, and on the first level there was a concourse that looked like a suburban shopping mall. Down below they were dug in for falling megatonnage, but if he did it right, Truong could send the Nightwind creeping down to them before anyone noticed.

The neon lights from Edge City were flashing in his

head again, like Las Vegas-on-the-Styx, inviting him to come for a night and try his luck. He could help Truong, and if Truong faltered he might even inherit the mission. There was a time, he thought, when he might have done it. To fuck the Pentagon, to physically penetrate the sleazy bitch and give her a dose of cosmic clap—it was an awesome thought. Fragging carried to its one logical conclusion. Bring the war home, defoliate the cherry blossoms, sanitize the Capitol, launch a protective reaction strike on the Rose Garden; a righteous motherfucker of a thought. Make the bastards pay for what they did.

Was that Truong, or was it him? Dance too long to the other man's music, and whose coin ends up in the jukebox?

Kendall took a deep breath of the rushing wind and stepped back from the door. He was getting married in the morning.

It wasn't '68 anymore, and he didn't need to play mind games with Truong. He had him, now, in the next car. All he had to do was wait until they stopped the train.

Kendall opened the door and stepped inside the final car. A seat at the left rear was empty, and he took it. He closed his eyes for a few seconds and tried to find the balance again. It was still there, waiting for him.

He opened his eyes and began the search for Truong. He checked off the passengers, starting from the rear. Two nuns, a young couple, a teen-age girl, a black man, a middle-aged woman, some kids . . . and a rising nausea as he realized that Truong was not here. He tried again, backtracking, as if he'd misplaced his car keys. Had to be here somewhere.

But he wasn't. Kendall felt a cold wave moving up his spine. If he wasn't ahead of him, then . . . Reflexively, he whirled around, but saw only the rear wall of the car and a poster advertising bargain rates from New York to Philadelphia.

Where the hell was he? Could he have jumped already? But why would he do that? He didn't know he was being followed, Kendall was sure of it—unless, during all that time he'd spent in Truong's head, Truong had been in *his*.

No, he told himself. It was nitty-gritty time now, and the vibes were nothing but the clattering of the train's wheels on a worn out roadbed. His own head was the only one he needed, and Joe Kendall was its sole occupant. Truong was definitely on the train. He was tired and he was sick and . . .

And sick people spent time in rest rooms. Kendall mentally kicked himself. He'd forgotten all about the rest rooms. There was one at the front of the car. Truong could be in that one, or in any of the six others in the cars he'd already checked.

This would be tricky. He walked carefully forward, keeping his eyes on the door of the rest room. If Truong popped out and saw him, the shit could come down right here and now. But he had to find him, nail him to one spot so he wouldn't have a chance to bolt when they stopped the train—which should be any minute, if Ginsburg was on the ball.

Before he got to the rest room, he saw that the door was half open. He could see the mirror reflecting the empty stall. Oh for one.

Kendall returned to the rear of the car and went out onto the rocking metal platform between this car and the next. Coming back was going to be dangerous. If Truong had returned to a seat, he would see Kendall coming.

Kendall leaned close to the window. He started checking faces, but he saw the motion before he saw the face. Truong, three rows back on the right, was pushing his seatmate into the aisle and scrambling to get free. Kendall threw the door open and plunged into the car. Truong, a wild, desperate look in his eyes, shoved the surprised passenger who had been sitting next to him, sending him spinning into Kendall. Kendall shoved him back into the seat and ran after Truong.

The conductor suddenly opened the rear door and entered the car, blocking the aisle. Truong stopped short, just as Kendall launched himself in a flat dive. He misjudged it, thrown by Truong's sudden stop. He grabbed at Truong, clutching at his jacket—felt it for an instant, felt the hard round puck—but the momentum of his leap carried him by, assisted by Truong's flailing elbow. Kendall crashed into the conductor, and they were both on the floor.

Truong ran the other way, toward the front of the train. Kendall broke free from the conductor and got back to his feet. Ahead, Truong was already into the next car. Kendall got to the outside platform and caught a glimpse of Truong disappearing out the final door.

There was nothing ahead but the engine, no place left for Truong to go. Not on the train. Kendall leaned out the open exit door and saw a dark blur up ahead, falling away from the train. Kendall had no time to think about it. He flung the bottom part of the door open, took one too-quick look, and jumped.

His timing was so good that he wasn't ready for the impact. He was expecting gravel or concrete, and instead, hit Truong. The shock of collision took him right out of himself, and for a moment he was back on the edge, and the bright sparks were falling rockets. Then he was back, pain and recognition all at once, and Truong was pounding at him, thumping his fist into his gut.

Kendall tried to shield himself, on his back in the soft dirt, elbows out. Truong bounced his fist off one of the elbows, and gasped from the impact. Reaching out, Kendall got his hand on Truong's jacket. Holding him with his left, he drove his right fist straight out and missed everything. Truong was back on top of him, and for a moment everything stopped.

Truong's face, half-lit by some distant luminescence, hovered above him like a pale, desperate ghost.

"Kendall!" The single word came out like a volcanic explosion. "I knew it would be you!"

"Give it up!" Kendall cried.

Truong looked at him for a long, suspended moment, as if he were actually considering it. He felt light and brittle on top of Kendall, a Tinkertoy man. For a split instant

278

Kendall could have had him, but Truong was still looking at him, his eyes gleaming in the darkness like twin moons floating above a cloud bank. The instant disappeared and Truong was reaching into his pocket, his left hand pressing down toward Kendall's throat.

Kendall grabbed Truong's arm with both hands and forced it away from him. But Truong had the gun out now. He brought it up and Kendall swung his left arm to ward it off. His forearm smacked against the barrel and the gun went spinning off into the darkness.

Truong pushed himself away from Kendall and scrambled after the gun, on hands and knees. With Truong's dry, hollow weight off of him, Kendall rolled to his side and found he was up against the rough embankment of the railroad tracks. In another second Truong would have the gun, and Kendall knew he could never get away in time.

His hands clawed at the embankment. It was nothing but a loose rockpile. Kendall closed his right hand around a stone, and he whirled back toward his left. He released the rock, hard and true, and it hit Truong in the shoulder. With no other weapons, Kendall grabbed more rocks and fired a rapid, accurate barrage at Truong. With each throw, he pushed himself farther away, and finally he was halfway up the embankment, his heels digging into the dirt. Truong had the gun but the rain of rocks was hurting him. He couldn't turn to fire without exposing himself to a rock in the face.

It couldn't go on much longer. Kendall fired one last rock and dived over the railroad tracks. He heard the sharp crack of the pistol behind him but felt nothing except the sting of the jagged cinders on the opposite embankment as he hit the earth again.

He rolled onto his back and saw that the embankment shielded him from Truong. He couldn't get up to run, but if he stayed flat and low, he would be safe until Truong came after him. But Truong didn't.

"Damn you, Kendall!" Truong shouted.

279

Kendall didn't answer. He didn't know if he could. Breathing was almost more than he could manage.

"They're coming!" Truong yelled. "But it isn't finished yet, Kendall!"

Kendall risked a look, raising his head a few inches. He saw flashing red and blue lights in the distance, coming toward him. The train was stopped a half mile ahead, and a half-dozen police cruisers were bouncing down the railroad tracks. He could hear the sirens now.

"You can still quit," Kendall called. "They can help you, Truong. I know you're sick. They can help you."

Truong laughed, a staccato, bitter rasp that sounded like a machine gun firing into an empty oil drum.

"No, thank you," Truong said when the laughter died. "I've had enough help from Americans. Good-bye, Kendall. And beware of dragons." He laughed once more, and then there was silence, except for the lonely wail of the sirens.

Kendall got to hands and knees and peered cautiously over the rails. Truong was running again, out into the formless blackness beyond the rails. The garbage flats. Kendall got to his feet, and managed two steps before he felt something give way in his right knee. He pitched forward, skidded down the embankment, and came to a stop. He tried to get up again, but the leg refused to function.

Up on the tracks the first police cruiser, bobbing up and down on the ties, slowed and then stopped. The other cars were close behind. Kendall stood up, balancing unsteadily on his left foot. He called to the nearest policeman.

"He's out there!" He pointed to the direction he meant. He could still see Truong in the distance.

The cops didn't have rifles. They drew their pistols and leaned across the roofs of their cruisers, taking careful aim.

"No!" Kendall screamed. "You can't shoot him like that!"

"He's the one we're supposed to stop, ain't he?" one of the cops answered.

"But you might hit—"

280

It was too late. The first gun went off, and then the others were popping. It was a sound Kendall hadn't heard since the last firefight in Hue. And suddenly, the memory was complete. In the distance, out on the garbage flats, something exploded in a muffled, dying thump.

"What the fuck?" said one of the cops.

Kendall could have told him what the fuck, but it didn't matter now. It really was over. He took a step forward and the knee buckled again. He fell, hit the soft muck, and sank into the garbage and filth, to wait for the end.

Chapter Nineteen

"Did you really throw rocks at him?" Hodges asked.

Kendall, sitting in the left front of a police cruiser, looked up, out the open door, and nodded at the agent. "I really did," he said.

Hodges chuckled. "I like it," he said. "The last battle of the Vietnam War—a rock fight. I like it."

Kendall tried to ignore Hodges. He was being compulsively chatty this morning, as if he could paper over everything that had happened by good cheer. Hodges could afford to feel happy; he'd won, after all.

Out on the garbage flats, smoke was rising along with the sun. The dawn was rosy and brilliant, the first bright rays flashing across the horizon like laser beams. He could see the Statue of Liberty in the distance, between him and the sun. The old lady had had another rough night, but she was still standing. Tired, poor, huddled masses would still have a place to come, if they didn't wind up dead in the mud of Bidong first.

He watched Ginsburg making his way up the embankment, holding a white handkerchief to his nose. Hodges poured some coffee from a thermos and handed it to Ginsburg when he arrived at the cruiser. Ginsburg took it, then turned to Kendall.

"The doctors are going to want some of your blood," he said, "just to make sure."

"They can have all of it if they want."

Ginsburg checked Kendall's eyes, searching for that thousand-yard stare, but it was gone now. "You're just tired, Joe. You'll feel better when you get some sleep."

"On his wedding night?" Hodges cracked.

"Are you serious about that?" Ginsburg asked.

"Uh-huh. Soon as you get me back to the city."

"You got a license? Blood tests? Hey, maybe they can do that when they take the sample. Kill two birds with one stone."

"That's not the American way," said Kendall. "Better to kill one bird with two hundred stones."

Ginsburg looked back toward the flats. "I know," he said. "I know. We were lucky. If it had been one of the lethal strains, we'd probably all be dead now."

They stared at the burning garbage flats. When the decontamination team arrived, sometime before dawn, they concluded that the quickest, safest way to deal with the problem was to set fire to the area, before a wind could come up and blow the Nightwind into some populated region. They spread gasoline and ignited it, but a dropped cigarette would have been enough. There was something in this polluted mud that burned like brimstone. Within minutes the entire field was afire.

"The irony," said Ginsburg, "is that the stuff that's already here is probably more dangerous than the Nightwind."

"Yeah," said Hodges, "one hell of a strange fire. That's a fire that's gonna burn for a long, long time."

283

Still Missing

Beth Gutcheon

On a beautiful spring morning, Susan Selky kissed her six-year-old son Alex goodby and watched as he skipped down the street to the neighborhood school. She could not possibly imagine that what began as a cheerful morning would end as a hellish nightmare, for Alex never came home. He is ...STILL MISSING.

"Mesmerizing. Absolutely riveting." — *Newsday*

"Expertly harrowing. Gutcheon plays on our emotions with fiendish skill. The ending will leave you limp."
— *Cosmopolitan*

"Much more memorable than *KRAMER VS. KRAMER* —which this will rival in every heart-wrenching way and top in suspense." —*The Boston Herald-American*

A Dell Book   17864-9   **$3.50**

The controversial novel of the
world's most fearsome secret!

GENESIS

by W.A. Harbinson

First came the sightings, sighted by nine million Americans.
Then came the encounters. Then came the discovery of an
awesome plot dedicated to dominate and change the world.

An explosive combination of indisputable fact woven into
spellbinding fiction, *Genesis* will change the way you look at
the world—and the universe—forever.

A Dell Book   **$3.50**   **(12832-3)**

"Gruesomely effective.
A scary, engrossing book."
—Stephen King,
author of *Firestarter*

The Unforgiven
by Patricia J. MacDonald

Maggie tried to forget the body of the man she loved, the
murder trial, and the agonizing punishment. Now she was free
to start a new life on a quiet New England island—until the
terror began again.

"A terrific psychological thriller." —Mary Higgins Clark, author
of *The Cradle Will Fall*

"...one of those rare books that, once started, you can't put
down." —John Saul, author of *When the Wind Blows*

A Dell Book $3.50   (19123-8)